Between the Lines

TRACEY MAGRUDER

For Randy.
Thank you for being my Sadie.

Content Warning

The themes represented in *Between the Lines* are handled with care and sensitivity, and the story focuses on healing, resilience, and finding love after loss. However, if you would like more information or specific trigger warnings, please visit traceymagruder.com/books.

December 31, 2009

-Sadie-

All Sadie wanted was to get off the train. Sweat trickled down her back as more passengers squeezed into the already packed Northern Line train car in London's Underground.

The Tube's musty dampness clashed with the floral perfume wafting from a group of women nearby, ready for a night out. She clung to the cold metal pole for balance, the books in her Foyles shopping bag digging into her hip as the carriage jolted forward. Around her, she could hear her friends' chatter, their voices a low hum beneath the train's rumble as they headed back to their hotel to celebrate New Year's Eve.

"This is what Tetris blocks must feel like," Lila grumbled beside her, rolling her eyes as yet another commuter elbowed past.

Sadie smirked, adjusting her grip on the pole.

"At least Tetris blocks don't smell," she shot back, wrinkling her nose. Lila's giggle was a bright spot in the chaos, and Sadie couldn't help but join in, the sound cutting through the stuffiness of the carriage.

During the trip, the organizers had spoiled the high school group. A tour bus chauffeured them around London and its outskirts in comfort. Today, though, they had broken up into small groups to explore the city, and she wouldn't have traded it for anything. Dickens' house, with its faded wallpaper, the Globe

Theatre's weathered beams, and a pilgrimage to Foyles that had her inner bookworm buzzing were all worth it. Her college admission essays were writing themselves in her head, fueled by every literary landmark she'd soaked in.

"Would you mind letting the normal people through?" a smug voice snapped behind Lila. A middle-aged man in a crisp business suit shoved his way forward, his expression pinched with irritation as he surveyed the high school group.

Lila straightened, tilting her chin up in the same haughty manner. "Oh yes, do let the normal people through," she parroted in an exaggerated British accent, her eyes glinting with mischief. "Can't you see how utterly important I am?"

Sadie couldn't control her laughter, earning her a playful nudge from Lila. But her mirth died on her lips as a warm hand brushed hers on the pole, and a jolt of electricity raced up her arm. Heat flashed beneath her skin, the lingering tingle refusing to fade. She jumped, startled by the touch, and spun toward the source.

"Sorry, didn't mean to..." a warm, deep voice said, trailing off when his eyes met hers.

They were a stunning shade of blue, framed by sharp features and dark hair that fell over his forehead. He stared at her, wide-eyed, as if equally surprised, a soft smile tugging at his lips.

"No, it's fine," Sadie blurted, trying to sound casual as she returned his smile. Her heart kicked hard in her chest, an unfamiliar feeling of fluttering in her stomach.

For a moment, the cacophony of the Tube faded, and it was just her and this stranger. As his blue eyes continued to stare into her gray, she felt an invisible thread stretching between them. It was the kind of moment she'd only ever read about, never expected to actually feel.

His gaze flicked to the Foyles bag swinging from her wrist and asked, "Fellow bookworm? Find any good bits?"

Her nerves melted with his easy grin, and the excitement of finding someone who understood her passion for classic literature.

"*Poems on the Underground* and *London: A Literary Anthology*," she said, returning his smile. "If it all fit in my suitcase, I would have bought one of everything..."

"Totally get that," he said, leaning in a little, his enthusiasm matching hers. "So, who's your favorite? Like, desert island pick?"

"Austen, hands down," she replied, her smile turning into a bit of a smirk. "You?"

"Hardy," he quipped. "Less ballroom, more doom—suits me."

Sadie opened her mouth to respond when a sharp voice sliced through their bubble.

"Alessandra, come on!" Ms. Harrow's stern tone jolted her back to reality. The train slowed, brakes screeching as Tottenham Court Road approached.

Panic flared in her chest as she turned back to the handsome stranger, realizing she didn't even know his name. As she took a breath to ask, the crowd surged forward like a tidal wave, pulling her along. She tried to fight the pull, desperate for one more second—anything that would let her anchor this moment to something real.

"Come on, girl, move it!" Lila tugged her along as they exited the train. "We're gonna lose the group!"

"Wait," Sadie stumbled, twisting around to catch one last glimpse. He was still aboard the train, looking out the window, and those blue eyes locked on her. Then the train motor hummed to life as it pulled away, his face fading into the tunnel's darkness.

Sadie's heart sank, her hand still tingling where he'd touched her. She barely heard Lila's voice, her friend shaking her shoulders to break her daze.

"Earth to Sadie. You look like you've seen a ghost. You okay?"

"I'm fine," she murmured, allowing Lila to pull her toward the rest of the group.

As Ms. Harrow herded them toward the escalators, Sadie's mind raced. Logic told her that she would never see him again. Her heart, however, insisted this was different, and the ache in her chest insisted she'd just let something important slip away.

Looking over her shoulder, she felt like she was leaving a part of herself behind with the man with those beautiful blue eyes.

February 4, 2025

-Sadie-

Sadie jolted awake, the relentless buzz of her phone pulling her from her slumber. She burrowed into the blanket, groaning as a spring from the pullout mattress dug into her side. Outside she could hear the familiar honking and rumble of early-morning traffic bleeding through the thin apartment windows.

"At least I'm not sleeping in a cardboard box," she muttered when her phone buzzed again.

Forcing herself to sit up, she reached for the phone as it vibrated with a third text message. Her stomach churned as she saw the name on the screen. Her ex-fiancé, Nate, was nothing if not persistent. There were a half-dozen unread messages, and she had to fight the urge to toss her phone out the window.

She had ended things with Nate last month after nearly a decade. Their relationship had never been perfect, but in the last few years, any love she might have felt for him had shriveled and died as he started to reveal who he was beneath the fake charm. When he smashed her laptop in a fit of rage, she had packed her bags and sought refuge at her best friend's apartment.

Preparing herself for the inevitable, she unlocked her phone and opened the messaging app. Her brows drew together while she read Nate's latest barrage of texts.

> I miss you, Sades. Too quiet here without your nagging.

> Found some of those romance novels you love. Meet me later? Enzo's? Back where it all began?

Even with the way things had ended, she still felt a smile tug faintly at her lips. Enzo's had been the restaurant where he took her for their first date. Where he'd gushed about her writing and how perfectly they would complement each other with their styles.

That smile faded the moment she read the last two texts.

> Ignoring me again?

> Whatever, Sades, I'll torch the fucking trashy books.

"Well, that escalated quickly," she mumbled. Her tired, puffy eyes stung. This was her reality, and she wasn't quite sure how she had managed to miss so many red flags over the years.

"I don't need this first thing in the morning," she muttered under her breath, putting the phone face down on the table.

Slumping back on the pillows, she covered her eyes with her arm. Jess had been a saint for taking her in. Of course, having a front row for the entirety of the relationship helped her best friend understand just how toxic it had become.

The shuffle of slippered feet snapped Sadie upright. Jess breezed in, chestnut waves teetering in a messy bun, two steaming mugs of coffee in hand. The rich aroma cut through the room, and it felt like a lifeline Sadie couldn't resist.

"Morning, sunshine," Jess said, her voice carrying a forced cheeriness. There were dark circles under Jess's eyes, too. Sadie knew she had been up half the night preparing for a board meeting. In addition to being her best friend, Jess was also Sadie's boss, and the board of the publishing house was getting ready to hold their quarterly meeting.

Jess placed one mug on the cluttered side table, and added, "How's my favorite houseguest doing?"

Sadie tried to muster a smile, her voice croaking when she replied, "Oh, you know, living the dream. Not that I'm not grateful. You ready for today?"

"As I can be with the board breathing down my neck," Jess said, taking a sip of her coffee. The phone buzzed again, and Jess's eyebrows knitted together as she perched on the edge of the couch. "Let me guess," she said with a quirked eyebrow, "Captain Douchebag?"

Sadie shook her head in exasperation, looking at the phone on the table.

"Isn't it always?" she whispered, hating how weak she sounded. "I didn't answer him, so I'm sure he's now in a full rage spiral."

"That vile asshole doesn't get to win." Jess's expression hardened. "Not after everything he's put you through."

Sadie's stomach churned as she remembered the last time she had tried to share something she wrote with him.

Stick to editing, Sades, Nate had said, *your little stories don't exactly scream genius.* After years of hearing the same message from him time and time again, she had started to honestly believe it.

"Ignore him," Jess continued, gently turning Sadie's chin so she would look at her. "I have something far more worthy of your time to discuss."

Before Sadie could respond, Jess was in motion, disappearing into the living room. She returned with her sleek work laptop, unceremoniously plopping on the mattress next to Sadie.

"Right," Jess announced, rubbing her hands together eagerly. "I think I have the perfect distraction for you, courtesy of my favorite literary hermit."

"What?" Sadie blinked, momentarily thrown by the abrupt change of subject.

"Corbyn Pearce," Jess said, her fingers flying across the keyboard. "He's run off another developmental editor. I've been trying to buy him time to finish his latest manuscript, but the board is losing patience."

Despite herself, Sadie felt a flicker of curiosity.

"Wait... Corbyn Pearce? *The* Corbyn Pearce? As in the man whose last murder mystery sold a million copies on the first day?"

"You're the only one I trust to handle this, Sadie," Jess said, her tone serious though she avoided meeting Sadie's eyes directly. "Pearce is a handful, but you've got a saint's patience. I still remember how you saved Stella Adkins' book last year when everyone else was ready to toss it."

"You're not telling me something," Sadie said, recognizing the avoidance and the attempt at flattery. "How many editors has he gone through?"

Jess winced, her tone sheepish when she replied, "You're the fourth since New Year's. But I genuinely think you can reach him where the others couldn't."

"Jess, please tell me you're not asking what I think you're asking," Sadie groaned, knowing her friend too well.

"You, my dear couch surfer, are my editing ace," Jess said with a smirk. "You've tamed worse than Pearce. Plus, the board is convinced that his comeback novel could be the title of the decade. You are the only one who can drag this project across the finish line."

Sadie couldn't help but snort at that.

"Plus," Jess continued, "here's your shot to wrangle someone who actually gets things done, instead of just whining about it."

She meant Nate. Sadie had spent years trying to help him find the inspiration to finish a project... any project. It had never ended well.

"I..." Sadie started to protest, but stopped when she saw the hopeful look on Jess's face. "So, how do I do this? Call him up? Or does he only do smoke signals and carrier pigeons?"

Jess's expression turned sheepish, and she replied, "I thought it might be better if you took a little all-expense paid working vacation. You know, Great Missenden's supposedly very quaint."

The words cut through Sadie's mental fog, and she blinked, trying desperately to process what Jess had said.

"Great... Missenden?"

"Yep," Jess said, popping the 'p' with relish. "Cute little town in Buckinghamshire. Roald Dahl country. Just imagine the inspiration!"

Sadie's mind whirled, and she stammered, "But... Corbyn Pearce? There?"

"He's holed up in some rickety cottage, probably scribbling with quills by candlelight," Jess chuckled, typing something on her computer. "Your job is to drag him, kicking and screaming if necessary, into the 21st century and finish his book. You would be saving me from an early grave, and who knows? Maybe you'll find your own muse while you're at it."

"I don't know, Jess, this is pretty sudden," Sadie began, doubt gnawing away at her gut. Nate's voice rang through her mind again, her confidence faltering. "I have a pile of manuscripts on my desk..."

"Which I am currently working on reassigning to the rest of our team," Jess interrupted as Sadie's phone buzzed with an email notification. "Surprise! Your chariot to Heathrow awaits. You leave tonight."

Sadie's eyes widened as she looked at her phone. The email was from British Airways confirming her travel plans.

"Tonight? But..."

"Your lease with Nate doesn't end for another two months," Jess interrupted, her voice gentle but firm. "And as your best friend, I think you need to get off this sofa before you sprout couch potatoes."

Sadie glanced around the cluttered space, over the stacks of books and half-unpacked boxes. She had tried to settle in and wait out the lease, but the truth was that being surrounded by the mess had kept her in a spiral of self-doubt for the last month.

"I need you on this project, Sadie," Jess's uncharacteristically serious tone pulled her from her thoughts, "and you need to do something other than mope on my sofa bed."

A watery chuckle escaped Sadie's lips. "Gee, thanks."

"I mean it," Jess insisted. "This isn't just about Pearce and his book. It's about you, too. It'll give you a chance to heal, without having to worry that Nate might be lurking around the next corner."

"Not to mention I'd be saving your ass with the board," Sadie replied before exhaling sharply.

Jess grinned, laughing a bit when she responded, "Yes, that too. Come on, Sadie, you used to talk all the time about going back to England. Back in freshman year, we couldn't get you to shut up about the trip you took in high school." Jess's smile turned mischievous before she added, "Do you remember that red hair you used to rock? Before Mr. Moody convinced you it was 'too attention-seeking'?"

Despite herself, Sadie felt a smile tugging at her lips.

"God, I haven't thought about that in ages. I looked like a deranged matchstick."

"You looked fierce," Jess corrected. "You were fierce, and you will be again. Great Missenden won't know what hit it."

"Okay, I'll go," Sadie told her, her voice shaky.

Her eyes stung with unshed tears, but beneath that, she felt something stirring in her chest. Something she hadn't felt in a very long time.

Jess didn't miss a beat, yanking her into a hug. Sadie half-collapsed into it, the smell of coffee and faded lavender shampoo grounding her.

"You're gonna nail this," Jess muttered, words muffled against Sadie's rat's nest of hair. "No one else I'd bet on, not even close."

"What if I screw it up?" Sadie's voice came out small, mashed against Jess's shoulder, doubt clawing at her. "Pearce'll probably despise me."

Jess eased back, hazel eyes glinting with that troublemaker spark.

"Then we'll pin it on jet lag and mail him a pigeon with an apology note. But you won't tank it—you're Sadie Reed, the writer-wrangler extraordinaire."

A ghost of a smile flickered across Sadie's face. "I think that title's a bit much."

"Nonsense," Jess declared. "I'm having business cards made."

"Thanks," Sadie whispered, her breath unsteady.

Jess squeezed her hand. "That's what friends are for. Now, let's get you packed. Great Missenden awaits, and it's your chance to show that sad excuse of an ex what Sadie Reed is really made of."

Sadie rose and met Jess's gaze, a spark of hope lifting the weight she had been carrying around for months, possibly even years. Jess was right; she did need this, and Corbyn Pearce was about to be beaten at his own stubborn game.

February 5, 2025

-Corbyn-

The sounds of the stationary bike's grinding wheels and heavy breathing were the only noises bouncing off the concrete walls of the basement gym. Using a towel, Corbyn wiped away the sweat that traveled down his face only to snag on a network of rough scars that crawled up his neck to his right cheek. Annoyance had him pedaling faster as his mind drifted to the half-completed manuscript sitting on his desk, just a floor above him.

Before the accident, he would have sought to clear his mind in the steep trails around Great Missenden. His body would lean into steep descents, and wind would tear at his face as he pushed his high-end mountain bike to its limits. The burn in his muscles had meant freedom in those days. Now, though, it was just another reminder of how much had been stolen from him, of how he lived like someone much older than his thirty-six years.

His right hand clamped the handlebars, knuckles white, while his left, a mess of surgical scars, barely hung on. His fingers were cramped with pain that the February chill only made worse. The doctors had sworn he'd get movement back, but he had been left with a shaky claw that could barely grip a damn book most days. Not that he'd cracked one open lately, with his deadline breathing down his neck.

Riley, his massive Irish Wolfhound, sprawled across the rubber mat next to the bike, a mass of tan fur and lanky limbs. His soulful eyes remained fixed on Corbyn, patiently waiting for his master to finish so he could then go patrol the manor grounds. The hulking beast had become a tower of strength, only asking for a scratch behind the ear or to be taken for a walk to break up the monotony of lying on a rug watching him attempt to write.

"Almost there, boy," Corbyn rasped, his breathing slightly labored from the pace.

When the phone on the bench, one of the few pieces of technology he allowed himself out of necessity, buzzed, and the name Jessica Harper appeared on the screen, his scowl deepened.

The New York-based editorial director had been hounding him more often lately, and he was well aware of the reason. Her patience frayed a little more with every deadline he'd blown past, and in the wake of a third failed developmental editor, she had to be at the end of her tether. The bike's rhythm faltered as he lunged for it with his right hand, his left flopping to his thigh.

Corbyn swiped to answer, propping the phone on the bike's book ledge and tapping the speaker as his legs slowed to a sluggish pedal.

"What is it now, Harper?" he barked as soon as the call connected.

"Good morning to you, too, sunshine," Jess retorted, her voice too bright given how early it had to be in New York. "Tell me you've got something new on those revisions."

Tension coiled in Corbyn's stomach, and he hoped she didn't hear his grimace when he lied, "I'm working on it."

"You've been 'working on it' for a month. The deadline was two weeks ago."

"I told you I needed more time after..."

"After that train wreck that was the last draft, yeah, I haven't forgotten," Jess cut in, her edge softening a hair. "I know you think

I'm just calling to nag you, but I do get it; you're stuck. And that's exactly why I'm calling. I've lined up some help."

His feet stilled, the bike groaning to a halt. Riley's head lifted when Corbyn asked suspiciously, "What help?"

"I am sending you one of our sharpest developmental minds. She landed at Heathrow this morning so she can dig into *Echoes of Ash* with you and push through this block of yours."

Heat flared up in Corbyn's neck, embarrassment at needing help causing his scarred cheek to throb red.

"No," he snapped, climbing off the bike to pace along the length of the room he used as a gym. "I don't need some stranger pawing through my work."

"Her name's Sadie Reed, and after tomorrow, she won't be a stranger," Jess responded, unfazed by his tone. "She dragged Malcolm Chen's mess of a manuscript into a bestseller last year. She's quick, quiet, as stubborn as you are, and, most importantly, exactly what you need."

"What I need," Corbyn snarled, left hand jerking with a stab of pain as he clenched it, "is to be left alone to finish this bloody thing."

"Three months ago, sure, but that ship has sailed, Pearce," Jess retorted, her tone suddenly turning to steel. "I've bent over backward for you. I've given you space, pushed deadlines, made excuses to the board. Besides, she should be arriving at The Roaring Stag any minute, so she will be at your door tomorrow morning, ready to work."

His heart thudded hard, and this time it had nothing to do with the workout.

"Are you pulling my leg?"

"Not today," Jess replied, and he could almost hear her smirk through the phone. "I'm giving her the rest of the day to shake off the jet lag, then you and your book are her sole focus." Jess sped up, cutting off his growl when she added, "You're late. Marketing's chewing my ear off. We need this book, and you need a lifeline. Sadie's proven she can deliver."

His left hand balled into a fist despite the discomfort, and he stopped his pacing as he stared up at the ceiling.

"You have no right..."

"Clause sixteen, publisher's right to call for editorial intervention," Jess told him, and there was something in her tone that suggested she was as unhappy about this as he was. "Check your contract. I held off until now because I thought you'd claw your way out solo."

"Send her back."

Jess sighed, clearly exasperated with him, before she said, "She's on an open ticket. Look, give her a week. If she hasn't made any impact, fine, she's gone. But try it—she's the best I've got."

Riley whined low as he pressed his nose against Corbyn's hand, sensing his master's agitated state. He flicked a look down, those steady hound eyes pulling him back from the edge for a second.

"Does she know about..." he trailed off, waving at his scarred cheek, even though it was pointless over the phone.

"She knows you value your privacy, and that this book is in trouble." Jess paused, but then added, "She's a pro, Corbyn. She's there for the pages, not to poke into your personal life or make you uncomfortable."

A sharp, humorless laugh escaped him when he replied, "Everyone pokes, Harper. It's human nature."

"Not Sadie. I've known her since college and she's one of the most patient and compassionate people I know. Trust me, she is only there to help with the book."

Trust. The word sank like lead. The last time he'd trusted someone with his work, a draft was stolen and leaked online. It had spread like wildfire through the literary world, everyone weighing in on the unedited pages. It had been the last time he had sent his work through email.

"She's already in England," Jess said, her voice growing softer. "Just don't bite her head off, alright? I'll check in next week."

The line went dead, Jess's voice lingering in the basement's damp chill.

Corbyn glared at the phone and then chucked it back onto the bench. It skittered across the scratched wood, teetering near the edge. Riley nudged Corbyn's hand again, drawing his attention away from the phone and his anger at Jess.

"You'll probably love her, won't you?" he grumbled at the dog as his fingers worked through his shaggy fur. "You'll wag your tail and roll over for belly rubs when she walks in."

Riley huffed a wet snort that might as well have been a yes.

Corbyn returned to his pacing, running a hand over his face. Sadie Reed. The name alone grated on his nerves. It was too bright, too American, and he would have to tolerate her presence for at least the following week. A week of some stranger crashing his solitude. A week of her tiptoeing around his scars, tossing out fixes for a book he couldn't seem to finish. A week of this Sadie Reed, some Yankee editor, here to pick at the wreckage, thinking she could be the savior the book needed.

Like that was even possible.

The stairs creaked behind him, a slow, steady rhythm he associated only with his housekeeper, Edie. She and her husband, Paul, who served as the groundskeeper, had been more like parents to him than his own mother and father.

Corbyn caught her reflection in the dusty mirror across the way. Her diminutive but sturdy frame eased down the steps. Auburn hair, streaked with silver, hung in its usual loose bun, stray wisps brushing her face. She clutched a water bottle in her hands, her expression disapproving.

"You left your water upstairs," Edie said, holding the bottle out to him as she raised an eyebrow in his direction. "Again." That last word carried years of nagging in two tired syllables.

Corbyn's jaw locked, and he blew out a rough breath as he raked his good hand through damp hair.

"Thanks," he grunted, sharper than he meant.

Edie had always been unshakable, no matter how much he snarled or groused, and the scars that now marred his body had never once spooked her. She'd patched his scraped elbows and knees long before she'd bandaged the mess left behind by the car crash.

"You're overdoing it," she said, nodding at his shaky left hand. "Cold's chewing you up, isn't it?"

He clenched his left hand, trying to hide the shaking as he muttered, "I'm fine."

"Hmph." Edie's grunt called out his lie without a word. "Damp's in your joints. I can tell by that hunch alone."

He didn't argue. Winter always found his weak spots, and there was no sense in denying it. The pins in his hand, the fried nerves under grafted skin that never fit right, it was a constant this time of year. But admitting it outright would never happen, not even with Edie.

"Have you been doing those hand exercises Ellie's friend recommended?"

Corbyn's shoulders tensed, and the way she raised her eyebrow made him feel like he was ten years old again and caught stealing sweets before dinner. He knew his sister had meant well, asking her physical therapist friend at the hospital for more exercises that might help improve the range of motion in his useless left hand. After four years of exploring every possible option, he was simply done being disappointed when there was inevitably no improvement.

"That's what I suspected," she said, brushing off his silence. "I ran you a bath upstairs with that oil Ellie brought over. After, you'll have a proper breakfast. None of your coffee-only rubbish you like to spout."

Riley nosed his hip, backing her up like a furry nag. The dog's knack for sniffing out pain before Corbyn admitted it to himself was eerie.

"You're grumpier than usual," Edie continued, eyes narrowing. "What's going on?"

Corbyn grabbed the bottle, pinning it against his chest with his left hand to twist the cap off with his right. The hand's uselessness pissed him off every time. He gulped half before answering.

"My publisher is sending someone to work here in person. A developmental editor."

Edie's brows lifted over her glasses, and she asked, "Is that so?"

"To 'fix' it," he spat, the word burning his tongue. "Some Yank who turns trash into gold, supposedly."

"Ah. Well, that explains it." Edie nodded, calm as if he'd mentioned the weather. "When's she showing up?"

"Tomorrow," he told her, looking over her face and noting her lack of surprise, and his eyes narrowed. "I never said anything about it being a woman."

A flicker of guilt crossed Edie's face, but it was gone just as quickly as she replied, "I might have spoken to Ms. Harper about this before she called you."

"Of course you did," Corbyn replied, his irritation seeping into his tone. Edie had been Jess's point of contact when he had been recovering and unable to answer for himself. "So, everyone's plotting my rescue behind my back?"

"No one thinks you need rescuing," Edie said, voice even, as she began fussing with the towels on a nearby rack. It was a nervous tic, the need to straighten up, and it usually meant she was about to say something he wouldn't like. "But that book needs help. You've said it yourself."

"I can do it solo."

"Can you?" she asked, her question soft but blunt. "Months and your publisher hasn't seen a page. Paul says you're staring holes in your study walls more than writing."

That stung, but it was closer to the truth than he cared to admit. Words that used to pour out had clogged up, leaving him with scraps and dead ends.

"I don't need a stranger rooting through my stuff, gawking at..."

He waved at his scarred face, the mess that made eyes dart away and strangers whisper.

"Ms. Harper made her sound very professional," Edie cut in, sidestepping the real issue.

He snorted, collapsing onto the bench and taking another sip of his water.

"Probably some chipper American itching to brainstorm about my 'process.'"

The word dripped acid. His process had always served him perfectly in the past.

Edie's mouth twitched, almost into a grin. "God forbid we have a little cheer in this house. Maybe it's what you need, someone with fresh eyes. It's work, boy, not a love affair."

"Work turns personal when they're in your space every day," he shot back, but the fire in his eyes faded. Riley whined, resting his head on Corbyn's shoulder until he received the attention he desired.

Edie's hand came up to pat his cheek. Hers was one of the few touches he didn't shrug off. Her voice took on that motherly tone that he had come to know over the years, and she told him, "If she gets that book moving, isn't that worth a little nuisance?"

He didn't answer, and the basement went quiet for a long moment.

"Stubborn as a mule," Edie muttered, softening it with a half-smile. "Always were—digging in 'til the last second, then bending on your own damn terms."

That dragged a grudging smirk from him against his better judgment. "I haven't bent yet."

"You will." She nodded, sounding sure. "I know you want this book to be good. If this editor can help, you'll let her take a swing." She looked down at Riley, who was now seeking her affection. "Plus, this mutt could use fresh meat to con."

Riley's ears perked, tail smacking the mat slowly and hopefully.

"Bath's cooling," Edie called over her shoulder, heading for the stairs. "Coffee will be done shortly, and Paul's frying eggs the way you like."

She climbed back up, steps creaking steadily. Corbyn watched her vanish, her tread fading into the kitchen's clatter when she opened the door. Riley glanced between him and the stairs, clearly torn between duty and the promise of bacon.

"Go," Corbyn sighed, and the dog bolted up with a grace that his bulk shouldn't have allowed.

Alone, Corbyn snatched his phone, thumb hovering over Jess's number, itching to unload after realizing this was an ambush. But what would it fix? Edie was correct; there was no escaping this. Sadie Reed was coming, whether he liked it or not.

February 5, 2025

-Sadie-

The car door creaked open, a gust of wind slapping Sadie awake. Somehow, she had managed to not drive the rental car into a ditch, the shift to driving on the opposite side of the road clicking blessedly fast. She yanked her bag from the trunk, stumbling a bit on Great Missenden's cobblestones.

Taking a moment, she scanned the buildings along the narrow street. A row of cottages lined the road; their walls covered with ivy, giving off a quaint vibe that brought a smile to her lips. As the street curled around a bend, she noticed a butcher's shop with a red awning and a post office with a charming thatched roof. It was like stepping into a postcard, and part of her still couldn't believe she had actually let Jess convince her to leave New York.

Her phone buzzed in her pocket, and for a moment she expected another text from Nate. Instead, it was a calendar reminder:

> First meeting with C. Pearce—tomorrow, 10 AM

Reality crashed into her once more. She wasn't here as a tourist to take in the sights, but as a professional with a job most editors would kill for. Or run screaming from according to the rumors.

The last time she'd been in England, she'd been seventeen and carefree. She had been convinced that literary greatness was in her future if she could just survive her college years. Instead, she carried the weight of having to save the career of a man who wasn't exactly known for being warm and fuzzy toward his editors.

"Just don't screw this up, Reed," she muttered to herself, drawing a curious glance from a passing local.

She forced herself to focus on the misty charm of Great Missenden, with its weathered buildings and winding lanes. If she thought about all the things that could go wrong for too long, her anxiety would only overwhelm her.

"Right," she muttered. "Check in at the inn. Sleep for approximately one million years. Then... save a book and figure out life?" It wasn't much of a plan, but it was hers, and Sadie felt the faintest flicker of hope for the first time in years.

She hefted her bag and turned toward the building behind her. The Roaring Stag looked like the very picture of a quaint pub in the English countryside. It was a Tudor-style building, with window flower boxes and a small courtyard on one side of the pub area. Above were a line of windows she assumed belonged to the guest rooms.

Sadie's lips quirked into a tired smile.

"Straight out of a British rom-com," she laughed under her breath. "Maybe Colin Firth's waiting inside with a cup of tea."

She stumbled through the creaking door, her carry-on thumping against the worn threshold. The mingled scent of wood smoke, ale, and baking scones hit her like a comforting blanket.

Behind the polished oak bar stood a woman with a platinum blonde bob that caught the glow of low lights. Her dark brown eyes were sharp, sizing Sadie up. It was clear this woman was the sort who would know all the comings and goings in the small village.

"You must be my last-minute reservation," the woman said, her voice brisk but not unkind. "Rough flight?"

Sadie opened her mouth to respond, but found herself too exhausted to form words. Instead, she nodded mutely and slumped onto a nearby bar stool, her bag thudding beside her on the floor.

Great first impression, Reed, she thought.

"I'm Maggie," the woman told her, leaning a bit over the bar as she tossed a rag over her shoulder.

"Sadie."

Glancing around the pub, she noticed a few men gathered in one corner. They eyed her warily, turning back to their breakfasts when she made eye contact. It wasn't exactly the warm welcome she had been hoping for, but she supposed it was normal for the locals to be cautious around outsiders.

"What's dragged you all the way to Great Missenden?" Maggie asked, sliding a cup of tea toward Sadie.

She took it gratefully, sipping a small amount of the hot liquid and letting it ease the dryness the flight had left in her throat.

"Work, actually," she told Maggie, mustering up a small smile despite her exhaustion. "I'm here to help a local author with his book."

"Only author around here would be Corbyn Pearce," the other woman replied, raising an eyebrow slightly. "Last I heard, he isn't open to visitors."

"So I've heard." Her shoulders drooped a bit. Apparently, Pearce had a reputation in the village as well. "But, I'm here to try."

"Well, I wish you the best of luck, love. He's pricklier than a hedgehog in a huff these days," Maggie said, a small smirk tugging at her lips. "He had a real spark once. Hopefully, you can sort out his scribbles."

Sadie leaned against the back of the stool, taking another sip of her tea. It was clear that Corbyn had been a regular fixture in the village at one time. She had read something on the plane about him being in a horrific car accident several years ago, and he had all but dropped off the face of the earth after that. It made her wonder exactly what she should expect when she arrived at his door the next morning. She had seen an old black-and-white headshot; he had been handsome in a rugged sort of way, with his chiseled features and sharp eyes. It was clear there was more to the story, as most people didn't just shut themselves away without a good reason.

"His estate is just down the road," Maggie continued, drawing Sadie back to the present. "He lives there with his housekeeper, Edie, and her husband."

Sadie gave a little nod before changing the subject away from the dreaded meeting tomorrow. "So, what's Great Missenden like? Anything I should know about while I'm here?"

Maggie's eyes brightened, clearly pleased by being asked about the village.

"Ah, where to begin? Small but not dull, if you know where to look," she said before leaning in conspiratorially. "See that lane up there?" She nodded toward the window. "Roald Dahl used to write his tales just around the corner. Got a museum dedicated to him now."

"I loved his books growing up," Sadie replied, perking up a little at the thought of exploring the museum.

"Most do," Maggie replied with a knowing smile. "Museum's worth a visit when you've got time. The trails leading up to the hills are lovely, too, if the weather permits."

"I'm not sure how much free time I'll have," Sadie admitted with a slight shrug.

"Well, if you do have time, London's only an hour by train," Maggie offered. "Though between your author and our little haunts, I suspect Great Missenden might catch you off guard."

Maggie's chatter flowed on while Sadie finished her tea. She learned about village quirks and tucked-away corners, a little mental list of places to visit forming in her mind.

A brass key slid across the bar and into Sadie's vision just as a yawn escaped her.

"Right, that's enough chinwag for now, love," Maggie told her, the woman's expression suddenly turning sympathetic. "You look knackered. Your room's upstairs, number 7. Get some rest, eh? Dinner starts at 5, and tonight's special is shepherd's pie. You don't want to miss that."

"Thanks, Maggie," Sadie replied, the weight of her fatigue slamming into her. "I'll see you tonight then."

She hoisted her carry-on off the floor, its straps digging into her palm like someone had snuck a stack of books in it while she chatted with Maggie.

The narrow staircase moaned under her feet as she forced herself to climb. Doubt flickered for a moment. Could she really do this? Could she actually be the salvation everyone seemed to think Pearce needed?

When she reached the door with the number 7 on the left side, she used the key to let herself in. The room was snug, with sloped ceilings and faded floral curtains, but it was quiet and cozy. A quilted bed stood before her, and her shoulders dropped with relief.

"Oh, thank God," she rasped, her bag thudding to the boards. Jet lag hit hard with a wave that buckled her knees. She staggered to the bed, shoes kicked off in a clumsy tangle, and crashed onto the quilt. The softness of the mattress threatened to swallow her whole, and she sighed in contentment.

The quilt smelled faintly of lavender, and she was being pulled under almost instantly. All thoughts of Corbyn Pearce and his book vanished as her body and mind gave in to sleep.

February 6, 2025

-Corbyn-

Corbyn glared at the blank page before him, willing the words to flow from his pen. The late morning sunlight filtering through dusty windows only illuminated the mess of papers strewn across his oak desk. He ran a hand through his dark hair, a nervous habit he had picked up after the accident when touching his face became something to avoid, pushing it out of his eyes as he hunched further over the page. He'd been sitting here for three hours, and the page remained stubbornly, infuriatingly blank, like the current state of his mind.

"Bloody useless," he muttered, tossing the pen onto the desk where it rolled against a stack of research notes he hadn't touched in days, his left hand clenching in his lap.

Leaning back, he rubbed his left hand, massaging the stiff fingers that no longer cooperated. His mind kept circling back to the editor who would be arriving any moment. Arriving so she could "fix" his disaster. Four bestsellers, critics falling over themselves with praise, and now he was stuck.

He wondered if she would see right through him. Would she realize the accident hadn't just mangled his body but had stolen whatever spark had made his writing worth reading? The thought churned his stomach more than the pain ever could.

"Stop it," he growled to himself, shaking his head as if to dislodge the thoughts. "Focus, you git."

Riley huffed near the fireplace, a sprawling tangle of long limbs and wiry tan fur. The Irish Wolfhound's tail thumped against the warped floorboards as if trying to draw him from his internal spiral.

"At least one of us is content," Corbyn muttered. The dog's ears perked at his voice, as he watched him with unwavering devotion.

His shaggy hair fell forward again, partially obscuring his eyes. They narrowed in frustration, strands brushing his stubbled jaw. He needed a cut, but that would mean submitting to Edie's mother-hen routine and listening to her go on about how he should take better care of himself. With an impatient gesture, he pushed the hair back once more.

The sound of distant tires on the gravel drive pulled Corbyn from his thoughts as he glanced at the clock. It appeared Jess's miracle worker was right on time. Deep down, he knew his book needed help; however, admitting that to anyone else was something that would not happen.

The sound of a car door slamming shut caught Riley's attention, the hound's massive head lifting from the ground. Pushing up from the seat, Corbyn bit back a swear as his frustration with the situation grew. He worked alone, and he liked it that way. Alone was much more straightforward than having someone constantly hover over your shoulder, making suggestions.

"Stay," he commanded Riley, as the doorbell chimed. The hound looked up at him with puppy-dog eyes that said, *You can't be serious*, and Corbyn sighed. "Fine. Come on then."

Each step toward the heavy oak door felt like a march to the gallows. Corbyn's mind raced, conjuring up a dozen sharp remarks to drive away this intruder before they could breach his sanctuary. If he was lucky, she'd be gone in a day or two instead of the week he promised Jess.

He yanked the door open, an insult ready on his lips, but it never came.

A woman stood on his doorstep, long hair the color of butterscotch loose around her face, windblown and catching the weak February sunlight. It framed gray eyes that met his directly, steady and unflinching, where most people quickly looked away. A jolt shot through him, a tightening of his chest that he couldn't explain. He snapped back to attention when Riley pushed his head through the doorway, tail thumping eagerly.

"Mr. Pearce," she said, drawing Corbyn's attention away from the dog, "I'm Sadie Reed." She offered a small, professional smile as she extended her right hand. "Jessica Harper sent me."

Riley shoved fully past him, nearly knocking him off balance. The wolfhound's body trembled with barely restrained excitement as his tail whipped hard enough to sway his whole rear.

"Riley, no..." Corbyn grunted, but the dog was already focused on the newcomer.

The hound lurched forward, nose shoving at this stranger, tail smacking the door frame. Sadie quickly pushed her bag aside to dig her fingers behind Riley's ears. Her smile was wide as she practically cooed, "Hey, big fella. Look at you."

Riley did his best to charm a potential new source of scratches and snacks by nuzzling against her side. She looked back up, and something sharp twisted in Corbyn's chest once more; it was damn annoying.

"Come in then," he said, stepping aside, left hand clenching again.

Sadie stepped over the threshold, and Corbyn felt a twitch in his gut. The way she didn't shy away from meeting his gaze threw him off, and he refused to let that be the reason he caved.

"I don't need help," he barked before she could open her mouth, his voice cutting through the still house. "I work alone, and the last thing I need is an editor breathing down my neck."

Sadie's eyes popped wide, his snap clearly catching her off guard. For a second, he thought she'd bolt, but then her stare steadied, and her chin raised defiantly. With a grunt of frustration, he turned and trudged through the living room back toward the hall that led to his study.

"My boss seemed to think otherwise," Sadie replied, her tone neutral but firm as she followed him. "She mentioned you missed a few deadlines."

His right hand tightened on the study door handle, opening it with more force than was strictly necessary. She wasn't wrong. He had missed several deadlines as he sat staring at the page day after day, hoping *Echoes of Ash* would write itself.

Undeterred, Sadie crossed the threshold, her tone taking on a patient, calming tone that both soothed and annoyed him as she said, "She believes in your work. We *both* do."

Riley nudged her hand with his nose, eliciting another small smile from her, and Corbyn leaned against the side of the desk, feigning casualness as she took her first look at the state of his study. Riley flopped by the fireplace as Sadie stood a few feet away, lower lip caught between her teeth. There were manuscript pages scattered, reference books stacked precariously, and pens strewn everywhere but where they belonged. He gritted his teeth, suddenly aware of how unkempt he must appear.

Finally, he broke the silence, his voice rough when he said, "No matter what Harper thinks, I don't need a babysitter."

Sadie shifted her weight but didn't retreat from his harsh tone.

"Jess thought you needed a developmental editor to help finish *Echoes of Ash*. The deadline was..."

"I know when the bloody deadline was," he cut in, jaw tightening, the muscles in his neck tensing. "What I don't know is why she thought sending someone to hover over me would magically produce words that aren't coming."

"I don't hover," Sadie said, her voice level. "I collaborate."

He made a dismissive sound in the back of his throat.

"I don't do collaboration. I work alone. Always have," he insisted, shaking his head.

"That stops now."

The simple statement hung between them. Corbyn straightened from his casual pose, wincing as his spine protested before he moved behind his desk, his left hand clenched into a fist at his side.

"Ms. Reed…"

"Sadie," she corrected.

"Ms. Reed," he continued, gritting his teeth. "I appreciate that Ms. Harper is in a difficult position. The publisher wants the book. I'm contracted to deliver it. But having a stranger in my space, telling me how to write my own characters, frankly, is not going to work."

Sadie, to his amazement, stood her ground, steadfast in the face of his frustration. She was several inches shorter than him, but a certain defiance in her stance made him wonder just how hard he would have to push before she simply threw in the towel.

"I'm not here to tell you how to write your characters," she said, crossing her arms over her chest as she looked up at him. "I'm here to help you navigate whatever's blocking you from finishing this book."

His scowl deepened as he made a point to study one of the half-written pages lying on his desk.

"Nothing's blocking me except the constant pressure from people who think writing is like flipping a switch."

"From what I understand, you've been stuck at chapter fifteen for months," Sadie replied, her voice closer now. She'd moved toward him, scanning the paper that had grabbed his attention.

Corbyn whipped around, eyes narrowing as the truth of just how screwed his writing was washed over him.

Leaning forward, his hands rested on the surface of the desk as he argued, "She had no right."

"She's the one ensuring your book gets published," Sadie insisted, a hint of steel beneath her calm exterior, and she matched his stance on the opposite side. "And she believes in this book. In you."

"She believes in her profit margins," he countered, but the words didn't quite ring true. Jess was the only reason he still had this opportunity, allowing him time to heal even though he was under contract. She had defended him to the board when deadlines slipped, fighting for extensions he didn't deserve, all while he did everything to make Jess and her team's lives as difficult as possible.

"Let me be clear about something," he told her, his voice dropping to a lower register as he leaned closer still. "I don't trust editors. I don't trust their so-called 'process.' And I especially don't trust that."

He pointed to the tablet he saw peeking from her bag. When she turned her head, a familiar scent he couldn't quite place hit him. Realizing how close they were, he shifted back quickly.

"My tablet?" she asked, raising an eyebrow when she straightened her posture and looked back up at him.

"Aside from my phone, technology and I aren't on speaking terms."

"So I've heard, though that might be difficult in this century," she quipped back, a little smirk tugging at her lips.

"I manage," he replied, his tone making it clear the subject was non-negotiable. That smirk of hers had drawn his attention to her mouth, and his gaze dropped to look for a moment all on their own, much to his irritation. "Pen and paper first. Typed after, but nothing gets saved to your magical cloud, emailed, or put anywhere else someone might gain unauthorized access."

He watched her consider his words, her head tilting a bit when she said, "Jess mentioned you had some issues with..."

"An intern hacked into one of the editor's emails," he cut her off, his voice tight. "Three chapters of my last book were leaked online before it was even half-written, to be torn apart by anyone with a web browser. Do you have any idea what that does to a writer?" His right hand slammed against the desk for emphasis, the sound sharp in the quiet room.

The sudden movement caused Sadie to jump. Shame flooded him almost instantly, hot and unwelcome, and he stepped back and moved to the window. He'd never been that man. The one who acted out angrily, causing fear in those around him.

Sadie straightened her shoulders, quickly regaining her composure.

"I understand your concerns about digital security," she said, the professional mask slipping back into place. "We can work with paper copies. That's not an issue."

"There is no 'we,' Reed," he insisted, his voice taking on a sharper edge.

"You promised a week," she countered, the quirk of her eyebrow a challenge. "At least give me that, let me prove that I can help you not only push this book over the finish line, but make it your best work to date."

There was something in her tone that caught him off guard. She wasn't trying to flatter him; it was clear she truly believed every word, and it was... disarming.

Riley's soft whine drew both of their attention. The dog had raised his head, soulful eyes moving between them as if following the volley of words.

"Even your dog knows you're just being willful," Sadie said, the faintest smile touching her lips.

"Only because he sees you as a new source for treats," Corbyn muttered, shaking his head at the giant dog. Riley's tail thumped faster in response as if it were a compliment. "Have it your way," he said, running his fingers through his hair again as he moved back to the desk. He sorted through stacks of paper, feeling his frustration grow as the lack of organization became apparent.

Finally, he located what he was looking for and thrust it in her direction as he added, "This is the first act of the book. You can look through it in the living room, but it's not to leave this house. And that tablet of yours stays in your bag."

She crossed the short distance with a single nod. When her fingers brushed his as she took the draft, his world seemed to tilt as a long forgotten sensation ran up his arm. He stiffened, his gut twisting. Sadie's eyes had gone wide as she stared at him, neither speaking nor seeming to breathe. It was another of Riley's soft whines that broke the spell, tail thumping as he maneuvered between them, looking for attention.

"You have the manuscript. The living room is that way," he growled, voice low and harsh, gesturing sharply toward the door. He caught her reaction, a flicker of hurt and perhaps fear making her eyes stormy. Her lips parted as she stepped back, papers clutched tight in her hand, and he saw her steady façade cracking just enough to sting him before she turned and walked toward the door.

He followed behind, holding the door open until she passed through and disappeared into the hall. With a satisfying bang, he slammed the door shut, leaning against it momentarily as he caught his breath. Another one of Riley's plaintive whines broke the silence.

"Don't start," Corbyn grumbled at the dog.

He forced himself to move back to his desk, collapsing into his chair with a grunt of pain. The unfinished pages on his desk swam before his eyes, the words blurring into an indecipherable mess.

"Bloody hell," he hissed, running a trembling hand through his hair. "Get it together, Pearce."

But try as he might, he couldn't focus. He'd allowed her to take the manuscript. The walls he'd built around himself suddenly felt a little less solid, a little less impenetrable. And that terrified him more than he cared to admit.

February 6, 2025

-Sadie-

Sadie leaned against the wall at the end of the hallway. Corbyn's demand that she leave the study had reverberated through Pearce House. Her body melted against the wall as the adrenaline from the confrontation drained away.

Her fingers still felt the ghost of that brief contact with Corbyn's hand while taking the manuscript. A strange feeling had run through her, something she hadn't felt in years.

Between that spark and the fright from the moment he slammed his hand on the desk, she felt her heart racing. It had been an automatic response carved into her by years with Nate and his temper tantrums, but Corbyn had immediately stepped back, and something that looked like regret had flickered across his face. Unlike Nate, who would press closer and use her vulnerability as a weapon, Corbyn had given her space.

It was a small thing, but it was unexpected. And in that moment, something fragile and hopeful fluttered beneath her frustration. That hope hadn't lasted, though.

The back of her head hit the wall, a dull thud that matched her deflating spirits. Perhaps she had really gotten in over her head with this assignment.

"Come on, Reed," she coached herself, trying to summon an ounce of the determination that had propelled her across an ocean. "You've dealt with worse."

But her pep talk did nothing to steady her as another wave of exhaustion crashed over her. The five-hour jump from New York felt like a leap across worlds, leaving her body confused and her mind foggy. No amount of sleep would cure the fatigue weighing her down.

Nate had often told her she could be a nagging know-it-all when it came to editing. Corbyn seemed like the sort who would bristle the moment she tried to offer any kind of criticism, and she couldn't help but wonder if she'd made a monumental mistake in coming to Great Missenden. But then she looked down at the stack of papers in her hand. The confrontation hadn't been a complete failure; he'd given her everything he had completed thus far, which was a step in the right direction.

The smell of rich, savory food hit her, followed by the sound of clanking pots. She followed the scent through the living room toward the back of the house, and her weary eyes landed on the figure standing at the stove in the kitchen. The woman wiped her hands on her apron as she turned at the sound of Sadie's footsteps. Her silver-streaked hair was gathered in a loose bun, and her warm brown eyes peeked at Sadie through wire-rimmed glasses, framed by the kind of laugh lines that only come from decades of smiling at other people's chaos.

"Rough go with him already, love?" The woman's voice carried a no-nonsense lilt that made Sadie wonder how she put up with Corbyn's mood swings.

"You could say that," she replied, offering her a tired smile. "But I did manage to secure this before he tossed me out of his office."

Sadie held up the manuscript pages like a prize and received a knowing look in return. She had a feeling she wouldn't have to pretend with this woman that things hadn't been tense with the manor's resident grump.

"Oh, you poor thing," the woman clucked, her motherly concern washing over Sadie like a balm. "Come on, let's get some tea before you melt into the floorboards. I'm Edie, by the way."

"Sadie," she said in return.

Her bag slid to the floor with a soft thump as she sank onto one of the stools lined up along the kitchen island.

Edie bustled over, sliding a steaming mug of tea and a warm scone across the counter, the scent of bergamot wrapped around her.

"Thanks," Sadie rasped, gripping the mug tight. The heat seeped into her hands, a jolt against the cold sting of Corbyn's brush-off.

"Eat up, love," Edie said, nodding at the scone. "Clotted cream's better than moping over his nonsense."

"For a moment I thought things were starting to go well," she mumbled, taking a tentative bite. Her cheeks warmed, and she closed her eyes, savoring the flavor. The scones Maggie had served that morning had been good, but Edie had a gift.

"He's prickly, that one." Edie leaned against the counter, a wry smile playing at her lips as she regarded Sadie with sympathy and amusement.

The click of nails on hardwood announced a new arrival, and the estate's Irish Wolfhound padded into the kitchen. He trotted over to Sadie, soulful eyes glinting as he nosed her hand with a soft whine. She couldn't help but smile at the gentle giant, sure he would be her favorite manor resident.

"Well, hello there," Sadie murmured, scratching behind his ears. The wiry fur was warm under her fingers, and the dog leaned into her touch with obvious pleasure. "At least someone's glad I'm here."

"That's Riley," Edie explained. "Corbyn's bark might be worse than his bite, but Riley here's all love, and no teeth."

Sadie's smile grew as she replied, "I think Riley and I are going to get along just fine. Any chance he's looking for an editor?"

Edie laughed, turning to stir the stew that was simmering on the stove. The aroma evoked a sense of comfort that washed over her body.

"When he plants himself," Edie said over her shoulder, her voice dropping like she was letting Sadie in on a hard-won trick, "you've got to hold your line and stare him down 'til he shifts. He'll test you, push you to see if you'll bend. But once he sees you're not running, he starts to listen. Don't let him scare you off."

Sadie blinked, unconvinced as she replied, "I have a feeling I'll be lucky if he doesn't toss me out on my ear by sundown."

"Nonsense," Edie tutted, turning to face her. Those warm brown eyes crinkled with a knowing glint that made Sadie squirm. "You've got more fire in you than you let on, I'd wager. You managed to get him to hand over those pages."

Sadie's lips twitched, a tired half-smirk. "Guess I'll give it a try," she rasped, tea warming her hands. "Not much left to lose."

Edie's mouth curved, approval flickering in her eyes. "That's the way, love."

A slow tread echoed from the hall, and Riley practically pranced in place with anticipation, earning a soft chuckle from Sadie. Corbyn appeared a moment later, hair mussed from raking hands through it. He didn't glance Sadie's way, just jerked his chin at the dog.

"Walk, boy."

"Mind the puddles this time, eh?" Edie called from the kitchen. "Last go nearly did me in with the scrubbing."

"No promises," Corbyn grunted. It was a rough huff that might've been amusement. His blue eyes met Edie's for a beat, softening just enough to hint at affection before he tugged the door open and stepped out, Riley trailing into the mist.

Edie watched them go, then turned to Sadie, wiping her hands on her apron. "Make yourself at home. Kettle's on if you need more."

Sadie nodded, clutching the tea and the pages Corbyn had left in her care. She made her way into the living room and sank onto the comfortable sofa, fighting back a sigh. She placed the mug on a nearby table, giving *Echoes of Ash* her full attention—scrawled lines, crossed-out chunks, and a tangle of ink. She rubbed her eyes and flipped the first page.

"Alright, Pearce," she muttered, her voice firm despite the jet lag dragging at her. "Let's see what I'm dealing with."

February 7, 2025

-Corbyn-

In the soft morning light that filtered in through the study's ivy-covered window, Corbyn stared at the blank page like it was an old enemy. He had hoped that the words would flow magically this morning, if only to prove to everyone that he didn't need Sadie Reed meddling in his work. Yet, here he was, still stuck, frustrated, and dreading the appearance of a certain American editor.

When Riley's head lifted from the floor, tail thumping, he knew his solitude had ended. Her footsteps echoed down the hall a moment later, and he quickly hunched over and grabbed a half-finished page to make it *seem* like he'd been writing.

In his peripheral vision, he saw her pause in the doorway. Looking up, he found Sadie standing there, his manuscript pages held tight against her chest, a tense look on her face, undoubtedly preparing herself for another round of verbal sparring. Riley's tail thudded against the floor, breaking the silence, and Corbyn's jaw tightened as she stepped through the door to greet the dog.

"You're early," he muttered, his words clipped, hoping she'd take the hint and retreat to the kitchen, where she had been talking to Edie.

"Not by much," she replied, her voice steady and unshaken by his tone. She crossed the room, pausing before his desk, and then placed the marked-up manuscript in front of him. "I thought we could have a quick chat about the flashback scene."

"What's wrong with it?" Corbyn asked, already feeling his patience waning.

"Nothing is *wrong*, exactly," she said, shifting her weight. "It just slows the pacing."

His shoulders stiffened at the sight of all the red ink on the page. His gaze sharpened as he looked at her, ready to defend his work. He was used to his editors focusing on grammatical issues and making broad comments about structure and pacing. What was staring up at him from the page went well beyond that.

"The pacing is fine," he said, looking down again at the page he had been pretending to write in an attempt to dismiss her from his office.

"It's a little heavy-handed, don't you think?" she asked calmly, her voice causing his eyes to snap up to meet her gaze. "You could hint at Shaw's past instead of spelling it out. Also, the arson timeline doesn't add up."

A muscle in his jaw twitched, irritation tightening his voice.

"There's nothing wrong with my timeline." The words were rough with the various emotions he was trying to keep in check. The frustration he felt toward himself and his inability to put pen to paper was the one most desperately trying to break free.

She leaned in, clearly unshaken by his snapping tone.

"But you see what I mean, right? If you shift this scene earlier, it makes more sense."

"It's fine as it is," he repeated, knowing it was a lie. He could feel his control slipping. He rose, crossing his arms over his chest as he stared at her from the other side of the desk.

To his surprise, Sadie held her ground, her steady gaze met his as she posed a question that felt like a punch to the gut.

"Fine isn't what you're really after, is it?"

The question hung there, the air between them tightening. Riley lifted his head, a soft whine cut through, clearly sensing the storm brewing between them. Corbyn's face flushed, whether with embarrassment or anger, he wasn't sure, and he clenched his left hand to stop its trembling. He managed to fight back a grimace of pain as his joints and muscles protested the sudden movement.

The next words out of his mouth were a snarl. "You've been here for one day and already you're hovering, poking around like you own the place. It's not even nine in the morning."

Once again, she didn't flinch. Instead, she stood taller, a little more defiant when she replied, "I'm not hovering, I'm doing my job."

Her steadiness only fueled his frustration. "I don't need you managing my every thought like some bloody nanny." His voice came out in a harsh bark, and he paced toward the window. "Leave your notes. I'll look at them later."

His back was to her, but he could feel those gray eyes boring into him. If he turned and faced her hard stare, she might see right through all his posturing to the real problem. He was terrified that she would see a washed-up has-been who would never complete another work for the rest of his life.

"No time like the present," she said, her voice taking on a slightly sharper edge that hadn't been there before. Apparently, even Saint Sadie Reed had her limits. "You're the one dragging your feet."

He heard her sigh, and the sound caught his attention. He found himself turning to look at her, and he saw a nearly imperceptible shift in her expression. There was a tightness around her eyes, and her shoulders started to round forward in such a way that suggested this was more than professional frustration. It was gone almost instantly, but Corbyn caught it, filing it away to ponder later when the infuriating woman wasn't standing just a few feet away.

"My role here is to help you, Mr. Pearce, not to make your life more difficult," she said, her voice steady, hiding the troubling thought that had just flashed through her mind. "You don't strike me as the type to settle for mediocre work, and neither am I. Either work with me to make this book the best it can be, or we can waste precious time bickering. Your choice."

Finally, he exhaled, a ragged sound—more exasperation than surrender—as some of the urge to fight drained from his body. She was right, he would burn the bloody book before he'd let them publish anything that came close to mediocre.

"If we must, we'll try it your way. But I have conditions," he said, his eyes pinning hers, and he silently dared her to push further.

The only sign she had heard him was the lift of one eyebrow. He took that as a sign to continue.

"We can have brief meetings," he said, feeling the need to regain some control over this situation. "Mornings only. And no more than ten minutes."

"You and I both know that isn't nearly enough." She crossed her arms, staring him down. "We're going to need longer sessions. Ninety minutes three times a week, as well as daily check-ins."

Corbyn's jaw tightened. "Once a week. One hour. No more."

"Twice a week, ninety minutes each session and twenty-minute morning check-ins," she countered.

Surprised by her counteroffer and how she looked up at him as if challenging him to argue further, he found himself raising an eyebrow.

"You're negotiating with me in my own house?"

"I'm ensuring this process has a chance of success," she told him evenly. "One hour a week isn't enough time to make meaningful progress, especially with a project already behind schedule."

They stared at each other across the study, a silent battle of wills. Riley came to stand between them, gaze bouncing back and forth, his tail beating faster with the tension. A soft whine cut through the tension, and her eyes dropped to the Wolfhound before calling him over to scratch behind his ears.

"Once a week, ninety minutes." He found himself grudgingly feeling a small amount of respect for how she handled his mood. When she simply stared at him, his shoulders dropped in defeat. "Twice a week. Sixty minutes each and ten-minute morning check-ins. That's final."

She nodded, the corners of her mouth lifting in a small smile. He felt a sense of déjà vu as he looked at her, something funny twisting in his chest. He quickly lowered his gaze as he returned to his chair.

"Agreed," she said simply, before leaving his study.

He looked up, his eyes lingering on her back as she left. A mix of irritation and confusion flooded his mind as he tried to figure out what had just happened. That smile of hers made it clear she had won this round, and apparently not just in terms of the book.

Looking down, he found she had left the manuscript on his desk, her red ink staring up at him, almost daring him to look at her suggestions. Slowly, cautiously, he picked them up—as if expecting them to bite him. With a sigh of defeat, he began flipping through the pages to find out what the formidable Saint Sadie, savior of lost and broken authors, had suggested.

✳✳✳

-Sadie-

Sadie fell back onto the quilted bed that evening. The faint scent of lavender, combined with the steady patter of rain against the windowpane, eased the lingering tension from her body. She kicked off her boots and let herself sink deeper into the mattress with a contented sigh.

Her body was weary from a day spent trying to wrangle Corbyn's scribbles into something closer to the work she knew he could produce. It was a strange juxtaposition to the buzz of success. He had reluctantly agreed to her terms, but only after careful negotiation. She had suspected his pride in his work would be the key to breaking down his resistance, and she had been right.

It had come at a cost, though. His comment about not needing a nanny had struck a familiar chord within her, conjuring up arguments from her past. She had quickly pushed those feelings aside, not wanting him to see the moment of doubt and weakness, but it didn't change the fact that his words had hit their mark.

A cheerful chime broke the silence, and she pushed herself up so she could retrieve her tablet from her bag. Jess's name appeared on the screen, and she felt herself perk up at the prospect of talking to her best friend. If anyone could ease her fears, it was Jess.

Accepting the call, she leaned back against the headboard of the bed, a smile forming when she saw Jess's familiar face on the screen. She hadn't realized how much she had missed Jess already, as she propped the tablet against a pillow.

"Sadie! There you are," Jess exclaimed, her smile brightening Sadie's mood even further. "Well? How'd it go with our recluse?"

"I survived the first two days," she said. "He tried to fight me this morning when I said we needed regular meetings to discuss edits. But, I got him to commit to check-ins and a couple of longer meetings each week."

"Well, you're already miles ahead of everyone else who's worked with him," Jess said, and Sadie watched a proud smile tug at her friend's lips. "I told you that you were a miracle worker."

Sadie couldn't help but laugh, although she wasn't sure she deserved the title. Corbyn had already managed to stumble upon her buried insecurities.

"I wouldn't go that far," she replied, studying the way her fingers twirled around a loose thread from the comforter. "He hasn't actually taken any of my notes yet."

"Just keep doing what you're doing," Jess advised, her face softening in understanding. "He'll come around once he realizes your process works."

Sadie hesitated, doubt flickering like a shadow in the back of her mind.

"I hope so. This book truly does have the potential to be a bestseller, but what if I push too hard? He's just... he can be tough to read, and I don't want him to shut down because he thinks I'm nagging him."

Jess tipped her head slightly, her voice softer when she replied, "So, you let him stew until he realizes you're right."

She dipped her head in a quick nod, the hard knot in her chest loosening as she exhaled. Jess always seemed to know exactly what to say when Sadie doubted her abilities.

"Thanks, Jess. I was running on empty after today."

"Always got your back," Jess said, her grin widening, bolstering Sadie even through the screen. "Alright, enough shop talk," Jess said, leaning closer to the screen. "How's my favorite world traveler holding up in the wilds of England? Found any cute pub locals to sweep you off your feet yet?"

Sadie snorted, a sound somewhere between a laugh and a groan, as she tugged the quilt higher over her knees.

"Oh, sure, between wrangling Pearce and dodging rain puddles, I'm a regular Elizabeth Bennet."

"Well, as long as you're not letting your thoughts be haunted by a certain asshole back here in New York, I fully support you using your free time to be just that," Jess said with a little smirk. "You need to find your spark again, Sadie... and maybe England can do that for you."

"God, I miss you," Sadie admitted, voice soft. "This place is growing on me, but it's not going to be the same without your terrible singing on karaoke night."

"Rude!" Jess gasped, clutching her chest in mock offense. "My 'Bohemian Rhapsody' is a masterpiece, and you know it."

"Tell me what's been going on with you," Sadie laughed, needing to change the subject.

"I went on a date the other night and it ended up being one of those creepers who doesn't look one bit like his profile photo," she replied, making a disgusted face that caused Sadie to snort. "I'm thinking of giving up and just getting a cat."

"No, you can't do that," Sadie said, trying to give Jess a pep talk. "You are a brilliant, successful editor. There's nothing you can't do."

Jess's smile faltered at the mention of her job title, and she looked away for a moment.

"I know that look," she said softly. "What's going on, Jess?"

"It's nothing for you to worry about," Jess replied, and Sadie raised an eyebrow at her friend's face on the screen. Jess hesitated for a moment, and then said, "Marketing is getting antsy about Corbyn's book. They're talking about pulling the budget if we don't show substantial progress soon. They're looking for someone to blame if this fails... and that someone would be me."

Sadie could hear the stress underlying Jess's typically confident tone. This wasn't just about Corbyn's book; it was about the entire publishing ecosystem balancing on a knife's edge.

"We need this book," Jess continued, her voice dropping. "I've been assuring them that if they're patient, he'll deliver for so long they no longer believe me."

"I promise you, I'm working on it," Sadie assured her.

Jess nodded, letting out a slow breath. "Get some sleep, Sadie. You sound like you've been running on fumes. Tomorrow's another day."

"Yes, boss," Sadie replied, the familiar banter a comfort.

"And Sadie?" Jess's voice caught her before she could end the call. "You've got this. I wouldn't have sent you if I didn't believe that completely."

The call ended, leaving Sadie in the stillness of her room. She couldn't help but replay what Jess had told her about the marketing cuts. So much was tied up in making sure this book succeeded.

Glancing at the bedside table, she looked at the leather journal Jess had given her a few days after she had left Nate. It had been a silent challenge from her best friend that she needed to reclaim everything Nate had stolen from her, especially her writing.

She picked it up, trailing her fingers along the leather spine, hesitating for a moment before reaching for a pen from her bag. Taking a breath, she let herself write whatever came to mind. She didn't worry about structure or flow. She just let the words pour out for the first time in years.

It was nearly an hour later when she finally stopped, looking down at the pages she had filled with her thoughts. It wasn't much, and to anyone else the ramblings wouldn't make sense, but it was a start.

February 12, 2025

-Sadie-

Sadie stepped out of The Roaring Stag into a crisp February morning, appreciating the fresh air. After nearly a week of trying to work on Corbyn's manuscript in his living room, her shoulders ached. He had made some progress, and her mind had begged for a break to explore the village.

She looked down the street, taking in the picturesque village. In the distance, she could see red brick cottages, smoke rising from their chimneys. Across the street were several Tudor-style buildings that housed various local shops. There was even a small bookshop a few doors down, where she had stopped the previous evening and fallen into an easy conversation with the man who owned it.

She wandered past the butcher's shop, its red awning waving in the breeze. Sausages and cuts of meat sat in the window, and the sign above the door read *Williams Family Butchers—Est. 1937*. Next door, the tea shop's windows were steamed up, shapes of people hunched over mugs barely showing through the haze. The tea shop was even older, serving the village since 1908.

The village felt both timeless and lived-in. Sadie pulled her notebook from her bag and quickly noted: *Great Missenden—time moves differently here. Not slower, just... different.*

As she returned the notebook to her bag, her gaze caught on a splash of pastel blue further down the street. The Roald Dahl Museum seemed to call to her, and her feet carried her toward it. She paused outside, studying the quirky façade. A small smile curved her lips, and she decided there was no better way to spend her day off than to explore the creative space of an author who truly understood the magic of something unexpected.

Inside, children were darting between exhibits, parents trailing behind them. This place celebrated imagination rather than the hushed reverence of a more traditional museum, and the energy was infectious.

Sadie drifted through the galleries, occasionally pausing to look more closely at photographs or read some of the papers on display, items from his childhood. She wondered if he had foreseen what his words would become. Or had he simply been a boy with a pencil and a head full of wonderings?

She continued into the Solo Gallery, where her steps slowed involuntarily. Dahl's Writing Hut stood before her. It was a meticulous replica of the space where he'd created worlds. Yellow pencils sharpened to stubs lay arranged beside sheets of paper, as if waiting for genius. A foil ball fashioned from chocolate wrappers perched like a strange metallic planet among the ordered chaos of the desk.

Sadie's throat tightened. This was what a writer's life looked like. It wasn't glamorous or extraordinary in its components, yet the space felt sacred.

She lowered herself into the green armchair that had been set up for visitors, its worn fabric cradling her as she tried to imagine what it must have been like for him to sit for hours just creating. Her eyes fluttered closed momentarily, and she could almost picture Dahl leaning over his writing board, scribbling the first lines of *Charlie and the Chocolate Factory*.

It had been months, maybe years, if she was being completely honest with herself, since she'd written anything. Editing was safe. Editing was useful. Editing hadn't left her vulnerable to critiques or led her to believe her writing wasn't worthy enough to be read by anyone. But sitting here, she felt that urge to put words on a page that were her own. To create rather than correct.

In the museum shop, she paused before a display of notebooks and pens, tempted to add to her collection. Instead, she picked up a Village Trail map from a stack near the register.

"The green trail takes you up to the hills," the cashier offered when she saw Sadie looking over the map. "There are good views of the Misbourne Valley."

Sadie studied the simple map, noting the path leading from Church Street to the Chiltern Hills. Open space. Fresh air. It sounded glorious after days cooped up with Corbyn's tightly plotted murder mysteries.

She passed by the crowded courtyard café, stepping back onto the street. The village continued its quiet Thursday morning routine around her, unaware that something had shifted inside Sadie while visiting the museum. There was a flicker of an idea for a story, something she hadn't felt in a very long time. Perhaps it wouldn't amount to anything, but the fact that she felt it at all gave her hope.

Reaching the top of the trail, Sadie took a moment to catch her breath. Her calves burned, unused to the drastic change in elevation, and she leaned against an old oak tree for support.

"Not as fit as I thought," she murmured, her words forming clouds that dissipated into the cool air.

When she regained her ability to breathe, she climbed the last few feet to a lookout point she had spotted up ahead. The beauty of the English countryside sprawled out before her, and for a moment, she was lost to the majesty of it. The Chilterns and the

Misbourne River below looked almost unreal, and part of her wished she could stay in this very moment forever.

She spotted a bench sitting nearby, its wood gray from years of exposure to the open air. The bench creaked beneath her weight, but it seemed solid as she settled in. Placing her bag beside her, she pulled out her notebook, opening to the next blank page.

Even though she had been writing all week, she hesitated. Most of what she had written had been more stream of consciousness than actual storytelling. The idea of filling the page before her with a creative piece had her frozen in terror.

What if the words wouldn't come? What if they did, but were terrible?

"Stop it," she whispered, the breeze carrying the command. "Just write something. Anything."

She uncapped her pen, and she took a deep breath, letting the fresh air calm her nerves. Perhaps this was a bit like what Corbyn was going through, that fear that whatever went onto the paper somehow wouldn't be good enough. A wave of empathy washed over her, a sort of understanding that she had been lacking before.

Taking a breath, she closed her eyes. She saw a pair of familiar eyes, Corbyn's at first, the way they watched her with a quiet intensity when she spoke. Then, another pair. These eyes were full of life, light dancing within their depths at the idea of finding another literary buff on a train.

Opening her eyes, she began to write.

New Year's Eve, London Underground, 2009. The train car swayed, bodies pressed together like sardines as the Northern Line rumbled beneath the city. She hadn't meant to meet his eyes, but once she did, the world seemed to slow. Blue eyes. The bluest she'd ever seen, like a clear winter sky or the ocean on a perfect day. His hand brushed hers on the pole, and something electric passed between them, a spark she'd never forget.

She was pulled away too soon, never to learn the stranger's name. Instead, she was left always wondering: what if?

She paused, surprised by how easily the words were flowing. She wasn't sure why she had chosen that particular moment. It had been so brief, practically over before it even started. Yet, it had stuck with her all these years later. She'd never told anyone about that moment, about the stranger on the train or the way she had felt when his fingers brushed hers.

Looking down at the page once more, she continued writing. She wrote without judgment, without her internal editor questioning word choice or metaphor strength. This wasn't for Jess, or Nate, or anyone else. There was no one here to call it "pretentious garbage." This was for her alone, and that made it feel all the more precious.

Years later, she would imagine him sometimes and wonder if he remembered the girl with red hair clutching poetry books. Or if he too had felt that jolt, that spark that passed between them? She'd secretly imagined him living a thousand different lives. A writer, perhaps, or an artist. Someone who sees the world in all its beauty and pain. Someone who would have valued her words instead of burying them.

Sometimes, she even allowed herself to dream that they met again. No crowded train this time, but a quiet spot. A bookshop, maybe, both reaching for the same volume. Their fingers would touch, and when they felt that spark, they would look at each other and just know that they had been given a second chance.

After what might have been ten minutes or an hour, she paused, hand cramping slightly. She stretched her fingers, then returned to the beginning of what she'd written, curious to see what had emerged.

The words weren't perfect. Some lines felt rushed, others relied on clichés she would circle in red if they appeared in someone else's manuscript. But there was an authenticity, a glimpse of a voice she'd nearly forgotten was hers.

She flipped to a blank page, pen poised to keep going when her phone's buzz cut through the quiet. The noise instantly pulled her out of the overlook's calm. She stared at it, half-tempted to let it go to voicemail while she continued her communion with the page. But years of being available to her boss, authors, and even Nate, with his demands and emergencies, had conditioned her to respond. With a sigh, she reached for her bag, the spell of the moment breaking.

The screen lit up with a name, causing her smile to vanish instantly. Nate.

Sadie stared at the screen for a moment, wondering if she could simply ignore him and return to her writing. She glanced back at her notebook, at the words that had flowed so freely moments before. Now, though, all she could think of was the sneer on his face when he would read something of hers that she felt honestly had potential.

Before she could decide whether to answer or let it go to voicemail, the buzzing stopped, only to start again immediately. Whatever he wanted, he wasn't going to give up easily, and with a reluctant sigh, Sadie answered the call.

"Hello, Nate." She aimed for neutral, missing by miles as her voice emerged tight and thin.

His voice spilled out immediately, no greeting, no preamble, just a slurring growl that confirmed he'd been drinking. Based on the time difference, he had likely been out all night at the bar. Some things never change.

"You think you're better off, huh? Hiding in some nowhere dump?" The words tumbled over each other, thick with spite.

Sadie's stomach clenched. That particular tone usually preceded thrown objects or a lengthy lecture on her flaws and how everything was her fault. She glanced around at the peaceful hillside, suddenly feeling exposed despite being completely alone.

"Got yourself a cute little country vacation, playing editor to some hack writer?" he continued. "What happens when your little holiday is over?"

Sadie pressed her back against the bench, seeking its solid support as Nate's poison tried to seep through the phone.

"I've been ignoring you for a reason," she said, glad to be alone where no one could witness her side of the conversation. "What do you want?"

"Want?" He snorted, the sound wet and ugly. "I want to know why my fiancé's suddenly playing house in England with some hotshot writer when our lease isn't up for another two months. I paid the rent, by the way. You're welcome."

"Always good to try something new, isn't it?" Sadie snarked before she could stop herself. She had been covering the entirety of the rent for years while Nate worked on 'finding his inspiration.' She pressed on before he could rage at her for her comment, "I told you I took care of my portion with our landlord. And it's ex-fiancé, Nate. We've been over this."

"Right, right. Ex. Such a drama queen." His voice dropped into the wheedling register she knew too well. "Come on, babe. This temper tantrum's gone on long enough. What, I get mad over your nagging, and you move across the ocean?"

The casual rewriting of history wasn't lost on her, as if he hadn't smashed her laptop against the wall when she had the nerve to send him the listing for writing gigs so he might earn some money. As if the scar on her calf hadn't come from dodging a thrown coffee mug. As if years of systematic belittling could be dismissed as a single moment.

"You know that's not what happened," she said, surprised by the steadiness in her voice.

"Whatever. So you're what, finding yourself? Playing in the mud with the sheep?" His tone sharpened, the false concern evaporating. "Or is it this author guy? You fucking him, Sadie? Is that it?"

The crude accusation hung in the air, intended to shock and wound. Old Sadie would have rushed to explain, placate, and defuse his jealousy with reassurances. But something about being on the other side of an ocean made her brave. She was tired of making herself smaller to accommodate his insecurity.

"I'm working, Nate," she said, each word cool and clipped. "You don't get to ask those questions anymore. You don't get to wreck this."

"Working." He infused the word with disdain. "Right. Fixing comma splices for some British prick who couldn't finish his book. That is what you reduced yourself to? I mean, I know Jess always rolls shit downhill to you, but sending you across the ocean?"

"Corbyn Pearce has sold millions of books," she said, though she owed him no explanation. "And I was sent because I'm good at my job."

"Corbyn Pearce?" Nate's laugh returned, uglier than before. "He hasn't published anything in years. Jesus, Sadie, are you editing airport paperbacks now? What's next, ghostwriting celebrity cookbooks?"

Sadie felt her spine straighten, a flash of unexpected anger rising in her chest. "You don't know the first thing about Corbyn Pearce or his work."

"Whoa, a bit protective are we?" Nate's voice dripped with mock surprise. "Wasn't he in some sort of accident a few years back? What, is he tragic and misunderstood? That's pathetic even for you."

"What's pathetic is tearing down someone who's survived what he has," Sadie shot back, surprised by her own vehemence. "The man has more talent and determination in one finger than you have in your entire body."

The silence on the other end told her she'd hit a nerve. But the dismissal of her career choices had been a cheap shot, one that preyed on the lingering fear that she was wasting her talent fixing other people's words instead of creating her own. Looking down at the notebook on her lap filled with her morning's writing, gave her confidence. She was more than her job title, more than Nate's narrow definition of success.

"Eventually, everyone, including Jess, will realize you're not as sweet and charming as they think you are," he continued, filling her silence with more venom. "When this gig crashes and burns, don't come crawling back to..."

Her index finger stabbed the end call button, cutting off the tirade mid-sentence. For a moment, she sat motionless, waiting for the familiar wave of guilt to crash over her, but it didn't come. Taking a breath, she found his number in her contacts and quickly blocked it before he could call back—a long-overdue action.

She shoved the phone into her pocket and tipped her head back, letting the cold air wash over her heated face. The wind swept back in, clean and crisp, as her pulse slowed from a gallop to a canter. Closing her eyes, she made an effort to release the tension in her muscles, wiping away the tears that had managed to escape.

When she opened her eyes again, she looked down at her notebook, at the words she'd written. Lifting the pen once more, she continued to write, forgetting about Nate, her fears, and even Corbyn and his stalled manuscript. Jess had sent her here to heal, and for the first time in a very long time, she felt like it might just be possible.

February 14, 2025

-Sadie-

The soft sound of a pen moving across paper and the patter of rain on the window were the only two things to interrupt the silence of Pearce House's living room. It seemed fitting to Sadie as she circled yet another paragraph in Corbyn's latest chapter of *Echoes of Ash*, on a page that was already bleeding with red ink.

The mystery was turning into a gripping work featuring a burned-out detective investigating arson cases that mirrored his own tragic past. The premise was solid, and Corbyn's prose could be devastatingly good, but his tendency to wander into tangents killed the pacing.

"The reader doesn't need three pages on the butler's childhood," she muttered, scribbling a note in the margin. "He doesn't even show up again until chapter twenty-four."

It had been eight days since she first arrived in Great Missenden. Most of those days included stilted morning check-ins with Corbyn, each a test of her patience. Their first hour-long meeting about the manuscript had gone surprisingly well and miraculously concluded without raised voices or slammed doors. She'd taken Edie's advice, met his glare evenly, and offered a well-thought-out explanation as to why her advice should be taken seriously. He'd growled and grumbled, but by the end, he'd muttered a grudging "not bad" that had felt like she had won something monumental.

She didn't hold much hope for a repeat performance today. She had been up until the early morning hours working on a freelance editing project for a self-published romance author. She needed a new laptop to replace the one Nate had smashed, but it would take about three more projects to afford the one she had her eye on.

The peaceful atmosphere was broken when her phone buzzed suddenly on the coffee table. Her brow furrowed as the text showed it was from an unknown number, and curiosity had her unlocking the screen.

> Miss you, babe.

Her eyes narrowed. There was only one person who could have sent that message. Nate had figured out she had blocked him and took it upon himself to get a new number.

And of course, because today was Valentine's Day, the man who'd called her "unlovable" and a "waste of space" mere weeks ago was reaching out. She snorted, flat and humorless, as another message appeared.

> I keep thinking about our first Valentine's. Remember that workshop we went to about crafting the perfect love letter?

For a moment, her mind slipped back to that night all those years ago. There had been wine and laughter, and they had both crafted beautiful letters to each other. He had seemed so sincere at the time, and just thinking of it made her chest ache.

> I found them in a box under the bed.

A photo popped up on her screen. Two letters, one in her neat cursive and the other in his somewhat messy scrawl. She took a shaky breath, trying to will away the mix of emotions that flooded her at seeing those letters. That had been a moment she had treasured, those letters an anchor to the early days.

> It's a shame these letters are here with me and you're not.

Deep down, Sadie knew she shouldn't have been surprised by the turn this conversation was taking. Nate was a master at manipulating situations and emotions so he ended up looking like the victim.

"Nothing says I love you like a holiday guilt trip," she muttered, staring at the words.

> I'm not doing well without you, Sades. I need you here, my writing isn't the same without you.

She rolled her eyes. The last time she had tried to offer him any sort of suggestion, he had told her that she had been spending too long reading novels written by authors who had sacrificed true art to appeal to the masses. That her input only stifled the emotional depth of his genius.

She slipped the phone into her pocket, then leaned back on the sofa, rubbing her brow to ease the tension that had formed there. She inhaled deeply, catching the scent of something rich and savory from the kitchen. She could hear Edie moving about behind her, preparing dinner. Deciding to seek out the housekeeper's motherly presence, she forced herself to stand and move to the kitchen.

"You alright, dear?" Edie asked, turning to look over her shoulder at the sound of Sadie's footsteps. "You look knackered."

Sadie managed a smile, and sat on one of the stools at the island before answering, "I'm fine, just preparing myself mentally for another hour of grumbling."

"He's been muttering about your notes since this morning," Edie lowered her voice to a conspiratorial whisper. "That's good. It means you've gotten under his skin."

"Are you sure?" Sadie asked, doubt creeping in. A moment ago, she had been able to ignore the uncertainty Nate's text had conjured, but now she couldn't help but wonder if he had a point. If he did, eventually Corbyn might also figure out she wasn't the miracle worker everyone proclaimed her to be.

"Trust me, love, he's obsessing over your feedback. That means you got through to him," Edie said with certainty, waving her away. "Go on then. Best not to keep him waiting."

When she reached the entrance to the hallway, she paused, preparing herself mentally for whatever was to come. In the study, she found a fire crackling in the stone hearth, and Corbyn lounging on the worn leather sofa, a stray lock falling across his forehead as he wrote something in a notebook. Riley lay at his feet, sprawled out in canine contentment. The dog noticed her first, his tail thumping against the floor in lazy welcome.

Corbyn looked up, the cool blue of his eyes cutting through the fire-lit room. The scarring on the right side of his face caught the firelight. She had never spent much time looking at the scars that trailed down his jaw and neck before disappearing beneath the collar of his shirt. She had noticed early on that he had a tendency to turn that side of his face away from her as much as possible, as if to hide it. Once she had noticed, she had gone out of her way to do things that wouldn't add to whatever psychological discomfort her presence brought.

As she approached, she dropped the marked-up chapter onto the coffee table before sitting in the armchair opposite him. Riley stretched before padding over to her, his head landing in her lap as he demanded attention. She let out a breathy laugh before scratching behind his ears.

"Round two," she said, looking up at Corbyn, who was watching her with what she hoped was curiosity. She was pleased that her voice emerged steady, despite the nervousness fluttering in her stomach.

A grunt was Corbyn's only response, and he set aside his notebook to reach for the pages. He flipped through them, pausing at a particularly red-soaked section, and she saw his jaw tighten.

"This better not be a hatchet job," he muttered, looking over her notes.

Sadie squared her shoulders, recalling Edie's advice. *Don't back down.*

"It's strong, Corbyn," she said, keeping her voice even. "Your voice cuts like a blade, and your characters stick with readers. Detective Shaw is compelling, and the arson cases are intricate and well-researched."

His expression remained guarded, but something in his posture eased slightly even as he said, "But?"

"But," she continued, leaning forward, "it's bloated. The pacing drags here..." she reached across as best she could with Riley's head still in her lap to tap a heavily marked section. "And this subplot with the mayor's wife is a snarl of loose ends. Streamline it, and the whole narrative hits harder."

She saw him bristle, his jaw ticking with tension, before he ground out, "It works perfectly well as is. The mayor's wife subplot adds depth to the town's corruption."

"It adds confusion," Sadie countered. "It's too disconnected from the rest of the book. If you show how it directly impacts his investigation of his brother's death..."

Her phone vibrated in her pocket. For a moment, she felt her shoulders draw up toward her ears, but she forced herself to relax and ignored the phone, focusing on the page before her.

"This section here," she pressed on, pointing to a crossed-out chunk. "Three pages of Shaw remembering his childhood. It takes away the tension you've built with the warehouse discovery. Cut it, and the tension spikes."

She flipped to her suggested restructuring, letting him read her notes.

The phone buzzed again, and her hand twitched toward her pocket despite her resolve before she caught herself.

Corbyn's expression became pinched, eyes motioning towards her hand before he asked, "Problem?"

"No," she said quickly. Too quickly, her voice was more of a squeak than she intended. She tapped the manuscript again, hoping to redirect the conversation. "Chapter three has a timeline hole. Shaw couldn't have seen the fire chief at the station and then driven across town in ten minutes to meet his informant. The geography doesn't work."

Buzz. Another text.

Sadie clenched her jaw, but curiosity and dread won out. She pulled the phone far enough from her pocket to read what was on the screen.

> Figures you'd ignore me. You always were spiteful, just like your mother.

> You're trying to punish me, aren't you?

> Never mind. I'm tossing those stupid fucking letters.

Her throat tightened. She tried to remind herself that this pattern was exactly why she had left. First came the charm, then the guilt and manipulation, and if that didn't work, then it was anger.

Clearing her throat, her voice was a little less steady when she continued, "Fix the timeline, or the whole sequence unravels."

Corbyn was watching her now, his gaze more intent. She folded her fingers around her phone to try to hide the slight tremor she was sure he noticed. His pen tapped a rhythm against the armrest of the sofa.

"You're gutting it."

"It's surgery, not slaughter," she shot back, meeting his glare. The words came with a heat that wasn't purely meant for him. "Surely you've heard the saying 'Kill your darlings?' Some of these scenes are darlings, Corbyn. Beautiful but unnecessary."

Buzz. Her phone lit up again.

> You'll be back when you're no longer hiding behind Pearce's words.

Her fingers twitched, and a slow breath escaped her. Nearly six weeks free of him, and still, his words could reach inside her chest and squeeze. She swiped the phone to silent before shoving it back into her pocket and turning her attention back to Corbyn.

He had leaned forward, and for the first time, his eyes remained locked with hers. He studied her, as if tracking every flicker of hesitation, and she shifted in her seat under the weight of it.

His voice emerged gruffer than before, but with an undertone that wasn't entirely hostile when he asked, "Your phone's having a fit. What's that about?"

Sadie felt heat rise to her cheeks, and she aimed for a casual dismissal when she replied, "My ex. He's throwing a Valentine's Day tantrum because I'm not answering him." She tapped the page again, desperate to turn his attention away from Nate. "This subplot is pulling focus from your main narrative arc. If you tighten it, connect it more directly to Shaw…"

"Is that normal, these tantrums?" Corbyn interrupted the word hanging between them.

Sensing the shift in mood, Riley gave a soft whine, looking up at her from where his head rested against her thigh. She gratefully scratched behind his ears again, glad for a reason to look away.

"It's nothing," she said firmly. "Just…toxic history. Not worth discussing."

She felt him watching her a moment longer before returning to the manuscript. Sadie waited, her chest tightening as she hoped the dismissal of Nate's childish behavior would be enough to return them to the safety of their professional roles.

"Maybe…" he said slowly, as if the admission cost him, "that bit does drag." He frowned at the page. "Still don't agree with cutting the mayor's wife entirely."

"Not entirely," Sadie clarified, seizing the opening as relief rose in her chest. "Just reshape her role. Make her connection to the arson cases clearer earlier. Right now, readers will forget about her between her appearances."

He looked back up, and for the first time, he seemed to truly consider what she was saying.

"And the timeline in chapter three?"

"Easy fix," she told him, a little smile pulling at her lips at the victory. "Extend the time frame or move the informant meeting location closer to the station."

He nodded slowly before leaning back on the sofa once more. Sensing the easing of the tension, Riley flopped down with his large head on Sadie's foot, emitting a little grumble of contentment that made her chuckle.

"The core mystery is strong," Sadie said, gentler now. "Shaw's discovery that his brother staged his own death, that he might be behind the arsons, is compelling. All these changes do is bring that core into sharper focus."

Corbyn's eyes lifted from the manuscript and looked at her with an expression she had never seen before. She wasn't sure if it was surprise or the beginnings of respect, but she didn't question it.

"You actually read it," he mused, and she thought she might have seen what could be the beginning of a smile tugging at his lips. "Not just skimmed, but you read it."

"That's my job," she replied, slightly confused as to why that would be surprising.

"You have no idea how many don't," he told her, looking at her like he was seeing her for the first time. "They look for obvious errors and make generic suggestions." His finger tapped one of her more detailed notes. "This isn't generic."

The compliment, backhanded as it was, caught her off guard. Warmth bloomed in her chest, and she had to fight back a grin, knowing that would certainly ruin the moment.

"I'll think about these," Corbyn stated, placing the pages on the table. It wasn't an agreement, but it wasn't dismissal either. "Your ex sounds like a git."

The blunt assessment, and the fact that Corbyn had been the one to say it, startled a laugh from her.

"That's... accurate."

Riley's tail thumped against the floor as if in agreement.

Before Sadie could respond further, Edie appeared in the doorway, a little smirk tugging at her lips as she looked between them. It was a look Sadie had learned meant the housekeeper was up to something.

"Shepherd's pie is ready," she announced, her knowing gaze traveling between them. "Paul set the table for four. No arguments; you both could use a good meal."

Corbyn rolled his eyes, but there was no heat in it. Edie seemed to be one of the few who could honestly get away with bossing him around.

"Apparently, we're eating," he told Sadie, tucking the manuscript under his arm. "Then I have... questions. About these edits."

Sadie hesitated, caught off guard by the unexpected invitation. Dinner with Corbyn and his makeshift family hadn't been part of her plan for the day. There was something disarming about the way he was looking at her while he waited for her to follow him to the kitchen. Corbyn wasn't just tolerating her professional presence in this moment. Even though it was Edie's idea, he was including her in something more personal. The realization sent a strange flutter through her chest.

"Okay," she said simply, not trusting herself with more words.

As she followed Corbyn and Riley toward the kitchen, Sadie felt something shift. Somehow, she had managed to put a crack in the walls he had built around himself. He'd listened. He'd actually considered her suggestions, and that felt like winning a small but significant battle.

February 19, 2025

-Sadie -

"Two weeks down," Sadie murmured, smiling as she approached the front door to the manor, "and look at me actually excited about this."

There had been a change in her working relationship with Corbyn since Valentine's Day. The other day, during one of their sessions, he had shocked her when he simply nodded and replied, "That works," after she made one of her suggestions. She wasn't entirely sure what had caused the shift, but it had given her a sense of optimism she hadn't felt when she first arrived.

"Good morning," Edie called from the kitchen when Sadie used the key she'd been given to let herself in. "You're early today. Keen to get started in the lion's den?"

Sadie smiled, setting her bag on the island. "More like eager for your tea. The inn's is good, but yours is somehow better."

"Flattery will get you everywhere," Edie said with a chuckle, already reaching for an extra mug. "I made fresh shortbread this morning."

"You spoil me," Sadie said, settling onto a stool at the island while Edie prepared the tea. She retrieved one of the biscuits from the plate Edie had left conveniently in front of her usual stool. Taking a bite, she let the buttery flavor wash over her, a contented sigh escaping her.

This had become a bit of a morning ritual, and it was one Sadie was sure she would miss when this assignment was over. Edie had a way of making anyone in her kitchen feel at home.

"I'm just glad to have someone who enjoys it," Edie replied with a wink, placing the mug in front of Sadie. "Lord knows Corbyn wouldn't know good baking if it bit him."

Sadie took a grateful sip of tea, letting its warmth chase away the last of the morning chill.

"Is he already working?" she asked, knowing Corbyn had a habit of starting work at an ungodly hour of the morning.

"Been at it since dawn, I'd wager. Heard him pacing before the sun was even up," Edie told her, brow furrowing. "Seems in a state today, but more focused than brooding, if you know what I mean."

That was promising.

"So," Edie said, leaning against the counter with her mug, "how was your day off? Get out and about a bit?"

Sadie nodded, breaking off a piece of shortbread. "Actually, I had quite the adventure yesterday. I went for a hike up in the hills past the church, but I got turned around and ended up on someone's farm. Mr. Davies, I think. I've seen him in the pub a few times."

Edie's face lit up and she grinned. "Old Gareth Davies! Salt of the earth, that one. Been farming those hills longer than I've been alive."

"He was so kind," Sadie continued, warming to the memory. "I ended up spending most of the day there helping him with the lambs. He taught me how to bottle-feed the orphaned ones. I was covered in mud by the end, but it was worth it. I couldn't get enough of those little lambs with their wobbly legs."

Edie's eyes crinkled with genuine pleasure. "That's a proper Great Missenden welcome, that is. Gareth doesn't let just anyone get that close to his precious lambs."

"It was exactly what I needed," Sadie admitted. "After being hunched over manuscripts for days, holding something warm and alive was..." She trailed off, unsure how to articulate the simple joy of it.

"Good for the soul," Edie finished for her. "Remind you there's a world outside these pages we all fuss over."

Nails scrambling against the hardwood announced Riley's approach. The Irish Wolfhound bounded into the kitchen, his lanky frame vibrating with excitement as he spotted Sadie.

"Well, hello there, handsome," Sadie laughed as Riley shoved his massive head into her lap, nearly knocking her off the stool. She scratched behind his ears, his favorite spot. "Someone's happy this morning."

"Don't get too comfortable," came a gruff voice from the doorway. "We've got work to do."

Sadie turned to find Corbyn leaning against the entrance to the kitchen, arms crossed over his chest. His hair was disheveled, and there was a restless look about him that suggested he hadn't slept well. But there was something different in his posture, as he rolled his shoulders to relieve some of the tension.

"Good morning to you, too," she replied, keeping her voice light. "I'm not due in your office for another ten minutes."

His gaze flicked to the clock on the wall, then back to her. "I need to ask you something about that scene in chapter eight."

"What about it?" she asked, still absently stroking Riley's head. Chapter eight contained a crucial revelation about Detective Shaw's missing brother. She'd suggested major restructuring, worried the impact was being diluted by too much exposition.

Corbyn shifted, clearly uncomfortable having this conversation with an audience.

"In the study. When you're done..." he trailed off, gesturing toward her tea.

Instead of retreating back to his office, though, he lingered in the doorway. His left hand flexed at his side. It was a subtle movement she'd come to recognize as a sign of either pain or agitation. Today, she suspected it was the latter.

"I can come now," she said, giving Riley a final pat and sliding off the stool. "Thanks for the tea, Edie."

The housekeeper nodded, her shrewd eyes moving between them with barely concealed interest as she called after them, "I'll bring more in a bit. Something tells me you two might need it."

Stepping through the study door, she was greeted by the now familiar scents: the faint trace of wood smoke from the hearth, the earthy smell of the old books that lined the shelves along one wall, and something uniquely Corbyn. At some point, she had memorized the scent of his cologne, and she told herself it was merely because she spent hours in this room with him and nothing more.

"So," she said, "chapter eight."

Corbyn circled his desk, picking up a marked-up page covered in her red ink and his cramped handwriting.

"This bit you circled," he responded, "about Shaw realizing his brother might have staged his death."

"Yes?"

"You said it comes too late. That I need to seed it earlier," he continued with a frown, pointing to a spot on the page. "But if I move it up, it undercuts the tension in the warehouse scene."

Sadie approached the desk, close enough to see the page but maintaining a professional distance.

"Not if you handle it right. Look, the reader suspects something's off with the brother from chapter three. But Shaw's too close to see it; it's the classic detective blind spot. If you show him picking up on the clues but dismissing them because it's his brother, then, when the warehouse revelation hits, it's not just shock but self-recrimination."

"I'll try it your way," he conceded after a moment. "But if it falls flat..."

"I'll personally rewrite it myself," she finished, a smile tugging at her lips.

He snorted, something close to amusement flickering across his face. "As if I'd let you near my draft."

"It's a bit late for that," she gestured to the pages between them, and actually earned a hint of a smirk.

Corbyn leaned back in his chair, studying her with an intensity that might have made her uncomfortable two weeks ago. Now, she met his gaze steadily, refusing to give in to intimidation.

"I worked on the next section last night," he said, sorting through stacks of papers until he found what he was looking for. "The arson investigation."

Sadie checked her watch, surprised to find that their ten-minute check-in had already stretched to fifteen.

"I should let you get back to work."

"Read it," he interjected, pushing the pages toward her. "Now, if you have time. I want to know if the timeline tracks."

The request caught her off guard. Usually, Corbyn guarded his fresh pages, reluctantly handing them over only after fussing over them for days.

"Are you sure?" she asked carefully.

A muscle in his jaw ticked, and she wasn't sure if it was nerves or annoyance at her hesitation.

"Wouldn't have asked if I wasn't."

They spent another half hour going through the new material. It was probably the best he had written since her arrival, and Sadie found herself genuinely engaged in the story rather than just its technical aspects.

"This is what you should aim for in the earlier sections," she said, tapping a particularly effective scene. "You've found Shaw's voice here. It's clean, sharp, and you can feel his desperation without spelling it out."

Something shifted in Corbyn's expression. He took the pages back, his fingers briefly brushing hers. The unexpected contact sent a flutter through her, and her breath hitched. She waited for him to growl or throw her out of the office and then distance himself for the rest of the day, but it never came. He stayed silent, and for a moment, he looked up at her, his eyes searching hers. She wasn't sure what he was looking for, or if he found it, because he looked away just as suddenly.

"I've got more edits to work on," Sadie said, swallowing hard as she rose from her chair. "I'll be in the living room if you need anything else."

He nodded, already turning back to his work, not meeting her eyes again. Riley, who had been dozing by the hearth, scrambled up to follow her out, his loyalty apparently divided this morning.

As she walked down the hallway, Sadie found herself rubbing her thumb against her fingertips, tracing the path where his skin had touched hers. She had been so careful after that first meeting to keep her distance, having written off the initial spark as nerves. It was still there, though, and somehow it felt more significant than it should.

She shook her head, trying to refocus on the task ahead. There were manuscripts to edit, deadlines to meet, and a book to save.

But the memory of that brief contact refused to fade, no matter how much she tried to bury it.

Two hours later, Sadie was deep in concentration when heavy footsteps thudded down the hall. Paul, the estate's groundskeeper, trudged through the hallway with a toolbox and mud-caked boots on his feet.

"Afternoon," he grunted, noticing her presence.

"Hello, Paul." Setting aside her pen, she asked, "Busy morning?"

He shrugged his broad shoulders, telling her, "Greenhouse heater's on the fritz again. Old as sin, that thing." His Yorkshire accent wrapped around the words, a contrast to what she was used to from Edie and Corbyn.

Sadie had seen little of Paul during her time at Pearce House. He moved like a shadow around the estate, appearing when needed and vanishing just as quickly. Unlike the more maternal Edie, Paul maintained a gruff distance that might have convinced most people he was related to Corbyn himself.

"Can I get you some tea?" she offered, gesturing to the pot Edie had left. "It should still be warm."

Paul hesitated, then gave a short nod. "Wouldn't say no."

As she poured him a cup, Sadie ventured, "The greenhouse, is that the structure beyond the orchard?"

"Aye." Paul set down his toolbox with a heavy thunk. "Been there longer than the house, almost."

He accepted the tea with weathered hands, calluses and dirt ingrained in the lines, speaking of decades of physical labor.

"I noticed it on a walk with Riley," Sadie explained. "I've never been inside, though."

Something shifted in Paul's expression, a slight softening that she was taking an interest.

"Used to be Corbyn's favorite spot. As a lad, mind you."

Sadie's interest piqued as Paul took a sip of tea. "Really?"

"Aye. Precocious little thing, always had questions about the plants. Why does this one need shade? How come that one grows faster?" he paused, shaking his head, a ghost of a smile on his lips. "Notebooks full of observations he had."

The image of a young Corbyn, curious and eager rather than bitter and closed off, tugged at something in Sadie's chest. There had been a glimmer of that eagerness today, and the interaction suddenly took on an entirely new meaning.

Before Sadie could respond, Corbyn's voice echoed down the hallway. "Reed! I need you again!"

Paul's mouth twitched in what might have been amusement. "Duty calls. Mind he doesn't work you too hard. Man forgets others need rest, even if he doesn't."

When Sadie reentered the study, Corbyn stood by the window, staring out at the grounds in a way that suggested he wasn't seeing them. He turned as she entered, his expression more troubled than it had been before.

"The brother," he said without preamble. "Shaw's reaction when he finds the evidence that his brother faked his death. I can't nail it."

Sadie approached cautiously, still not sure how to read this version of him, the one that actually wanted her help. This was the book's emotional core, and she knew getting it right was crucial.

"What's the block?" she asked, keeping her voice soft.

Corbyn gestured to the pages scattered across his desk, voice tense when he admitted, "He's a detective. He should be able to look at the evidence logically."

Sadie settled into the chair across from his desk, considering. "Shaw can be both a detective and a brother in that moment. The conflict of logic and emotion is what makes the scene powerful."

He pulled his chair around to her side of the desk, and she had to try not to look at him as if he had suddenly sprouted a second head. They worked side by side, though, with Sadie suggesting approaches while Corbyn shaped the actual prose. The scene slowly transformed as it gained depth and nuance that had not been there before. Time slipped away as they passed pages back and forth, refining dialogue and pacing.

"There," Corbyn said finally, reading over the final version. "That works."

Sadie stared at the clock in surprise. They'd been at it for over an hour, completely absorbed in the creative process. It was, she realized, the first time they'd truly collaborated rather than just negotiated.

"I should let you get back to it," she said, gathering her notes. "I've still got those earlier chapters to finish."

As she rose to leave, Corbyn's voice stopped her.

"Reed..." he paused, as if shocked that he had spoken. "Stay. Work in here."

She stared at him for a moment, uncertain she'd heard correctly. Corbyn gestured awkwardly to the leather sofa near the hearth, where Riley often sprawled during their sessions.

"If you want," he added gruffly. "Might be easier... for when we're working together."

The invitation wasn't casual, though he'd tried to make it sound that way. This was his domain, a sacred space that wasn't meant to be shared. Yet here he was, asking her to stay. Perhaps it was simply that she had finally earned his professional respect, but it felt like something more fragile and precious. Either way, she recognized it for what it was, a risk he was taking, a test of trust neither of them had expected.

"Okay," she said, keeping her tone light despite the moment's significance. "Let me grab my things."

When she returned with her editing materials, Corbyn was already back at work, pen moving steadily across the page. Riley had claimed one end of the sofa and looked up with doggy contentment as she settled at the other.

The study was quiet except for the scratch of pens, the occasional rustle of paper, and Riley's soft sighs. Something had shifted, creating a warmth in Sadie's chest. She couldn't help but think that this was the beginning of a partnership that might actually save this book.

February 20, 2025

-Corbyn-

Corbyn sliced through the water, the feeling of weightlessness combined with the warmth of the indoor pool allowing a moment of reprieve from the constant aches. After a particularly trying editing session with Sadie yesterday, he had overdone it on the stationary bike, and his body was paying for it in addition to the usual aches from the February chill. Here, though, he could still maintain some level of activity and normalcy.

Riley sprawled across the tiles at the pool's far end, tracking Corbyn's movements with sad eyes. The Wolfhound had been reluctant to leave the study, or more specifically, to leave Sadie. His massive head had been nestled in her lap, her hand occasionally scratching behind his ears while she worked. When Corbyn decided he needed a break, Riley had looked up at him for a moment as if to say, *Really?* before heaving a sigh and following him toward the door that led to the lower level.

Sadie had been here for over two weeks already, despite his grumbling and best efforts to send her fleeing back to America. That meant two weeks of clipped good-mornings, two weeks of her red pens, and two weeks of her suggestions.

Somehow, she'd surprised him. He'd expected another mediocre editor with an eye on the clock and general notes that even an intern could muster up. Instead, she'd walked into his study with a stack of pages marked with precise notations, her gray eyes unflinching when he'd growled at her critiques.

Other editors hacked at his prose, trying to make the book more "marketable," more "accessible." They had tried to strip away the heart of the story. But Sadie was different. She didn't want to change his voice; she wanted to strengthen it.

Corbyn made another turn, his pace finally catching up with him, and his left hand refused to cooperate. Pain shot up his arm, and he cursed under his breath as he stopped and his feet hit the floor of the pool. Riley's head lifted, concern evident in the slight whine that carried across the water.

"I'm fine," Corbyn muttered, even though the dog wasn't asking. It was a force of habit after years of everyone asking if he was okay any time he so much as grimaced.

His thoughts drifted back to Sadie as he trudged toward the pool stairs. Three editors had come and gone before her, each causing his frustration and doubts to grow. She saw through his posturing to the man underneath, and the realization that she had begun to crack through the armor he'd welded around himself unsettled him more than he cared to admit.

As he moved toward the bench where dry clothes waited, Riley trotting behind him, Corbyn caught himself wondering what Sadie might be working on this morning. He'd left her in the study with the stack of papers to read through for the afternoon session. To his surprise, he actually found himself looking forward to it, to the sharp back-and-forth of literary debate. She was one of the few who could keep up with him, and that had his mind drifting down a dangerous road.

She was only here temporarily. She would inevitably return to her life in New York, and he knew better than to get attached.

His swim shirt clung uncomfortably to him, and getting it off would be a battle. It was a familiar one, but still one he never won gracefully. Knowing there was no way to escape the inevitable, he reached for the hem with both hands, grimacing as his left refused to fully cooperate. His fingers fumbled against the wet fabric, and the first tug brought a hiss through clenched teeth as the material dragged across hypersensitive skin.

"Bloody hell," he growled, trying again with more force. The shirt rolled up his chest, catching on the raised ridges of scar tissue that crisscrossed his torso. Each pull was just another reminder of how simple tasks had become complex negotiations with pain.

When he finally managed to drag it over his head, his left arm twisted at an awkward angle, sending a fresh spike of agony shooting through his shoulder and down his spine. The shirt hung from his right hand, his breathing heavy from the exertion.

He caught his reflection in the mirror across the way. Welts stretched across his chest and abdomen, ranging in colors from silver to red, puckered and uneven. The worst ran from his right shoulder to his left hip, a jagged line where his clothing had first caught fire. Others radiated outward, smaller but no less vivid. They'd faded somewhat over the years, but not enough. Never enough.

He reached for his towel on the bench beside his dry clothes. The motion stretched tender skin, but he bit back another curse. Riley watched, patient and unperturbed by the marks his human bore. To the dog, scars were another part of Corbyn, neither more nor less important than any other.

Scowling in disgust, he turned, towel half-raised to his chest, and stopped cold.

Sadie stood at the bottom of the stairs. Her eyes widened for a fraction of a second as they took in his exposed chest. Time froze, and Corbyn couldn't move or breathe. He felt a bit like he'd been pinned under glass.

Her eyes met his, a direct gaze that didn't flinch away from what she saw. There was surprise there, but not the revulsion he'd learned to expect. Not pity either, that poisonous emotion that cut worse than any physical pain.

"Edie sent me... she says lunch is nearly ready," she said, her voice remarkably steady, betraying nothing of what must be churning beneath.

Heat shot up Corbyn's spine, and the moment stretched in silence. Riley sensed the tension and stood between them, his gaze swinging between the two humans.

Corbyn snatched his dry shirt from the bench, sending water droplets flying. His fingers fumbled with the fabric, clumsy with haste and humiliation. The shirt snagged on his damp skin, and a hiss escaped his lips as his left hand seized again, his anger boiling up to the surface.

"Get out," he barked, the words slicing through like a blade.

Sadie didn't move. Her jaw tightened, a small muscle jumping near her temple, but she stood her ground. The manuscript pages crinkled slightly in her grip, the only sign that his words had landed.

"Now, Reed," he growled, yanking the shirt down, teeth gritted against the pain that radiated from his shoulder. "I don't need you staring."

"Corbyn," she started, taking a step forward. Her voice was even and controlled, and that somehow made it worse. It was threatening to further breach the walls he'd so carefully constructed. "I didn't mean..."

"You didn't mean to what?" he cut her off, snarling the word. "Gape? Piss off, Reed, I don't want your damn pity."

"It's not pity," she said, and he saw the flush creeping up her neck in either embarrassment or anger. "I was just..."

"Just what?" he snapped, his voice rising. "Wanted to satisfy your curiosity? Did Jess not warn you what you'd be dealing with when she sent you here?"

Her spine stiffened, her voice tense as she breathed, "That's not fair."

"Life isn't fair," he spat, his scarred hand curling into a fist at his side. "Or haven't you figured that out yet? Now get out before you see something else you don't want to."

"Corbyn, I..."

"I said GET OUT!" His roar echoed against the tiled walls, making Riley jump. "This isn't part of your job description, Reed. You're here for the book, not to inspect the damaged goods. Or did your contract include being my therapist, too?"

The color drained from her face, her expression shifting from concern to something more challenging, colder.

"Fine," she said, her voice tightly controlled. "If that's what you want."

"What I want," he said, each word precise and cutting, "is for everyone to stop pretending they can fix what can't be fixed. Including you."

She stepped back, stunned, the hurt in her eyes cutting through her professional mask.

"Message received," she said quietly. Then, she turned on her heel, her footsteps quick and sharp as she headed for the stairs.

"And don't bother coming back tomorrow," he called after her, the words flying out before he could stop them. "I worked alone before you arrived. I can damn well continue without you."

For a moment, the only sound that echoed through the room was his ragged breathing. Then, Riley gave a low whine, a sound of distress that cut through the sudden silence. The dog padded closer, pressing his warm bulk against Corbyn's leg, offering comfort that wasn't deserved.

"Don't," Corbyn muttered, though he didn't push the animal away. His hands were shaking now, the adrenaline crash leaving him unsteady. "She shouldn't have come down here."

He knew he shouldn't have snapped at her like that, that she hadn't come down with any sort of malicious intent. But the shock of being caught exposed and vulnerable had triggered a defensive response so ingrained he couldn't have stopped it. Better anger than weakness. Better to push her away than see the moment when her professional politeness gave way to revulsion.

It always happened eventually. Always.

He finished dressing with clumsy movements; the look on Sadie's face before she fled played over and over in his mind. Riley watched, head tilted slightly as if trying to parse the complexities of human behavior that made no sense to his canine brain.

"Come on," Corbyn said finally, his voice rough. "Let's go upstairs."

Riley's tail gave a hesitant wag, relieved they were moving past whatever storm had broken over them. The dog led the way to the stairs, pausing at the top to look back, ensuring his human followed.

Corbyn climbed slowly, and that brief moment of hurt on Sadie's face before she masked it played in his mind over and over again. He'd have to face her again at lunch. Sit across from her at the table and pretend that nothing had happened while the weight of his outburst hung between them. At some point, he would have to find a way to apologize for his behavior, although his wounded pride bristled at the very idea.

He rounded the corner at the top of the stairs and stopped short. Edie stood there, arms crossed over her flour-dusted apron, her small frame somehow blocking the entire space between the stairs and the kitchen. She wore an expression on her face that he hadn't seen since he was fifteen and got caught sneaking alcohol out to the greenhouse to drink with his friends.

"Sadie just bolted out of here like the house was on fire," Edie said without preamble, her voice low and hard, the gentle lilt of her accent sharpened by disapproval. "Face white as a sheet. What did you do?"

Corbyn moved past her, slumping onto a bar stool at the kitchen island. His body suddenly became too heavy for his legs to hold upright as shame washed over him. He scrubbed a hand across his jaw, feeling the rough stubble there, a reminder of how long it had been since he'd made himself presentable.

"She caught me half-stripped," he muttered, the words grinding like gravel. "Told her to get out."

Edie's stare bore into him, steady and unyielding. Her eyes, a warm brown that usually held a maternal twinkle, were now flat and hard. She said nothing, just waited, the silence that stretched between them worse than her yelling.

Riley trotted back around the island, sensing the tension. The dog paused halfway between them, head swiveling, before settling on the floor with a heavy sigh that seemed to express the weariness of dealing with humans more eloquently than words.

"What?" Corbyn growled, uncomfortable under Edie's scrutiny.

"You've told her to get out before, and it didn't send her running," Edie replied, continuing to stare at him in that way that told him she was just waiting for him to admit to what she already knew.

"I... snapped," he admitted grudgingly. "I said things I shouldn't... but she shouldn't have come down to the pool."

"She went down there because I sent her," Edie replied, her voice clipped. "To tell you lunch was ready. Not to be barked at like some trespasser."

Corbyn shifted on the stool, pain flaring in his lower back.

"She saw everything," he said, gesturing vaguely at his chest, the words coming out more defensive than he intended. "All of it."

"And?" Edie's eyebrow rose, a perfect arch of skepticism. "Did she run screaming? Point and laugh? What exactly did she do that warranted you sending her off like that?"

The question hung in the air, uncomfortable and pointed. Corbyn glared at the floor, unwilling to admit that Sadie had done none of those things. She'd simply looked at him. There had been surprise, but without the reflexive disgust he'd grown accustomed to seeing, without the careful pity that somehow hurt worse.

"She stared," he said finally, the accusation sounding weak even to his ears.

"For about two seconds, I'd wager," Edie countered, unmoved. "You have scars. There's no getting around that fact. A moment of being surprised is natural, and knowing that girl, that's all it was."

Corbyn's jaw tightened. Edie had been with him through everything, the accident, the surgeries, the long, brutal months of recovery when the pain had been his constant companion. She'd changed bandages without flinching, helped him dress when his hands wouldn't cooperate, and seen the worst of his physical and emotional wounds. She had earned the right to her bluntness, but that didn't make it easier to swallow.

"It's not that simple," he said, hating the defensiveness in his voice.

"It never is with you," Edie replied, but some hardness had left her tone. She moved closer, uncrossing her arms, her expression softening into something more familiar.

"Corbyn, she isn't here to gawk at or pity you. She's here for your book, and you've just treated her like she committed some terrible crime by doing exactly what I asked her to do."

As was usually the case, Edie was correct about everything. After the initial moment of shock at taking in the extent of his scars, Sadie had simply gone back to looking at him as she always did, steady and unflinching, like he wasn't some broken thing to gawk at, and he'd acted like a bloody jackass.

"What exactly do you expect me to do?" he asked, his voice unable to hide the edge. "Chase after her? Beg her to come back?"

"I expect you to act like the man I helped raise," Edie replied evenly, her hand coming to rest on his shoulder. "The one who understood the difference between pride and foolishness."

"This isn't about pride," he shot back.

"Isn't it?" Edie's eyebrow arched perfectly. "Tell me, then. What is it about?"

Corbyn opened his mouth, then closed it again. The truth was too raw, too close to the surface. The humiliation of being caught exposed had shattered the fragile trust he'd just begun to place in her. In his usual self-destructive way, he had shoved the only person to truly understand how to get him past his mental blocks right out the door.

"She's probably halfway to London by now," he grumbled, not answering the question.

"Nonsense," Edie replied. "The Roaring Stag is her home here. She'd at least have to go pack her things, and you know Maggie would try to talk her out of leaving first." She wiped her hands on her apron, fixing him with another hard look. "The question is, are you going to sit here, or are you going to get off your stubborn arse and do the right thing?"

Riley whined softly, chiming in. His massive head nudged Corbyn's hand, seeking reassurance.

"And what if she doesn't want to see me?" Corbyn asked, voice dropping lower. "After what I said..."

"Then at least you'll know you tried," Edie said simply. "That book needs her, Corbyn." She turned back to her cooking, adding over her shoulder, "First time in years I've heard you argue about something you care about instead of just shutting down."

The silence stretched between them, and Corbyn felt the weight of Edie's words settle. His outburst in the pool hadn't just been about Sadie seeing his scars. It was the fact that she saw past his carefully curated persona, and that scared him more than he cared to admit.

"You made your point," he grumbled, not wanting to admit she was right, even though she clearly was. "I'll go talk to her."

Edie's face softened a bit, and she responded, "Good. But for heaven's sake, go change first. You smell like a bucket of bleach, and those clothes are damp." She gestured to his rumpled appearance, continuing, "Not exactly the picture of contrition, are you?"

Despite himself, a flicker of something almost like amusement tugged at Corbyn's lips.

"Wouldn't want to add insult to injury."

"Exactly," Edie said, turning back to her cooking with renewed vigor. "Clean shirt, proper shoes. Maybe even run a comb through that bird's nest you call hair."

Corbyn pushed himself to his feet, Riley immediately at his side. The dog looked up at him with those soulful eyes, as if understanding the importance of the mission.

"Best do as she says," he muttered to the hound. "A lifetime of nagging has perfected her technique. No man or beast stands a chance."

"I heard that," Edie called, not turning around.

As Corbyn headed for the stairs, he felt a knot settle in his stomach. He had no idea what he would say to Sadie when he found her; his pride would only let him go so far. He couldn't let her leave like this, though; the book deserved better from him. She deserved better from him.

February 20, 2025

-Corbyn-

For the first time in months, Corbyn found himself outside the safety of his estate. Riley bounded ahead, and guilt prodded at him. Riley's world, like his own, generally did not extend beyond the estate grounds. That meant Riley stopped to sniff nearly every patch of ground while Corbyn hauled himself up the trail that stretched before him.

He'd gone to the Roaring Stag first because it was the logical place to start. He'd steeled himself for the conversation, rehearsing hollow apologies and professional half-truths on the drive over, while his hands clenched around the steering wheel. But she hadn't been there, and her rental car was nowhere to be seen. Maggie, when she'd finally returned from her errands, had also been no help at all.

"Haven't seen her since this morning," Maggie had said, once she got over the shock of seeing him. Her eyes had lingered on Corbyn's face a beat too long, as if reading the tension there, before asking, "She left early from your place? Is something wrong?"

He'd muttered some noncommittal answer about a miscommunication and felt the weight of Maggie's stare on his back as he walked out the door.

He chose to check the hiking path Edie had mentioned before he left. Apparently, it had become Sadie's favorite place to go when she wasn't at the manor working.

Now, slogging through the damp trails of the Chilterns, Corbyn second-guessed his decision to come here. Sadie's phone was going straight to voicemail, which only spiked his worry. She could be anywhere, including halfway to London to catch a flight back to New York.

Riley paused ahead, nose twitching as he sniffed the damp air. The path forked here, one trail leading deeper into the woods, the other climbing toward the hills that overlooked Great Missenden.

He'd walked these trails more times than he could remember as a boy, escaping his parents' empty house and hiding from his little sister. Later, as a teenager, he'd come here with books tucked under his arm, seeking solitude to read and eventually to write. His first short story had been scrawled in a notebook while sitting on a bench overlooking the Misbourne Valley, the words pouring out of him with an urgency he'd never experienced before.

After university, he'd returned to these hills whenever London's frenetic pace became too much. Even as success found him, as his books climbed bestseller lists and his name became recognizable, he'd retreated here to think, to plot, to breathe.

Then the accident happened. Fire and glass and screaming metal. Months of surgeries, of physical therapy, of looking in mirrors and not recognizing the patchwork person staring back. He hadn't walked these trails since. The pain became an excuse to never even try. Until today. Until Sadie.

His breath came harder as the path steepened, a testament to how much his fitness had declined since the accident. Before, he'd have bounded up this incline without a second thought. But he pressed on, following the trail as it curved around a massive oak tree as he approached the final bend that would lead to the familiar bench and overlook.

He stopped, unease pooling low in his stomach.

A solitary figure sat on that bench, her back to him. The wind tugged at her dark blonde hair, wisps of it blowing gently around her face and neck. She was hunched slightly, writing in a notebook. Her pen moved steadily across the page, completely unaware of his presence.

Relief surged through him, so sudden it disoriented him. She was still here. She hadn't fled Great Missenden and abandoned the book.

Hadn't abandoned him.

That thought came unbidden, and he shoved it aside. She was here to help him finish the book, nothing more.

Before he could move, Riley's ears perked up. The dog had spotted Sadie, too, his wiry body starting to wiggle as his tail whipped from side to side. Corbyn reached for his collar, but it was too late.

"Riley, no," he hissed, trying to keep his voice low, but the hound was already bounding forward, an unstoppable streak of tan fur.

Sadie turned at the sound of approaching paws, her surprise brightening into delight as Riley reached her.

"Well, hello there, handsome," she laughed as he licked her face, and the sound caused a weird tingling sensation in Corbyn's chest. "What are you doing here?"

Her gaze lifted, searching, until it landed on Corbyn. The smile faded from her face, replaced by something more guarded. She said something else to Riley that he couldn't hear, her hand absently scratching the dog behind his ears, but her eyes remained fixed on Corbyn's approaching figure.

He made his way over slowly, suddenly acutely aware of how he must look, disheveled from the climb, cheeks flushed with exertion, the scars on his face standing out more sharply in the cold air. He swallowed, mouth dry.

"Sorry about him," he said gruffly, gesturing to Riley. "No manners."

"Better than most," Sadie said, leaning into Riley's enthusiastic greeting. Her gloves lay beside her on the bench, her bare fingers still buried in Riley's fur. "No 'get out and don't come back' from him. He's just genuinely happy to see me. It's a refreshing change."

Her words landed like a direct hit, making him wince. The accusation wasn't subtle, and he knew he deserved her ire.

Corbyn shifted his weight, hyperaware of how exposed he felt here, away from the familiar shelter of his study. No desk to put between them. No manuscripts to focus on. Only her steady, steel-eyed gaze.

"What are you doing up here?" Sadie asked finally.

"Needed air," he replied, the half-truth slipping out easily. He glanced at the notebook now closed on her lap, a pen marking her place. "You're writing."

She nodded, one hand still absently stroking Riley's head. "Just thoughts. Nothing important."

"You left," he said, not quite a question.

"You told me to. Quite emphatically."

Corbyn looked away, focusing on the view instead of her face, taking a breath before saying in a rough voice, "I thought you might be booking a flight back to New York after what happened."

"The day is young," she said, her tone light. "And flights run until midnight."

Corbyn felt himself stiffen at her words, the casual way she implied she might still leave landing like a physical blow. The thought of her actually going and him having to return to his empty study sent a wave of something close to panic through him.

"I wouldn't blame you," he said, clearing his throat to try to eliminate the roughness. "Probably show good judgment on your part, actually. But I'm hoping you won't. I..." he started, then caught himself. "The book needs you."

The slip was slight, but in the quiet of the hillside, it hung between them. When he looked over at her, she was studying him with that quiet, unyielding intensity that made it difficult to focus.

"The book shouldn't be collateral damage to whatever the hell happened today," she said firmly. "It has too much potential."

Corbyn noticed how she'd shifted the focus from herself to the book. It was subtle. She wasn't asking for validation, but there was something in her measured response that suggested she wanted more than just professional acknowledgment.

"My writing... it's better with you there," he confessed, the admission coming easier than he expected. "Your perspective helps."

She nodded once, a small smile tugging at the corner of her mouth before she looked away, back toward the valley below.

"We make a good team when you're not throwing me out of rooms."

The gentle jab held no malice, just a reminder that they still had ground to cover in their working relationship.

"May I?" Corbyn gestured to the empty space beside her on the bench.

Sadie hesitated, then slid over slightly, making room. The wooden slats creaked as he lowered himself down, and the soreness in his body from the climb became more pronounced. Riley flopped at their feet with a contented sigh, clearly pleased that his humans seemed to have resolved some of the tension.

"I used to come up here as a kid," Corbyn said softly, surprising himself by offering her a personal detail. "To read. To think."

Sadie glanced at him, curiosity evident in her expression.

"It's beautiful. Peaceful."

"It was. Is," he corrected and then paused, choosing his words carefully. "I haven't been up here since before the accident."

The admission hung between them, like a peace offering. Sadie seemed to understand its significance, her expression softening slightly.

"Why today?" she asked quietly.

Corbyn looked down at his hands, his right one normal, the left a mess of scars with limited mobility. The truth was too raw, too close to the surface. *Because your notes push me harder than I push myself. Because in two weeks, you've seen through the flaws I've been blind to for months. Because with you challenging my work, I finally feel like a writer again instead of just a has-been hiding from the world.*

"Motivation," he said simply, not ready to examine any of the thoughts racing through his mind too closely. "This morning," he continued, changing course, "at the pool... I handled it badly." He paused, his jaw tightening. "I'm not used to... I could have done better."

Sadie was quiet for a moment before she replied, "I should have called out before coming down the stairs. Edie sent me to tell you lunch was ready, but I should have announced myself."

"No." The word came out sharper than he intended as he looked over at her. "It wasn't your fault. I..." He broke off again, the right words elusive. "I'm not used to being seen like that. Without warning."

"You made a lot of assumptions at the pool. I wasn't invading your privacy, nor was I guilty of any of your other accusations." Her voice was steady, and she held his gaze, unflinching. "You don't get to decide what I think or feel, Corbyn."

"I know." Corbyn's hand clenched against his thigh, the fabric of his trousers rough under his palm. "I'm..." He paused, his gaze briefly meeting hers before sliding away. "I'm trying to do better. I want to."

The words were difficult for him to say. It was as close to an apology as he could manage at the moment, and he hoped she would understand the true meaning behind it.

Sadie nodded slowly, seeming to accept the olive branch for what it was, much to his relief.

"Where do we go from here?" she asked, her voice gentle enough that he had to look back at her.

"Back to work," he said, his voice steadier now. "If you're willing."

He held his breath as he waited for her answer. Even with his attempt to smooth things over, she could still decide to leave and return home. The very thought caused a pit to form in his stomach.

"I am," she told him hesitantly before adding, "but things need to be different."

He tensed slightly, wary, and asked, "Different how?"

Turning to face him fully, she explained, "I am your partner in this, not your servant. I was sent here because I'm good at what I do, and because I'll push you to be your best self." Her voice remained firm as she continued, "I've been patient and understanding, more so than most would be, but even I have my limits, Corbyn. No more shutting me out when the work gets difficult. No more ordering me to leave when I challenge you or things get too personal for your comfort. I deserve better than that, and so does this book."

Partners. The word landed heavily. He'd worked alone for so long, even before the accident, and collaboration had never been his strength. Letting someone else into his creative process felt like standing naked in a crowded room. But she was right. The book deserved better. And if he was honest with himself, so did she.

"Agreed," he said finally, the word a commitment he wasn't entirely sure he could keep, but one he would try to honor.

A drop of rain landed on the bench between them, then another. The clouds that had been threatening rain all afternoon were finally making good on their promise. Riley stood, shaking himself preemptively.

"We should head back," Sadie said, tucking her notebook into her bag and pulling on her gloves, "before it really starts coming down."

Corbyn nodded, rising from the bench with a wince he couldn't quite hide.

"I, ah, drove to the inn first," Corbyn said, aware of how the admission revealed more than he'd intended. "My car's still there."

Sadie's eyebrows lifted slightly, and he saw a flicker of surprise crossing her face before she schooled her expression.

"I'm parked at the foot of the trail," she told him, her voice neutral despite the small smile threatening at the corners of her mouth. "I can give you a lift back to the Roaring Stag."

They started down the path together, Corbyn setting a careful pace. The raindrops became more insistent, pattering against the leaves and their jackets. Riley trotted ahead, occasionally looking back to ensure they were following.

"I read your notes on chapter eleven last night," Corbyn said as they walked, needing to reestablish their professional boundaries, to bring them back to safer territory. "Your point about the arson scene having too much exposition... you were right."

Sadie glanced at him, the corners of her mouth tugging up ever so slightly. "I thought it slowed the pacing too much."

"It did. I've been reworking it. Showing more through Shaw's reactions, less through the technical details."

"That sounds promising," she said. "I'd like to see it when you're ready."

It wasn't long before they reached the end of the trail. Corbyn found himself chuckling along with Sadie as they watched Riley try to squeeze his bulk into the back seat of her tiny rental car. When they pulled into the Roaring Stag's parking lot, it felt as if they were truly back on solid ground once more.

"I meant what I said," Corbyn found himself saying as she parked next to his rarely used Range Rover. "The book is better because of your input."

Sadie's eyes found his, those stormy orbs of hers studying his face for a moment before she replied, "Thank you. That means a lot, coming from you."

For a moment, their eyes locked, and he was very aware of how close they were in the confines of the small car. From here, he could smell the citrusy scent of her shampoo, something he hadn't admitted to himself that he had noticed until now. He could also see the details he had missed: the freckles across her nose, the flecks of green in her eyes.

His musings were interrupted when Riley wedged his head between them, rewarding them both with sloppy kisses. Groaning, Corbyn pushed him away, muttering about the dog not having any manners.

"So," Sadie laughed, bringing his attention back to the present, "tomorrow morning. Nine o'clock?"

"Nine," Corbyn agreed. He made no move to exit the car though, something keeping him rooted to the spot. He knew there was more to say. Words that might bridge the remaining distance between them. Words about trust, vulnerability, and the fear of being seen. But they wouldn't come, not yet.

Instead, he said, "Bring your red pen. Chapter fourteen needs work."

A smile ghosted across Sadie's lips, understanding what he couldn't quite express.

"I figured it might. The mayor's wife scene again?"

"Among other things," he admitted, his hand reaching for the door handle. "Riley and I will see you tomorrow."

"I'll be there," she promised, and for the first time that day, Corbyn felt something in his chest loosen. A knot of tension unwinding, and a feeling settling over him that everything might actually be okay.

February 21, 2025

-Sadie-

The crunch of gravel under the rental car's tires was the only sound as Sadie approached Corbyn's estate. For just over two weeks, this drive had filled her with a sense of dread as she prepared herself for the inevitable clash of wills. Today, that familiar knot of tension had loosened, replaced by something that caused a fluttering in her chest whenever she remembered their conversation on the ridge.

The book needs you.

He'd almost slipped—she was sure of it. For a split second before he'd corrected himself, she'd heard the beginning of "I" form on his lips. *I need you.* The thought sent an unexpected warmth spreading through her, one she had been trying very hard not to think about.

And then there had been his unexpected appearance not only on the ridge, but also at The Roaring Stag. Corbyn Pearce, who by all accounts barely left his property, had come looking for her. He had driven into the village and walked into a public establishment, risking stares and whispers, because he'd wanted to what? Apologize? Make amends? The importance of that gesture wasn't lost on her, especially after what Maggie had told her.

***

"There you are," Maggie called, wiping her hands on a dish towel tucked into the strings of her apron. "I was beginning to wonder if you'd run off for good after whatever had Corbyn Pearce darkening my door this afternoon. He came in here looking for you, all worked up."

Sadie shrugged off her coat, draping it over the back of a bar stool. "Worked up how?"

Maggie grinned, pouring a glass of red wine without a word and sliding it across the bar.

"He was waiting for me when I got back from shopping," she told Sadie, a little smirk tugging at her lips. "He was frantic to find out where you had gone."

Sadie wrapped her fingers around the glass stem, taking a moment to gather her thoughts, before answering, "We had a rather... tense moment earlier. He wanted to apologize. Or rather, offer the closest thing to an apology I'm going to get from him."

"Well, I'll be," Maggie murmured, leaning her elbows on the bar. "He hasn't crossed through that door since before the accident. You know, when I took over this place about twelve years ago, he'd come in most evenings when he was working on his first novel. Always sat at the same corner table by the window. Polite, but kept to himself."

"Keeping to himself sounds familiar," Sadie said wryly.

"Oh, but he was different then," Maggie insisted. "He was quiet, but he was... approachable. He'd listen to the locals' stories for hours, jotting notes in that little book of his. Never invasive, just... curious. Observant. Used to help Mr. Davies bring in firewood when his arthritis was playing up. Walked Mrs. Whitfield's terrier when she broke her hip." A soft smile played on Maggie's lips, and she continued, "Not the sort of things that makes headlines, mind you, but they tell you something about a person's character."

Sadie tried to reconcile this image with the man he was now. Perhaps somewhere beneath all his prickly edges was the one Maggie remembered.

"It's hard to imagine, but I think I saw a bit of that today," she confided after a moment.

"And?" Maggie asked, her gaze shrewd.

Sadie ran her finger along the glass's edge, stalling a little while she gathered her thoughts.

"I think that under all that anger is someone who's been through hell, and is guarding their heart."

"People are complicated," Maggie counseled, patting Sadie's arm. "Fear makes cowards of the best of us sometimes."

Sadie took another sip of wine, digesting Maggie's words of wisdom.

"He was different today," she said. "By the ridge. There was a moment when..." She trailed off, uncertain how to describe the shift she'd felt between them.

"Go on," Maggie prompted gently.

"He told me my perspective helps," Sadie said, still slightly amazed. "After weeks of fighting me on every suggestion. And there was this... I don't know, sincerity? Like for just a second, he let the guard down."

"Is that so?"

Sadie met Maggie's knowing gaze, feeling her cheeks heat.

"We're working together. That's all."

"Mmm," Maggie hummed noncommittally as she refilled Sadie's glass. "You know, we all comment on him being this recluse, living in his big house on the hill. But I can still see him sitting right there," she nodded toward the window seat, "helping old Mrs. Hutchinson with her crossword every Sunday afternoon. Patient as a saint, even when she'd ask him the same clue three times over."

"I'd pay good money to see that," Sadie said, and she couldn't help but smile at the image.

"He's still in there, you know," Maggie responded softly. "That man who took the time. The scars didn't change who he is at his core; they just buried him a bit deeper."

Sadie swirled the wine in her glass, watching the ruby liquid catch the light.

"I think I saw him today," she admitted quietly. "Just for a moment."

"And?" Maggie pressed again, a smile playing at the corners of her mouth.

"And..." Sadie hesitated, searching for words. "I'd like to see more of him." As soon as the words left her mouth, her cheeks heated again. "Professionally speaking," she added hastily. "It would make the editing process easier."

Maggie grinned, not fooled for a second.

"You know," she said, leaning her elbows on the bar, "some people put up walls just to see who's stubborn enough to scramble over."

Sadie laughed quickly, shaking her head as she said, "Sounds like a line from those paperbacks you've got stashed back there."

Maggie chuckled, low and warm.

"Doesn't mean it's wrong, love."

***

Dropping her bag on the sofa, Sadie made her way to the kitchen, drawn by the comforting aroma of fresh bread. She found Edie at the island, flour dusting her forearms up to her elbows, a smudge of it across one cheek as she kneaded dough.

"Morning," Edie called, looking up with a warm smile. "You're earlier than usual. Eager to clash wits with our resident grump?"

Sadie grinned, heading straight for the cabinet where she knew Edie kept the mugs, grabbing one before replying, "Up with the birds. It's hard not to be when the inn's roosters think dawn is a competitive sport."

Edie laughed, the sound rich and full.

"Ah, Maggie's roosters. They've been the bane of this village for years. Even Paul tried to bribe her to relocate them once."

"Let me guess, she told him exactly where he could stick that suggestion?"

"You're learning our ways." Edie nodded approvingly as she gave the dough a final fold and covered it with a clean cloth. "Sourdough today. Paul's favorite, though if you asked him, he'd grumble that anything edible is his favorite. Man would eat bark if I buttered it properly."

Sadie laughed, pouring water over her tea bag. Paul was still a bit of a mystery to her, but she'd been picking up little tidbits of information from Edie. She got the distinct impression that they were a case of opposites attract. Where Edie loved to talk and gossip, Paul was quiet and chose his words carefully.

"Heard you and Corbyn had a chat yesterday," Edie continued after a moment. "Sorted some things out, did you?"

"We managed the conversation without bloodshed," Sadie replied with a wry smile. "Progress, I'd say."

"More than progress from what I can tell," Edie's eyes twinkled. "He came in and worked for hours. Even accepted a cup of tea and a slice of my lemon drizzle cake without acting as if I were poisoning him. Whatever you said on that ridge, it worked."

Sadie felt her cheeks warm, and she insisted, "I just reminded him we're supposed to be partners, not adversaries."

"Hmm." Edie's expression suggested she saw more than she let on as she bustled around the kitchen, putting away the ingredients. After a comfortable moment of silence, she added, almost casually, "You know, he's never been an easy man. Brilliant, yes. Kind, when he remembers the world doesn't revolve around whatever stories are in his head. But no, never easy."

"I've noticed," Sadie said dryly, making Edie chuckle. "How long have you and Paul worked for the Pearce family?"

She had gotten the feeling after watching Corbyn and Edie interact that it had been many years. There was an easy familiarity between them that made Edie feel more like family than an employee.

"Oh, I'd say it's been about thirty years now," Edie replied. "Corbyn's parents hired Paul, but when their housekeeper quit unexpectedly it seemed only natural that I step into the role, as the children were already comfortable with me. They were left in my care more often than not."

The pieces started to fall into place for Sadie. She had learned early on that while Edie had a niece and nephew who lived nearby, she and Paul had never had children of their own. Stepping into the role of caretaker and ultimately surrogate parents seemed to have been a natural progression. It also explained why Corbyn never seemed to take issue when Edie stood up to his grumbling.

"The accident changed him," Edie continued, her voice softening. "Not just the scars or the pain. It was like..." She paused, searching for words. "Like he lost faith in everything at once, his body, his talent, other people."

"That must have been awful," Sadie murmured, a heavy feeling settling in her chest.

"Hardest on his sister, Ellie, I think," Edie said. "Being a doctor and all, she took it personally when she couldn't fix him. Tried everything under the sun for his hand and his pain." She shook her head. "It was a lot for him to take in."

Sadie nodded, sensing there was more to the story but not wanting to pry. There was no way something of that magnitude could happen without affecting every member of Corbyn's family, and even though Edie had lived it, it wasn't entirely her story to tell.

"But lately with you here, he's different," Edie continued, looking at Sadie in a way that made her want to shift in her seat.

"I'm just doing my job," Sadie said quickly, taking a sip of her tea to give herself somewhere else to look other than Edie's knowing gaze.

"Maybe so," Edie conceded with a knowing smile, "but you're doing it differently than the others who've tried." She checked the clock on the wall. "Speaking of which, he'll be pacing his study by now."

Sadie drained her tea and stood, trying to shake off the storm of thoughts swirling around in her mind. Finishing the book was her reason for being here, and to blur the lines of personal and professional could easily spell disaster. Eventually, the book would be finished, and she would have to return to New York. That meant no matter what anyone else saw, she had to be careful to maintain boundaries for all their sakes.

"Thanks for this," she said, gesturing to the empty cup.

"You're welcome, love," Edie replied, patting Sadie's shoulder as she passed. She turned back to her bread dough, lifting the cloth to check its rise, then added almost casually, "And Sadie?"

"Hmm?"

"Whatever you said to him yesterday..." Edie glanced up, her eyes warm with genuine gratitude. "Thank you."

Sadie felt her cheeks flush as she nodded and slipped out of the kitchen, retrieving her bag from the sofa. Today would be about reestablishing professional boundaries, about ensuring nothing drew their attention away from the book. She couldn't let a brief glimpse of who Corbyn was behind his carefully constructed walls derail that.

Riley appeared at the end of the hallway, his lanky form wiggling as he walked toward her with evident delight. He circled her once, his tail sweeping in wide arcs, then pressed his head against her side in a gesture of greeting.

"Morning, handsome," Sadie murmured, pausing to scratch behind his ears. He leaned into her touch, eyes closing in bliss.

Riley huffed softly and then trotted ahead toward the study, looking back once to ensure she followed. All of it, the dog, the warm kitchen conversation, the way she was beginning to navigate the house with growing familiarity, meant that keeping that balance of professionalism would be that much more difficult. She was already getting attached, and that would only mean heartache when this assignment was over.

At the study door, she paused and took a deep breath. She wasn't entirely sure what awaited her on the other side. Despite her muddled thoughts, for the first time since arriving in Great Missenden, she was truly curious to see where the day would lead.

February 21, 2025

-Sadie-

The study door creaked, breaking the silence and making Sadie grimace as she pushed it open. Riley had gone ahead, disappearing through the gap that had been just wide enough for him to come and go as he pleased. By the time Sadie had crossed the threshold, the dog had already flopped onto the carpet by the fireplace.

Corbyn was at his desk, and she noticed that he had stopped writing, his pen hovering just above the page. Neither of them spoke for a moment, and she could feel the tension lingering even after yesterday's conversation.

"Morning," Sadie said, her voice neutral as she crossed to her usual chair across from him.

"Morning," Corbyn replied, not quite meeting her eyes.

Sadie set her bag down, unpacked it slowly to buy herself a beat to gauge the atmosphere. Silence stretched between them, and she could feel Corbyn's penetrating gaze without even looking up. They were no longer quite enemies, but they also weren't friends. It seemed neither was entirely sure how to proceed with this tentative truce.

Corbyn broke the quiet with a rough throat-clearing.

"I changed a few things," he said abruptly as he slid a stack of papers her way. "The warehouse scene, mostly."

Looking at the pages, surprise flickered through her as she noted the neat annotations in the margins. Throughout the manuscript, Corbyn had highlighted sections with small notes: *Expanded this as you suggested* and *Reworked dialogue here—see if it addresses your concern*, and even one that said, *You were right about this transition.*

"Oh," she said, thumbing through the pages. "That's... thorough."

"Don't sound so shocked," he said, a hint of his usual dryness returning without the former edge. "I do occasionally listen."

A small smile tugged at Sadie's lips, and she teased, "I've seen little evidence of that so far."

"Then consider this Exhibit A," Corbyn replied, the corner of his mouth quirking upward slightly.

The tension had eased a fraction, and Sadie leaned back in the chair to review the changes. Corbyn incorporated many of her suggestions, sometimes with his own twist, and her slight smile only grew the more she read.

"Don't look so smug, Reed," he said, drawing a soft chuckle from her.

"I'm not smug, just... pleasantly surprised."

"Pleasantly surprised that I can be a reasonable human being, or pleasantly surprised that you were right?" he shot back, a playful glint in his eye.

Sadie glanced up briefly, her smile widening, and teased, "Can it be both?"

He chuckled softly, shaking his head.

"I suppose that's fair."

When she looked up again and met his eyes, her breath caught. Instead of his usual scowl, there was a real smile. It was small and tentative, but the way his eyes seemed to light up told her it was honest. She had to force herself to look away, the faint amusement flickering in his eyes, making it difficult to focus.

Giving herself a little mental shake, she went back to her reading. Corbyn resumed his writing, and the sound of his pen scratching against the paper filled the study. They continued to work that way for the next several minutes until Sadie came to a scene that caused a crease to form between her brows.

Looking up, she watched him write for a moment, trying to work up the courage to test this newly minted peace treaty. She knew he was proud of the work he had done, and she didn't want to cause a setback. She felt her shoulders tense in anticipation of his reaction as she took a breath.

"I think spacing out this reveal sequence might make it hit harder," Sadie said, her voice steady but careful.

Corbyn's frame went rigid for a split second. It dawned on her then that this was a scene he had spent weeks crafting before her arrival, and she may very well have stumbled on to a hornet's nest.

"What's the issue now?" Corbyn asked, his tone taking on an all too familiar edge.

"There's no issue," Sadie told him, keeping her tone as light as possible. "The writing's tight and really strong, but I think readers need a breather to digest one jolt before we hit them with the next."

Corbyn's brow furrowed. "This scene's the backbone of the whole second act. I've torn it apart and rebuilt it three times, and it's *finally* right."

"The scene's got real weight," she said, nodding to his effort. She needed to get him back on her side, to try to see things from another perspective. "I'm just saying it might be good to reconsider its timing."

"It stays."

The words were clipped, and he immediately returned to his writing. The dismissal hit harder than an outright argument. This was his way of shutting down the conversation entirely rather than engaging, and Sadie felt herself coming close to snapping.

"Corbyn, you're not even listening..."

"I've already thought it over, Reed. There's nothing to listen to."

The words felt like a slap to the face, and Sadie felt her cheeks burn. It wasn't shame or embarrassment, but anger. She couldn't deny that this pattern felt all too familiar. With Nate, there had always been a brief period of harmony before the inevitable crash. She had spent years walking on eggshells in her personal life, and she refused to let it happen in her professional life as well.

"This is exactly what we talked about yesterday," she said, standing and placing the stack of papers she had been reading on the desk. "You're shutting down instead of engaging. You promised things would be different."

He looked up at her, and she saw his eyes narrow slightly, spine straightening as he prepared for the argument.

"Just because we agreed to be more civil doesn't mean I must agree with every suggestion you make," he replied. She noted instantly the coolness of his tone. "I am allowed to disagree with you, as this is still, in fact, my book."

"But you didn't just disagree, did you?" she fired back, throwing her hands up in exasperation. "You simply dismissed what I had to say. We are supposed to be partners, or did you already forget that?"

He stood then, and she could see the shift in his demeanor. She wasn't the only one losing her temper. She watched him stand, his eyes locked on hers as he leaned forward and braced his hands on the desk.

"I meant every word I said yesterday," he warned, his voice taking on a darker tone she hadn't heard before. "But it does not give you carte blanche to..."

"To what? Do my job?" Sadie cut in, mirroring his position as she leaned forward as well. "If we're going to make this work, we can't fall back into this dynamic every time we disagree. You need to trust me enough to hear me out."

"Trust works both ways. You could try trusting that I know what I'm doing with my own story!"

They stood there with their eyes locked, neither willing to back down. Sadie could feel a mixture of frustration and something else coursing through her. Something that had more to do with his proximity and the intensity in those blue eyes than with their disagreement about plot structure.

Before she could formulate a response that wouldn't escalate things further, Riley rose from his spot by the fire with a dramatic groan. The Irish Wolfhound padded over, tail swishing, and shoved his massive head underneath Sadie's arm and onto the pages they were arguing over. It caused several to flutter to the floor, and he looked up at them with a soft whine that seemed to say, *Enough, already!*

The absurdity of the giant dog's timing broke the tension, and Sadie couldn't suppress the laugh that escaped her lips.

"Impeccable timing, as always," Corbyn muttered, though his lips twitched with reluctant amusement as he tried to extricate the pages from beneath Riley's chin. "Some guard dog you are. You're supposed to take my side."

"Clearly, he's Team Compromise." Sadie reached out to scratch behind Riley's ears. "Wise beyond his years."

"Traitor," Corbyn told the dog, shaking his head. To Sadie, he added with a hint of resignation, "Go on, then. Make your case before he drools on the entire manuscript."

Sadie straightened, giving Riley one more scratch before meeting Corbyn's eyes once more.

"Actually, I have an idea that might solve both our concerns. May I?" she asked, gesturing toward the blank paper on his desk.

Corbyn pushed a sheet toward her, eyebrows raised in silent question.

"What if," Sadie began, sketching out a quick diagram, "instead of moving the reveal, you recontextualize it? What if he has this epiphany during the course of a conversation? With his sister, perhaps?"

Corbyn leaned forward again, and Sadie knew she had his full attention.

"Go on."

"Shaw's realization that he's been betrayed by someone he trusted is the heart of the scene," Sadie explained, glancing up to gauge his reaction. His brow was still furrowed, but his expression was thoughtful instead of angry. "What if, instead of being alone in his apartment and looking at evidence, he's talking to his sister about something seemingly unrelated, and she inadvertently gives him the piece he needs?"

"What about a gallery opening?" Corbyn countered, straightening and crossing his arms over his chest. "His sister's an art curator. Evening setting, public but intimate. White wine, pretentious conversations. She'd be distracted with managing the event, and might mention something about an acquaintance without thinking."

"Yes," Sadie nodded eagerly, her anger subsiding. She could picture it taking shape in her head: stark white walls covered with paintings, lights angled just so, a low hum of fancy voices tossing around words like brushwork and symbolism. "And, because it's such a public setting, Shaw's stuck holding it together. He's hit with this gut-punch of a realization, but he can't crack, not with so much on the line for her."

"What if," Corbyn grinned, and his eyes came alive as he looked at her, "she catches it anyway? His twitch or whatever, even though he's trying to play it cool. She could drag him off to some cramped back office, away from the suits, and push for an explanation."

The unguarded grin on his face caught her completely off guard, and it took a minute for her to realize she was staring. He was full of life and completely engaged, which caused an unfamiliar fluttering in her chest. Clearing her throat, she looked down at the pages on the desk, trying to recover her composure.

"Yeah, I think that's it," she murmured, her voice breathier than she would have liked.

Corbyn sat back in his chair, and she could feel him watching her. Slowly, she returned to her own seat, forcing herself to meet his eyes once more. The grin was gone, but it had been replaced by something softer, almost searching. He had been indifferent to her opinion, but she had also let her own insecurities get the better of her.

"I'm sorry if I came on a bit strong," she confessed, petting Riley, who had placed his head in her lap. "Having my thoughts dismissed... it's part of my baggage, but you shouldn't have to be held accountable for that."

"It's no secret I can be a stubborn arse, Reed," he admitted after a moment. "But we did agree to be partners, and I shouldn't have treated you like an adversary."

A comfortable silence settled between them, markedly different from the tense quiet after their previous arguments. Corbyn gathered the papers they had been working on, looking over their notes once more. She watched him lean back in his chair, lips pursing as he took everything into consideration.

"I'll draft this tonight," he offered after a moment. "I'll have something for you to review tomorrow."

"I look forward to it," Sadie replied, standing to head to the sofa where the pages she had been working on yesterday waited for her on the coffee table. Riley, now lacking her attention, wandered over to Corbyn and nudged his arm with his nose.

"He needs a walk," Corbyn chuckled, rising from his chair and flexing his left hand. She had noticed he tended to clench that hand when under stress, likely adding to any discomfort. "We've been at this longer than I realized."

"Time flies when you're locked in a creative disagreement," Sadie said with a small smile, looking up at him from the sofa.

Corbyn's mouth quirked in that almost smile, and he conceded, "Indeed." She watched as uncertainty suddenly crossed his features before he added, "Would you... like to join us? There's a path through the orchard that's pleasant this time of day."

The invitation surprised Sadie. Usually, he left for walks without even looking her way. It was a small thing, this social overture, but significant coming from a man who had initially resented her presence in his home. That flutter in her chest was back, and a slightly shy smile formed on her lips.

"I'd like that," she said simply, standing to follow him out of the study.

Later, as they walked the orchard path with Riley, their conversation flowed more easily than before. They discussed the book, but also the grounds, Riley's ridiculous squirrel obsession, and various other topics.

It was small talk, but for two people who had spent so much time trying to find common ground, it felt like a bridge being built... one unremarkable exchange at a time.

February 24, 2025

-Corbyn-

An unfamiliar anticipation tightened in Corbyn's chest the moment Sadie's rental car rounded the bend. He had settled into one of the weathered wicker chairs on the porch and found himself straightening in his seat when he spotted the car.

She didn't immediately exit the vehicle, and he found himself studying her from his spot through the windshield. She closed her eyes briefly, and her lips were moving in what might have been whispered encouragement. Then, she took a deep breath before opening the door and stepping out into the chilly February air.

The short ritual struck him, and he wondered if she still found working with him so challenging that she needed to gather herself beforehand. The thought caused an unexpected feeling of regret. He had been trying to control his temper since their last clash, keeping cutting remarks and dismissive behavior to a minimum. He had thought that they had reached some sort of common ground, but perhaps he had misjudged how much damage had been done during their earlier sessions.

Before he could dwell on this realization, a blur of tan fur ran across the lawn. Riley charged toward Sadie, tail wagging wildly as he nearly crashed into her. Instead of her taking a step back, as Corbyn expected, she opened her arms to the dog, who stood on his hind legs to put his front paws on her shoulders. He was prepared to correct Riley when he heard Sadie's laugh.

"Well, good morning to you, too, you big goofball," she exclaimed, a grin spreading across her face.

Corbyn leaned forward slightly in the chair, caught by the transformation. Without her usual calm, professional mask, her face was softer and more expressive. She roughed up the fur behind Riley's ears before giving him a gentle push so he stood on all fours once more.

"Alright, alright," she laughed as Riley nudged insistently at her hand. "Let's find you a stick, shall we?"

He watched as she scanned the frost-covered grass, spotting a branch nearby that she quickly retrieved before the hound could grab it. With an exaggerated wind-up that had Riley practically bouncing with anticipation, she tossed the stick in a high arc over the dog's head.

"Go get it, boy!"

Riley launched himself skyward, a graceful leap despite his lanky build. His powerful jaws snapped shut around the stick mid-air, and he landed with a triumphant huff that made Sadie clap her hands in delight.

"Good boy! That was impressive!"

Corbyn couldn't tear his eyes away from the scene. This version of Sadie Reed, playful, animated, and genuinely joyful, was miles from the woman who sat across from him in his study each day. Something about seeing her like this, with her hair slightly disheveled and her professional guard completely lowered, pulled at a forgotten part of him.

The game continued, Riley returning the stick for several rounds before deciding to change the rules. Instead of bringing it back, he planted his rear in the air, head lowered in a comical play bow, the stick firmly clenched in his jaws.

"Oh, so that's how it's going to be?" Sadie called, placing her hands on her hips in mock indignation. "You think you can out-stubborn me, huh?"

Riley's tail swished back and forth, stick clenched firmly in his mouth as if to say, *Bring it on, human.*

"Alright, you adorable menace," Sadie declared, crouching and taking a fake step toward the dog so he would spring backwards in excitement. "Let's see who wins this standoff. My money's on the one with opposable thumbs!"

Riley danced away as she playfully lunged for the stick, his body swaying gleefully. The standoff continued, Sadie laughing as she made increasingly theatrical attempts to retrieve the prize. They engaged in this light-hearted battle of wills for several minutes, with Riley always staying just out of reach.

As if sensing his gaze, Sadie glanced up suddenly, their eyes meeting across the lawn. Instead of immediately looking away, she held his gaze, her grin turning into a soft smile. For a moment, they simply looked at each other, neither moving nor speaking. The unexpected connection made Corbyn's pulse quicken, something it seemed to be doing around her more often lately.

"Enjoying the show?" she called, aiming for lightness but not entirely hiding a hint of something else in her tone. It wasn't quite embarrassment, but perhaps a bit of self-consciousness.

"It's not often I see Riley bested at his own game," he replied, surprising himself with the ease in his voice.

"Oh, I wouldn't say I've bested him yet," Sadie laughed, gesturing to the stick firmly clamped in Riley's jaws. "We're in a bit of a standoff."

Something in her relaxed posture and the way her smile remained when she looked at him felt like an invitation to join them. Before he could overthink it, Corbyn rose from the wicker chair and descended the porch steps.

"Then allow me to be the tiebreaker," he said, whistling once, sharp and clear. Riley's ears perked up immediately. "Drop it."

The stick fell to the ground as Riley bounded over, his loyalty shifting seamlessly. The Irish Wolfhound's tail wagged furiously as Corbyn scratched behind his ears.

"And here I thought we had a special bond," Sadie muttered with a chuckle as she approached them.

"He's fickle," Corbyn replied, surprising himself again with this easy banter. "Hard-won loyalty through years of table scraps and belly rubs."

Sadie's smile widened, and she laughed as she said, "A strategy I'll have to remember."

A rare, companionable quiet settled between them, so different from the tense quiet that usually filled his study. There was something striking about her features when animated by genuine emotion rather than careful professionalism.

"We should get started," Corbyn said, suddenly aware of how long he'd studied her face. "I made some progress on the warehouse scene last night."

"Lead the way," Sadie replied, bending to retrieve her bag from where she'd dropped it during the game with Riley.

As she straightened, Riley circled behind her and bumped against the backs of her knees. Sadie stumbled forward with a surprised "Oh!" as her balance failed her. Corbyn moved instinctively, closing the distance between them in two quick strides. His hands found her waist, steadying her before she could fall.

"Riley," he admonished, wincing a bit at the sudden movement. "Manners."

His attention, though, wasn't on the dog. It was on the warmth beneath his fingers where they gripped Sadie's sides, on the subtle citrus scent that reached him as she turned her face in surprise. His left hand, usually so stiff and uncooperative, seemed to have forgotten its limitations and curved perfectly against the soft fabric of her coat.

"Sorry," she murmured, her voice oddly breathy. "He caught me off guard."

Corbyn realized he was still holding her, though she had regained her balance. His hands lingered at her waist, the contact sending an unfamiliar warmth through his body. Time seemed to stand still as they stared at each other, until Riley's bark startled them both back to reality.

"Happens to the best of us," he managed, his voice rougher than he had intended, as he reluctantly released her and stepped back. "He forgets his size."

The moment stretched between them, loaded with something neither seemed prepared to name. Sadie tucked a strand of hair behind her ear, her cheeks flushed from more than just the morning chill.

Clearing his throat, Corbyn finally looked away, his attention drifting back toward the house. With an awkward sweep of his hand, he asked, "Shall we?"

Together, they walked to the house, Riley following them inside and then into the kitchen. Edie had left a pot of tea on the island with two mugs, and he watched Sadie immediately start to fix two cups of tea. Somehow, she had learned that he took his with a splash of milk, and she slid the perfectly made drink toward him on the island.

Riley sat next to her, his head leaning against her side until she reached down to stroke his fur while she poured her own tea.

"He's shameless," Corbyn commented, nodding toward the dog. "Always knows who to charm for attention."

Sadie glanced over, another soft smile playing on her lips.

"I don't mind. I miss having a dog around. My apartment in New York barely had room for my books, let alone a pet." She scratched behind Riley's ears, earning a contented groan from the massive hound, and added, "And my schedule was impossible when I was with Nate... it wouldn't have been fair to any pet."

"Nate?" Corbyn asked before he could stop himself.

A shadow flickered across her face, there and gone so quickly he almost missed it.

"My ex," she said simply, her focus returning to Riley. "My living situation has been... in flux while I wait for my lease to end."

Something in her tone warned against further questions, but it sparked Corbyn's curiosity nonetheless. Aside from the brief mention of her ex on Valentine's Day, this was the first personal detail she'd volunteered since arriving in Great Missenden. It felt a bit like venturing into uncharted waters, but something in him couldn't bring himself to discourage the conversation.

"Riley came to me during a period of flux," he heard himself saying, the words emerging before he'd fully decided to share them. "After the accident."

Sadie looked up, her expression neutral, but her gray eyes were looking at him with interest. She didn't speak, didn't push, just waited. He realized she was offering space for him to continue or retreat as he chose, and there was something incredibly refreshing in that approach.

"Ellie brought him home," Corbyn continued, his right hand moving to stroke Riley's flank. "She said he was a rescue and needed someone with patience. I think it was the other way around."

The corner of Sadie's mouth lifted slightly, and she asked, "He needed you, or you needed him?"

"Both, maybe." Corbyn's gaze drifted to his mug of tea on the island. "I wasn't in a good place. The surgeries kept failing to restore function to my hand, and the pressure started for the book I couldn't seem to write..." He trailed off, surprised at how much he'd revealed.

"And Riley gave you something else to focus on," Sadie finished softly.

"He needed food, walks, and attention. He didn't care about deadlines or scars or whether I could type properly," Corbyn explained, and he felt something tight in his chest ease as he spoke. "It's hard to stay in bed feeling sorry for yourself when a giant dog is whining to go outside."

Sadie smiled, and, to his relief, it wasn't the pitying look he'd dreaded. There was understanding in her eyes, warm and genuine, without the uncomfortable fake sympathy that made his skin crawl.

"I get that," she said. "Having something, or someone, who needs you can be grounding." A brief shadow crossed her face again, and she paused, absently tracing a pattern on Riley's fur. "I spent years supporting my ex's writing, Nate's novel drafts, his submissions, his rejections. I edited every word, managed his schedule, created space for his 'process.'" The word carried a hint of bitterness. "Even put my own writing on hold because he said we couldn't both be pursuing the same dream at the same time."

She looked up, seeming surprised at her own candor. "Sorry, I don't know why I mentioned that."

"Because some burdens get lighter when shared," Corbyn offered quietly, realizing how much this moment meant for both of them.

Sadie gave him a small, grateful smile, softly saying, "Maybe."

They fell into silence for a moment, both of them sipping their tea. Neither of them seemed to feel the need to fill it with small talk. It occurred to him then, somehow, without his noticing, Sadie Reed had coaxed him into an almost... normal conversation.

"We should probably get to work," she said, drawing him from his musings. "Chapter sixteen won't fix itself."

"No, it certainly won't," he agreed, and they both took their mugs as they made their way toward the study. "The revisions are helping," he added, surprised by how easy the admission was. "The book is... tighter."

Glancing over, he saw Sadie smile, and her whole face brightened at the acknowledgment. He felt his breath catch, and he tried desperately not to wonder what exactly that meant.

"It's a good story, Corbyn. It deserves to be told right."

At the door to the study, he motioned for her to lead the way, knowing if Edie saw him being anything less than a gentleman, he'd be hearing about it for the next week. As he watched her pass, he couldn't help but muse on this new development in their relationship. They weren't exactly friends, but they were certainly no longer adversaries. They were something undefinable, and that intrigued him more than he cared to admit.

February 25, 2025

-Sadie-

Sadie lingered in a cozy corner by the window of the Roaring Stag, enjoying the warmth of the morning sun as she continued the short story she had been working on in her journal. The memory of the brief moment on the Tube had taken on a life of its own, and it was turning into pages and pages of writing. The young man with those blue eyes had become a real character on the page, no longer just a dream.

The sound of an email notification broke the peaceful moment, and Sadie set down her pen. Her stomach tightened when Nate's name appeared on the screen. He'd been quiet these past few days—no manipulative texts or drunken voicemails—which had been a welcome reprieve. Now, though, as she stared at the phone screen, she felt anxiety crawl under her skin.

"Just delete it," she muttered, finger hovering over the trash icon. But curiosity won out, as it often did with Nate, and with a sigh, she opened the message.

She froze as she reread the message to be sure she wasn't seeing things. Instead of the usual vitriol, the email was surprisingly formal.

Sadie,

Hope England is treating you well. I've accepted an adjunct position at NYU, teaching creative writing. You always said I should consider teaching, and I'm tired of waiting for my masterpiece to come along. It's time I prove I can contribute, rather than just talking about potential.

The apartment feels empty without your books everywhere. I was cleaning out the bedroom and found your college journals. Let me know if you want me to bring them to Jess for when you return.
Take care,
Nate

Sadie stared at the screen, so many conflicting emotions washing over her at once. This was precisely the sort of message that had worked in the past when he had felt her slipping away. She found herself unconsciously analyzing each word, searching for genuine change while still trying to guard against hope.

"Just delete it," she whispered again, but her finger hovered over the screen. She recognized the pattern. It was what Jess had called "hoovering," where he conceded just enough to suck her back in when she was breaking free.

"Coffee?" Maggie asked, coming up beside the table with the coffee pot in hand. She glanced at Sadie, her eyebrows knitting together in concern. "You alright, love? You're white as a sheet."

"Email from my ex," Sadie said, shoving her phone into her bag. "Apparently, now that I'm finally free of him, he's decided to act like a grown-up."

Maggie snorted, pouring coffee into Sadie's cup. "Blokes like him? Same old spots, just better at tucking 'em under a rug when they're after something."

The blunt words hit their mark, the emotional turmoil easing a bit. "Yeah. I know you're right."

"'Course I am," Maggie said, flashing a grin. "Seen too many laps around this bloody block. Now, don't keep your grumpy writer waiting too long."

Sadie finished her coffee before gathering her things. Over the last several weeks, Maggie had grown into the confidant Sadie had sorely needed since arriving in England. She was grateful for the straightforward wisdom and support that helped her see things more clearly.

When she arrived at the manor, Riley greeted her at the door with his usual enthusiasm. The dog's paws landed on her shoulders, drawing a laugh from her.

"Good morning to you, too, handsome," she said, having to brace herself so she didn't stumble back under Riley's weight.

"He'd greet a burglar with the same enthusiasm," came Corbyn's dry response from the kitchen. "Worst guard dog in England."

There was a warmth beneath the sardonic tone that hadn't been there when she'd first arrived, and she could almost hear the playful smirk in his voice.

"Morning," Sadie replied, dropping her bag on the sofa on her way to the kitchen. "Sorry if I'm a bit late. Got caught up in... something."

"Edie's left tea and scones," he said, his back to her as she entered. "Apparently, we're being fattened for slaughter."

A soft chuckle escaped her, and she immediately reached for a scone from the plate on the island. Before she could even take a bite, Corbyn placed a steaming mug of tea in front of her. For a moment, she was taken aback. He was usually already tucked away in his study, hard at work, so to have him serve her a cup of tea rendered her momentarily speechless.

"Honey's there," he said, nodding toward the small bottle on the island, seemingly unaware of her surprise.

"Thanks," Sadie murmured, and she stared down at the mug on the counter.

It was such a simple act—pouring a cup of tea for someone else—but it was so different from what she had grown used to over the last decade of her life. There was no angle; Corbyn wasn't trying to use the tea to get something in return. It was just basic human decency.

Unconsciously, her thoughts drifted back to Nate's email, specifically to her journals. The leather-bound notebooks had been her favorite, and he'd known how much they meant to her. Now she couldn't help wondering: was his offer a genuine kindness, or just a carefully baited hook designed to draw her back into his orbit?

"Reed?"

She blinked, the kitchen coming back into focus. Corbyn was watching her, his head tilted slightly, a frown creasing his forehead.

"Sorry, what?" she asked, color blooming across her cheeks at being caught clearly lost in thought.

"I asked if you wanted milk," he said, his expression uncharacteristically concerned. "You've been staring at that mug for nearly a minute."

"Oh, I... I just... got caught in a thought," she stammered, cheeks heating even further. Quickly, she reached for the milk, turning away enough to hide the blush. "I'm fine."

From the corner of her eye, she could see Corbyn lean back against the counter. He was studying her, his silent observation slightly unnerving as she tried to regain her composure.

"You don't seem fine."

His comment stopped her hand as she stirred her tea with a spoon. The directness of the observation was new. A week ago, he wouldn't have noticed, or if he had, he wouldn't have said anything. Looking over, she saw his stance was less rigid, his left hand, usually tucked away in a pocket or clenched in a fist, was relaxed at his side. He was watching her with a curious, worried focus rather than annoyance.

"My ex emailed me," she replied, the words tumbling out before she could reconsider. "It's... thrown me a bit, I suppose."

Corbyn's eyes narrowed, but his expression was carefully neutral as he asked, "Bad news?"

"No, that's just it," Sadie told him, trying to put her jumbled thoughts into words. "It's sickeningly pleasant. He's taken a teaching position, which is something I suggested years ago. He's being thoughtful about my old journals." She shook her head. "I've been down this road with him before; it's just..."

"You're not sure whether to believe him," he finished for her, and she shifted under the weight of his stare.

"I know better," Sadie said firmly, taking a sip of tea. "Logically, I know exactly what he's doing. But there's this tiny voice that wonders if maybe this time..."

"If he's actually changed," Corbyn supplied, and she looked up to meet his gaze, surprised by his perception.

"It's stupid."

"It's human," Corbyn corrected, his voice gentler than she'd ever heard it. "Hope is persistent, even when we know better."

The understanding in his tone loosened something in Sadie's chest. Without thinking, she pulled out her phone and opened up the email. "Here," she said, holding it out to him. "You understand human nature better than anyone I know; it's what makes your characters so real. Tell me what you see."

Corbyn hesitated, his expression suggesting he recognized the significance of her request. Finally, he accepted the phone, scanning the message quickly. His jaw ticked as he read, the only outward sign of anything that might be running through his head.

"He's positioning himself as the reformed character," Corbyn said, returning the phone. "Taking credit for changes you suggested, implying he's stable now. And the part about your journals..."

He hesitated, almost as if he was unsure if he should continue, and she urged, "What about them?"

"It's a hook," Corbyn said bluntly. "Something he knows you'll want, something to keep you responding. And it's a reminder of your shared history, 'look at all we've been through together.'" His voice had hardened, and Sadie noticed his left hand had once more curled into a fist at his side.

"Well, I'm not planning on responding," Sadie said, tucking the phone back into her pocket. "Not yet, anyway. Maybe not at all."

"Good," Corbyn said, his tone sharp enough to make Sadie's eyebrows lift. He cleared his throat, modulating his tone when he spoke once more. "That is... You seem more focused when he's not intruding." The words came haltingly as if he were unused to expressing concern.

"I am," Sadie admitted, a slight smirk on her lips. "Which is surprising, given I'm spending my days with a notoriously curmudgeonly author."

The teasing comment broke the tension. She noticed a hint of a smile on Corbyn's face before he retorted, "Careful, Reed. I might start thinking you actually enjoy our battles."

"Now, let's not get carried away," she countered, relishing the moment of banter. "Shall we get started? I have thoughts on that scene transition in chapter fifteen you mentioned yesterday."

Riley trailed after them as they made their way to the study, and for the next two hours, they fell into their familiar working rhythm. They smoothed out the scene transition, fixed a character inconsistency, and tightened a bit of dialogue. Working with Corbyn when he was receptive to feedback was surprisingly satisfying. He still pushed back when he felt strongly about something, but the defensiveness that had been present in their early sessions was gone, allowing for a more collaborative approach.

"You have a remarkable eye for structure," Corbyn said unexpectedly as they solved a particularly thorny timeline issue.

The compliment caught Sadie off guard, and she shifted in her seat. She twisted her pen between her fingers, a little smile tugging at her lips.

"That's... thank you," she said, her voice soft.

When she looked up, their eyes met, and for a moment, she felt a sense of déjà vu. His gaze had softened, the blue becoming even more striking, and an image flashed in her mind of the young man from the Tube who had been haunting her memories for fifteen years. She quickly pushed that aside, though, telling herself it was simply because she had been working on a story based on that moment.

By mid-morning, Corbyn had settled in to work on new pages while Sadie reviewed what he'd written the day before. She curled up in the leather armchair on the opposite side of the desk, red pen poised over his manuscript, but she could not focus. The contrast between Corbyn's sincere appreciation earlier and Nate's manipulative email kept pulling at her thoughts.

Hope England is treating you well.

You always said I should consider teaching.

The apartment feels empty without your books everywhere.

Each sentence felt like an attempt to pull her back to New York and the old, suffocating patterns of their relationship. Sadie stared at the papers before her, not seeing the words. Instead, she was seeing the email, her mind overanalyzing every word.

"I can practically hear you thinking," Corbyn said, setting down his pen and breaking her from her thought spiral. "You're still dwelling on it."

Sadie sighed, leaning back in her chair, rubbing her temples as she groaned, "Sorry. I told myself I wasn't going to, and now I'm doing exactly what he wants, obsessing over his words."

Corbyn set his jaw, then looked away toward the window. He was silent for a moment, and Sadie figured he would simply return to his work. She looked down, trying to figure out where she had left off before her mind wandered.

"Just say it," he muttered. He was looking at her expectantly, and her brow furrowed in confusion. "If you need to talk about it... I can listen."

Sadie stared at him, caught off guard, and quipped, "Careful, Pearce. I might start to think you aren't a complete grump." The quip slipped out automatically, a shield against the vulnerability his unexpected kindness had triggered. She could have sworn his lips twitched in amusement, and she gave him a small smile before she continued, "You really want to hear about my ex?"

"We're not making much progress here anyway. And..." he hesitated with a shrug, then continued with what seemed like carefully chosen words, "sometimes it helps to speak things aloud. Makes them less powerful."

The moment felt significant. Corbyn Pearce, who had barely tolerated personal conversation a week ago, was now inviting her to confide in him. Sadie studied his face, the tension around his eyes suggesting he was as surprised by the offer as she was.

"I met him in college," she began slowly, testing the waters. "We had a few of the same classes our freshman year, and he'd already published a few short stories in literary magazines. I thought he was brilliant." She gave a short, humorless laugh. "He made sure I thought that."

Corbyn listened, his expression neutral but attentive, as she continued.

"He could be incredibly charming when he wanted to be, but his moods were..." she searched for the right word, "unpredictable.

Everything depended on how his writing was going. If he got rejected, it was somehow my fault for not supporting him properly. If he got accepted, well, that was all his talent."

Riley had gotten up as she spoke, stretching as he moved from his place in front of the fire. The dog settled at her feet, as if sensing the shift in her mood, his warm weight against her ankles providing silent comfort as the words poured out.

"The first time he destroyed my writing—"

"He what?" Corbyn interrupted, his voice suddenly sharp.

Sadie blinked, surprised by the strength of his reaction. When it came to things outside the realm of the book or his privacy, Corbyn usually showed as little emotion as possible.

"He... he was drunk," she stammered after a moment. "I'd been writing a short story in my journal that I was excited about. When I showed it to him, he told me I was copying him, that it was derivative of his writing style. When I disagreed, he ripped out the pages and tore them up." She forced her voice to stay even, despite the lump that had formed in her throat.

Corbyn's expression had darkened, his mouth set in a hard line, and he seethed, "And you stayed."

It wasn't a question, and Sadie bristled at what sounded like judgment.

"Yes, I stayed. Because he convinced me it was a one-time thing. He apologized for a week, and he seemed genuinely remorseful. He replaced my journal... and I..." she trailed off, the familiar shame washing over her, making her cheeks burn.

"You loved him," Corbyn finished, his tone softening.

Sadie looked up, startled as she whispered, "Yes."

A beat passed between them, allowing for a moment of understanding before he asked quietly, "What made you finally leave?"

Sadie stared down at her hands, a sharp memory surfacing. She wasn't sure she was ready to share it. Instead, she said, "I got tired of making excuses, and of feeling like I was losing myself more and more with each passing day." She looked up, feeling her expression harden. "I'd already given up so much... I stopped writing, stopped dreaming, stopped seeing friends. Everything revolved around his moods, his needs, and his writing. So, one day I went home with Jess after work instead of going to our apartment. I only went back to get my clothes when I knew he'd be out at his writer's group."

Corbyn was silent for a long moment, his expression unreadable. He leaned forward slowly, his elbows resting on his desk as he looked at her across the way.

"He sounds like a special kind of bastard," he told her, his voice tight with what Sadie was surprised to recognize as anger. It wasn't anger at her, though; it was *for* her, for what Nate had done to her.

"He wasn't all bad," Sadie said, the reflexive defense falling from her lips before she could stop it.

Corbyn shook his head. "Don't do that. Don't make excuses for him."

"I wasn't..." Sadie began, then stopped, realizing he was right, her shoulders dropping in shame. "Old habit. Sorry."

Riley picked his head up with a whine, looking between Corbyn and Sadie. Reaching down, she stroked the dog's head, the action soothing them both.

"It's okay, boy," Sadie murmured, and Riley leaned his head against her leg.

She heard the sound of Corbyn's chair scraping on the floor as he stood, and listened to his footsteps as he moved around the desk. Her breath caught when he crouched in front of her, forcing her to look at him. She saw him wince, but he didn't stand; instead, he just held her gaze.

"Listen to me, Reed," he said, his voice low and intent. "A man who destroys your work and who tries to extinguish your creativity... he doesn't deserve a second of your doubt. He doesn't deserve the space he's taking up in your head right now."

The ferocity in his tone caught her off guard, and she felt herself blink back tears. She refused to cry, not in front of Corbyn, and especially not over Nate.

"I know that," she whispered. "Rationally, I know that."

"But emotionally?" Corbyn pressed.

"That's harder," she admitted. "A decade is a long time to untangle."

"Yes, it is," he agreed, his expression softening. "But you're doing it. You left. Don't let him pull you backwards. Not even in your thoughts."

They were closer than they'd ever been, except for that brief moment when Riley had nearly knocked her over. He was close enough that Sadie could see the faint stubble along his jaw, the way the scars climbed his neck, and the golden flecks within the blue in his irises. The scent of his cologne flooded her senses, and she felt something electric humming between them. A pull low in her stomach stole her breath for a moment before she could respond.

"I won't," she promised softly.

His eyes dropped briefly to her lips, and for one dizzying moment, Sadie thought he might lean closer. Instead, he seemed to catch himself, and he stood before leaning back against the edge of the desk.

"Good," he said, his voice rougher than usual. "Because you deserve better."

Without thinking, she reached out, placing her hand over Corbyn's where it rested on the desk. His skin was warm beneath her fingers, and she felt the slight start of surprise at her touch.

"Thank you," she said simply.

Corbyn looked down at their hands, his expression a complex mixture of emotions Sadie couldn't fully decipher. When he looked up again, something shifted in his expression. There was a vulnerability that mirrored her own.

"Reed, I..."

The study door swung open as Edie bustled in with a tea tray, her cheerful voice shattering the moment. "Thought you two could use a..." She stopped abruptly, taking in their proximity and the way Sadie pulled her hand away from his. "Oh! I'm interrupting."

Corbyn stood quickly, moving back to his chair with false casualness, clearly something he had perfected over the years.

"Just discussing character motivation," he said smoothly. "Thank you, Edie."

"Perfect timing, actually," Sadie added, turning to mess with the papers in her lap to hide her blush. "We've hit a bit of a wall with chapter sixteen."

"Well then," Edie chuckled with barely concealed amusement that had Sadie fighting back a groan, "I'll leave you to your 'character motivations.' Lunch in an hour."

Riley followed Edie to the door, the lure of kitchen scraps stronger than his need to stay pressed against Sadie's leg.

As the door closed behind Edie, a slightly awkward silence edged around them. Sadie rose from the chair and busied herself with pouring tea. In the back of her mind, she wondered if this was another one of those moments, one that would further alter the way she and Corbyn interacted.

They would need to tread carefully. Blurring the lines between personal and professional any further could be disastrous. Yet, she had found a comfort in his presence she hadn't expected, and she wasn't sure what that would mean going forward.

"So," Corbyn said finally, accepting the cup she handed him, his fingers carefully avoiding contact with hers. "About that scene transition..."

It was an attempt to steer them back onto safer ground, something she knew was vital in this moment.

"Right," she said, gathering her notes. "The transition."

As they returned to the manuscript, Sadie felt more settled than she had before their unexpected chat. She wouldn't be responding to Nate's email because Corbyn was right: she deserved better than a man whose love had always come with conditions. She owed it to herself to reclaim what she had lost.

February 26, 2025

-Sadie-

The steady patter against the windshield had Sadie's unease growing as she drew closer to the manor. The cold front—and the rain it brought—had rolled in the previous evening. It was precisely the sort of weather that could set old injuries throbbing, and she suspected today might be especially difficult for Corbyn.

When she arrived, Edie greeted her in the kitchen as usual. She was wiping flour-dusted hands on her apron, but Sadie instantly noticed the way the other woman's lips pursed.

"Morning, love," Edie sighed, her voice taking on an edge she hadn't heard from her before. "He's in the study as usual. I've put the kettle on."

"Thanks," Sadie replied, hanging her coat on the rack by the door. "I'll take him some tea."

"Good luck with him today," Edie added, lowering her voice slightly. "Weather makes his hand act up something fierce, though he'd rather bite his tongue than admit it."

Sadie nodded, preparing two mugs of tea. She'd learned exactly how Corbyn preferred his, a splash of milk, no sugar, steeped precisely four minutes. It gave her a moment to collect herself, knowing that if Edie was on edge, then there had likely already been tension in the house.

When she approached the study, she paused at the threshold. Through the partially open door, she could see Corbyn hunched over his desk, his shoulders tense as he typed. His right hand tapped out a steady rhythm while his left hovered awkwardly over the keys, darting in every so often to tap a letter before retreating. A grimace flickered across his face as he flexed and stretched his scarred fingers, clearly trying to work through the stiffness.

Typing up the pages of his handwritten manuscript was a necessity, and he kept his laptop under lock and key. His fear that his work would be stolen once more meant it had to be hardwired to the printer, not connected to the internet.

Sprawled by the hearth, Riley lifted his head at her entrance, his tail thumping a gentle greeting against the floor. The sound caused Corbyn to look up, and Sadie caught the flash of pain that crossed his features before he could mask it.

"Morning," she said, keeping her voice light as she crossed the room. "Thought we could use some fortification before diving into the day's work."

"Thank you," Corbyn said, his voice rougher than usual as she set one mug on the desk where he could reach it. He flexed his fingers again, a barely suppressed wince betraying the cost of even that tiny movement.

Sadie settled into what had become her chair, angled slightly toward his desk, and kept her voice as neutral as possible. "Bad day?"

Corbyn's mouth tightened, his instinctive denial visibly forming. Then, surprisingly, his shoulders dropped, and he grumbled, "Blasted rain." That simple statement gave her all the confirmation she needed.

"My mom's hand acts up whenever a storm front moves through," Sadie told him, sipping her tea. That earned her a curious look, and she noticed that his expression seemed to soften.

She needed to be careful to not push too hard, but her familiarity with what he was experiencing seemed to ease his temper.

He gestured toward the laptop screen, his voice tight when he replied, "I've been trying to type up those edits we agreed on yesterday. It's going at a bloody snail's pace."

"I could type them for you," she suggested, knowing that her offer, no matter how sincere, would likely be rejected. "Since we've already decided on the wording..."

"No."

The word was clipped, definitive, and Sadie nodded, accepting the boundary without comment. His independence was something he guarded as closely as his writing, and she had come to understand how important that was to him.

"Alright then," she said, reaching for her notebook. "Why don't we talk through the climax of the book instead? We can work out where it's heading."

Relief briefly softened Corbyn's expression, though he tried to hide it behind his mug as he took a long sip of his tea. They fell into a productive rhythm, discussing how the various plot threads would converge in the climax. Sadie sketched a rough timeline on her notepad, capturing Corbyn's ideas and adding her own suggestions. The work absorbed them both, and for nearly an hour, the frustration with the laptop was forgotten.

When Sadie looked up to ask about a character's motivation, she found Corbyn grimacing, massaging the scarred fingers of his left hand with his right. After a moment, he pulled a small tube from his desk, and the name on the label was instantly familiar.

"Arnica was my mom's go-to as well," Sadie commented, keeping her voice soft. As their professional tolerance had shifted into something like friendship, she had been sharing more of these little asides, hoping to find more common ground.

"My sister's special blend," he said, looking up at her. To Sadie's surprise, the answer was delivered without the anger that had colored his tone earlier. "She left it during her last visit with explicit instructions that I'd better use it or face her wrath."

Setting down her notebook and pen, she asked, "She's a doctor, right? Your sister?"

"Surgeon," Corbyn confirmed. "Orthopedic. She had this particular formula made up by some herbalist colleague." A ghost of a smile touched his lips before he continued, "She once threatened to sedate me if I didn't follow post-surgical protocols."

"Would she have done it?" Sadie inquired, glancing over at him with a smirk.

"Without hesitation," he countered, returning her smirk with one of his own.

Sadie laughed, and she heard him huff a noise that might have been the start of a chuckle. There was a warmth that bloomed in her chest as she watched him relax for a moment. A fleeting thought drifted through her mind that she would like to bring out that smirk more often, and perhaps at some point even get him to laugh. She quickly pushed the thought aside, focusing back on the conversation.

"She sounds formidable."

"It's a Pearce family trait," Corbyn admitted with an amused shake of his head. He attempted to unscrew the cap with one hand, and she noticed his jaw tightened in frustration when the tube slipped from his grip.

Sadie watched his struggle, weighing her options. Three weeks ago, she would have pretended not to notice, respecting the walls he'd built around his limitations. But things between them had changed so drastically since those early days. Taking a breath, she decided to put that trust to the test, praying she wasn't making the wrong choice.

"May I?" she asked simply, holding out her hand.

Corbyn stilled, his blue eyes lifting to meet hers. A complicated series of emotions crossed his face: pride, resistance, and then, surprisingly, acceptance.

"If you insist," he said gruffly, sliding the tube across the desk.

Sadie uncapped it quickly, but instead of returning it, she hesitated, biting her lip as she worked up her nerve.

"It might be more effective if..." She paused, then gestured toward his hand. "I used to do this for my mom. If you'd rather not, that's completely..."

"Alright."

The single word hung in the air between them. Sadie glanced up, finding Corbyn watching her with an unreadable expression. All of his usual defenses were momentarily lowered, and she felt her stomach flutter as she realized he was allowing her to help.

She pulled her chair around to his side of the desk, the movement deliberate but unhurried. After she settled, she cautiously reached for his left hand, taking it gently in hers. The scarring was more extensive than Sadie had realized, angry red ridges extending across his fingers and palm, the skin pulled tight across knuckles that no longer bent with ease.

Sadie squeezed a small amount of the arnica cream onto her fingertips, its familiar herbal scent sharp, overwhelming the earthy aroma of paper that she was used to. She began working it into his palm with gentle pressure, carefully following the natural lines of his hand. When Corbyn stiffened slightly at her touch on a particular spot near the base of his thumb, she immediately lightened her pressure.

"Too much?" she asked softly.

"No," Corbyn said, his voice unusually subdued. "Just... sensitive there."

Sadie nodded, adjusting her technique. As she continued, she noticed the subtle shifts in his body language, allowing them to be her guide. In her peripheral vision, she saw his shoulders gradually relax when she found the correct pressure, and his breath eased when she worked through a particularly tight spot.

His hand was larger than she'd expected, the bones strong despite their limited mobility. She could feel the places where the skin had been grafted, the subtle differences in texture beneath her fingertips.

"You're good at this," Corbyn observed after a few minutes of silence.

"I had lots of practice," Sadie replied, focusing on a tight spot near his thumb. "My mom injured her hand when I was thirteen, and my dad traveled constantly for his job, so I became the designated massage therapist."

"That's a lot of responsibility for a thirteen-year-old."

Sadie shrugged slightly, her fingers still working over his hand. "It was what it was, but you adapt."

Something in her tone must have resonated with him because Corbyn's following words were softer than usual, and he murmured, "Yes, you do."

A comfortable silence fell between them as Sadie continued her careful ministrations. Every time she was this close to him, she was hyper-aware of every detail: the heat from his body, the scent of his cologne with its hints of sandalwood, the way her warmth spread through her body at the nearness. It created a heady mixture she found herself getting lost in as her fingers continued to move against his skin.

"How did it happen?" Corbyn asked suddenly, his voice pulling her back to the present. She blinked up at him, and he added, "Your mother's injury."

"She was a teacher, and she was trying to rearrange her classroom on her own," Sadie explained, looking back down at his hand. "She was so stubborn she refused to wait for the maintenance staff. A heavy bookshelf fell, and her hand got caught underneath. She went through multiple surgeries and years of physical therapy."

"Did it help? The physical therapy?"

"A bit," Sadie commented, her eyes still fixed on their hands. "She regained enough movement that she could manage basic daily activities. Typing was difficult, though, especially on days like today, and writing for longer stretches was impossible." She glanced up briefly, his blue eyes watching her intently. "She taught literature, and books were her life. Having to adapt how she interacted with them was... challenging."

Corbyn was watching her face now, his usual guardedness temporarily set aside. "How did she manage?"

"She learned to write with her left hand, though it was never as fluid. Later, when technology improved, she started using voice-to-text software." Sadie smiled slightly at the memory. "She hated it at first. She said it made her feel like she was talking to herself, but it gave her back something she'd lost."

"I'm impressed," he replied. "I tried to use one of those, but the words wouldn't come at all. I just sat there staring at a blank screen."

He shifted in his seat, and it drew him closer. His leg brushed against her knee, and she felt her breath catch. When she looked up, their faces were only inches apart, and this time she couldn't look away.

Something shifted in Sadie's consciousness; that strange sense of déjà vu returned, and with it came all those memories of another pair of striking blue eyes.

Corbyn tensed suddenly, and he drew his hand back, breaking the spell. Sadie found herself staring down at her now-empty hand, trying to calm her racing heart. She couldn't help but wonder if he had felt something too, and her mind was a whirlwind as she tried to figure out how to broach the subject. His dark hair and blue eyes certainly matched her memory from all those years ago, but what were the odds?

"That should be sufficient," he said, his voice noticeably rougher. He flexed his fingers experimentally, refusing to meet her eyes. "Thank you."

Sadie leaned back in her chair, giving him space as she wiped the excess cream from her hands with a tissue.

"Of course. Anytime."

Looking over, she noticed Corbyn's expression was closed again, the momentary openness gone. But when he finally looked at her, his eyes held something new, and she wondered if it was perhaps a touch of appreciation.

"You're the first person who's touched my hand without... flinching," he told her abruptly. "Besides my sister and Edie."

The admission hung in the air between them. Something tightened in Sadie's chest, and an ache formed at the thought that anyone would shy away from him because of his scars.

"There's nothing to flinch from," she answered, making herself hold his gaze, understanding the importance of this moment. She was being included in a tiny group of people he trusted, and that had her pulse quickening for an entirely different reason.

Corbyn studied her face as if searching for any sign that she might not be sincere. She knew he would find none, and he nodded once before turning back to his laptop.

Sadie watched as he positioned his hands over the keys, the left one still limited in its movement, but his fingers more relaxed than they had been earlier. His hands hovered, and she could sense his frustration building again before he even moved. The thought of the tediousness of the task clearly weighed on him.

"Wait," she said, sensing an opening as she reached for her bag. "I think I have something that might help."

She withdrew her tablet and stylus, setting them on the desk beside his laptop. His expression instantly changed, and he closed himself off, but she proceeded anyway.

"There's an app that will convert your handwriting to text," she explained, opening it to demonstrate. "You write with this, and it transcribes automatically. No keyboard required."

Corbyn regarded the technology as if it were a snake in the grass waiting to strike, and he practically sneered, "You know how I feel about that thing, Reed."

"Yes, I am well aware of your fear of living in this decade," Sadie quipped at the expected stubbornness, earning an eye roll in response.

He made no move to take the stylus she offered, instead countering, "My way works just fine."

"If you like redundancy," Sadie replied, raising an eyebrow as if challenging him to disagree. "With this, you only have to write it once. You can still edit and do everything by hand, but it would save you time transcribing it."

Corbyn's mouth tightened, his eyes narrowing. "And where exactly do these words go once they're transcribed? Some corporate server where anyone could access them?"

"It's all stored locally on the device," Sadie explained patiently. "No cloud backup unless you specifically enable it. Which you don't have to." Tapping the settings icon, she added, "Look, I've already disabled all the sharing features. Your manuscript stays right here, visible only to you."

He raised an eyebrow skeptically. "After what happened with the last leaked manuscript, I can't afford to take chances."

"I understand." She softened her voice in what she hoped would be a coaxing tone. "But technology isn't the enemy. Sometimes, it's just a tool that might make things easier."

Corbyn studied the tablet for a long moment, his brow furrowing as he considered the device before him. She could see all of the conflicting emotions playing on his face—apprehension, distrust, and even a bit of curiosity. It was the last one that had her breaking the silence after nearly a minute of his intense staring.

"Humor me. Keep it overnight and give it a try. If you hate it, I promise never to mention it again."

She knew this could potentially backfire, but if it ultimately helped him, then that was a risk she was willing to take. He looked up at her, his eyes holding hers for a long moment before he spoke again.

"You don't need it?"

"I brought it specifically for this. I thought it might help with the editing process. Plus, I've already set up all my files on my phone anyway," she told him with a shrug.

"This could be... useful," he admitted, his voice tense, like it cost him to say it.

Sadie had to fight back a grin. Even that small concession from him felt like a monumental win, but celebrating that fact would only have him rejecting the idea on principle.

The next few moments were spent demonstrating the app and how it worked. He watched curiously, although he said next to nothing, which she interpreted as a sign to continue.

"You just write normally," Sadie encouraged, writing a few lines and then angling the iPad toward him. "The app will do the rest."

She watched his eyebrows lift slightly when the words appeared as typed text on the screen, clean and immediate. When he leaned back in his chair with a soft, "Hmm," she hoped she had gotten through to him.

"When you're done, you can decide where the file is saved," she continued, encouraged by his lack of outright rejection. "It will save you hours of transcription time, and you can have complete control over the files."

Pulling her chair back around the desk, she managed to redirect his attention back to what they had been working on before she had helped him with the arnica cream. They spent the rest of the day planning with the sound of the rain as a peaceful backdrop.

Riley would occasionally get up and wander over to one of them for attention, breaking the monotony of the afternoon.

It was nearing five o'clock when she started gathering her things, glancing out the window. The rain was beginning to pick up, and the sky was growing darker, casting everything in a slightly ominous light.

"I should head back to the inn before this rain gets worse," she murmured, looking over at him, and giving him a small, genuine smile. When he returned it, she felt an ache in her chest and she quickly looked away under the pretense of focusing on packing her belongings. "If you run into any trouble with the tablet, my phone will be on."

"Reed..." he began, but she cut him off as gently as she could.

"Just try it, Corbyn. That's all I ask."

They stared at each other across the desk, and time seemed to slow. As was happening more and more lately, she was acutely aware of her heartbeat, and she found herself unable to break the gaze. He started to say something, but then settled for a nod, turning away. When the moment broke, she felt slightly off balance and had to shake her head to clear her thoughts.

"I'll see you tomorrow then," Sadie said, feeling the need to fill the silence as she slipped her notebook into her bag. "Same time?"

"Same time," Corbyn confirmed. He hesitated, then, when she stood, added, "Drive carefully on the way back. The bend near Miller's Farm floods easily in this weather."

Sadie blinked at him before she managed, "I'll keep an eye out. Thank you."

Swinging her bag over her shoulder, she turned toward the door. Riley trailed at her heels for a final goodbye at the front door, which had become a bit of a tradition in the last week. Corbyn's voice stopped her, though, and she turned back to look at him.

"Reed." Corbyn remained seated at his desk, watching her with an expression she hadn't seen before. It was vulnerable and almost soft. "What you did today," he told her, his voice low, "with my hand. It helped."

The words were simple, but his voice had roughened, his gaze had dropped to his hand rather than meeting her eyes. His scarred fingers curled slightly, and she remembered the way it had felt when she held it in her own.

"I'm glad," she said softly. "I'll see you tomorrow."

As she made her way through the quiet house and out into the rain, the navy umbrella keeping her dry, Sadie tried to make sense of the warmth blooming in her chest. It wasn't just the satisfaction of professional progress or the pleasure of a problem solved. It was more personal.

His eyes flashed in her mind once more. That shade of blue was so similar to the one that had lived in her memory for fifteen years. Part of her was desperate to ask him, to find a way to bring it up in casual conversation, but that thought also terrified her. They had managed to build a solid working relationship, which was slowly growing into a friendship. It was fragile, though, and the thought of upending that, of ruining everything they had built, had convinced her it was best to keep those thoughts to herself.

Slipping into the car, she let out a soft sigh. For the sake of the book and their careers, she knew she had to stay focused on the professional aspect of this partnership. Starting the engine, she shoved all her questions to the back of her mind and made her way back to the safety of the inn.

February 26, 2025

-Corbyn-

The stylus sat on the desk next to the tablet Sadie had left behind, taunting Corbyn. He'd spent the last hour trying to ignore it, but every time he so much as glanced in the direction of the infernal device, he could hear Sadie's voice in his head.

Humor me. Keep it overnight and give it a try. If you hate it, I promise never to mention it again.

She had said it so gently, without any of the usual condescension he had experienced from other editors when they had suggested a similar approach. When her eyes had met his, they were so caring, so full of encouragement, that he had very nearly caved and taken the stylus without complaint.

Slowly, as if it might bite him, he reached out and picked up the stylus. It felt cool in his hand, the sleek design fitting snugly between his fingers, much like his favorite pen; he could hardly tell the difference from the ones he used to scrawl his words on paper.

He eyed the tablet again; across the room, Riley heaved a sigh. The dog looked up at him from his spot by the fire, one shaggy brow raised in what seemed like judgment, as if to say, *Get on with it, human, you're being a daft idiot.*

With a sigh of his own, Corbyn slid the tablet closer, turning on the screen and launching the application Sadie had shown him earlier. The stylus hovered over the screen, ready and waiting for his words. He knew he was being stubborn; she had taken more precautions to ensure the security of his work than he had with his own laptop. Slowly, he lowered the stylus and began to write. The contact was almost frictionless as he wrote a test sentence.

Detective Shaw stood at the edge of the building, watching smoke curl into the night sky.

His messy scrawl transformed instantly into clean, typeset text. He marveled at it for a long moment. There was no waiting for his left hand to stop trembling enough to type, no smudged ink on paper. Just his thoughts flowing directly onto the digital page.

"Remarkable," he murmured, genuinely surprised by how easy the process was. He'd expected it to lag or horribly misinterpret his writing, yet his words were there, exactly as he had intended.

Riley lifted his head, ears perking up at the unfamiliar note in his master's voice. The soulful eyes of the wolfhound tracked the stylus in Corbyn's hand as he held it up to examine it.

"Don't get excited," Corbyn told the dog, his tone as dry as ever. "It's just a fancy pen."

Riley's tail thumped once against the floor, clearly unconvinced.

Corbyn returned his attention to the screen, adding another line: *The arson pattern had changed. The fire starter was evolving, becoming bolder, more precise.*

Again, his handwriting flowed into perfect text. It was... efficient. Unsettlingly so.

He jumped, dropping the stylus when his phone vibrated with an incoming call. Ellie's name flashed on the screen, accompanied by an unflattering photo he'd taken of her mid-sneeze last Christmas. He considered ignoring it, but capitulated on the fourth buzz. She would only keep calling until he answered.

"What?" he growled, more out of habit than irritation.

"There you are!" Ellie's voice burst through the speaker. "Thought you might be ignoring me again." The screen lit up as she initiated a video call, her dark hair bobbing into the frame.

Side by side, there was no denying the fact that they were siblings. They had the same dark, nearly black hair and the same sharpness to their features. Yet where he had inherited their father's icy blue eyes, Ellie had been born with their mother's hazel.

"I considered it," he replied, angling the phone to try to hide the tablet from view. "What do you want?"

"Charming as ever," Ellie laughed, her smile widening as she took the opportunity to get in a dig. "Just wanted to check in. Edie says the book is actually making progress? I half-expected her to call for an ambulance when she told me."

Corbyn scowled and said, "You two gossip too much."

"It's not gossip. We both worry about you," Ellie corrected. "Besides, how else would I know what's happening in your life? It's not like you're chatty."

He grunted noncommittally, shifting in his chair to position the phone at a more comfortable angle.

"Wait..." Ellie's eyes narrowed, a look he recognized all too well. She'd spotted something. "Is that what I think it is?"

Corbyn looked at the box containing his image and groaned. The tablet sat there partially visible at the edge of the frame. He looked up at the ceiling for a moment and prayed for patience while he dealt with his well-meaning, but annoying, younger sister.

"It's for work," he said defensively, knowing it was too late to move it out of view.

"It's an actual, honest-to-God tablet, isn't it?" she practically squealed in delight, making him cringe. "In your technophobic presence? That editor you've been working with got you to try using a tablet?" Her face split into a wide grin. "What sorcery is this? Did she hypnotize you? Blackmail? I need details immediately."

Corbyn scowled, telling her stiffly, "It's practical for the manuscript."

"Mmhmm," Ellie hummed, clearly unconvinced. "And how many editors have suggested 'practical' technology solutions that you've immediately shot down?"

"I'm just trying it out," he protested, but even he could hear how absurdly defensive he was being. "Today was... difficult. She simply asked me to give it a try this evening."

The admission hung between them, and Ellie's expression softened at his moment of vulnerability, the teasing fading to something warmer.

"She understands the work is what matters," Corbyn continued, the words coming easier now. "She wasn't trying to change how I write, just... making it possible." He stopped abruptly, aware he'd revealed more than intended.

"She sounds like she gets you," Ellie said quietly. "That's rare, Corbie."

"Don't call me that," he snapped automatically, hating that she still insisted on using the childhood nickname. "And don't make it into something it's not. It's a working relationship."

With a slight smirk, she fired back, "I would never make assumptions about your personal life."

"That's literally all you do," Corbyn said dryly.

Ellie studied him through the screen, her expression turning thoughtful before she wondered aloud, "You seem different. Less... prickly."

"I'm exactly the same level of prickly," he countered, which earned a genuine laugh. The last thing he needed was Ellie getting any sort of ideas regarding Sadie. She would undoubtedly scheme with Edie, and he would never have a moment's peace.

"If you say so," she laughed and then paused, her expression turning sly. "So... what's she like? She must be a bloody miracle worker."

Something in her tone made Corbyn tense; she was clearly fishing for information. Leaning back in his chair, he crossed his arms over his chest, one eyebrow raising slightly as they regarded each other through their phone screens.

"She's observant and annoyingly thorough," he answered carefully.

"Just observant and thorough?" Ellie pressed, her eyes sparkling with mischief, and he knew he wasn't going to get out of this with short one- or two-word answers.

Corbyn sighed, "She's... perceptive. Doesn't let me get away with lazy writing. Challenges the work without trying to remake it in her image. She's good at her job."

"I see," Ellie said, her tone suggesting that despite the careful answer, she was already making plans he wouldn't like. "And have you learned anything about her beyond her editorial skills? Where's she from? What does she like? Whether she has a cat or a goldfish?"

"Why would I care about any of that?" Corbyn scoffed, though he immediately thought of all the little things he'd noticed. Her preference for tea with honey rather than sugar, how she always had a book in her bag, and the fact that she had trusted him enough to open up about her ex. The memory of her quiet voice describing the torn journal pages stirred a protective anger he hadn't felt in years.

"Just curious if you've actually had a personal conversation," Ellie pressed. "You know, like normal humans do."

"She mentioned her mother had a hand injury," he said before he could stop himself. "Similar to mine. She used to help with physical therapy."

"Ah," Ellie said, her eyebrows rising with interest. "So you have talked about things beyond commas and character arcs." She leaned closer to the screen, not trying to hide her smile. "What else do you know about her? Is she married? Single? Originally from Mars? I need details, Corbie."

"Don't call me..." he began, but he cut himself off with a shake of his head. "Why do you care?"

"Because I haven't heard you talk about anyone like this in... well, ever," Ellie teased. "Not even Claire."

The mention of his ex-fiancée's name sent a familiar twinge through him, but it lacked the sharp sting it once carried. Claire was ancient history, and he had long ago accepted the fact that he was unlikely to find someone willing to look past the scars the car accident left behind.

"It's not like that," he insisted firmly.

He saw Ellie feign innocence, something she had always been good at, and she gasped, "I'm just curious about the woman who's accomplished what an army of editors, doctors, and one particularly stubborn sister couldn't. Getting you to try something new."

Corbyn ran a hand through his hair, grumbling, "She's American. Developmental editor. Early thirties. Temporary assignment. End of story."

"Mmhmm," Ellie hummed again. "And you've been working together for how long?"

"About a month."

"A month," Ellie repeated thoughtfully. "And in that time, she's got you using a tablet, making progress on the book, and..." she paused, studying his face, "something else has changed. I can see it."

"Nothing has changed," Corbyn insisted, though the words felt hollow even to his ears.

"You know," Ellie murmured, her voice gentling, "it's been four years, Corbie. Four years of shutting yourself away in that house, pushing everyone away except Riley, Edie, and Paul. You don't even take my calls half the time."

The words landed exactly as she had intended, and Corbyn looked away from the screen. She wasn't wrong; he had shut everyone out. It had been easier than dealing with the pity.

"I'd like to meet her," Ellie said after a moment. "Bring her to London sometime."

"She's not here to socialize," Corbyn protested, his eyes snapping back to Ellie's on his phone. "She's here to fix the book. Plus, you know how I feel about going into the city."

"And yet, you're using a tablet," Ellie pointed out. "Miracles do happen." She glanced at something off-screen. "I've got to go, I'm working the night shift. But think about it, okay?"

"You're a menace," Corbyn muttered.

Ellie grinned as she responded, "That's why you love me." Her expression softened, and she added, "I'm glad things are getting better, Corbie, and not just with the book."

The screen went dark before he could respond, leaving him staring at his own reflection in the black glass of his phone. He set it face down on the desk, unwilling to spend too much time trying to figure out what changes his sister had noticed.

Riley padded over, resting his shaggy head on the arm of Corbyn's chair. The dog looked up at him, and he was unable to resist running his fingers through Riley's coarse fur.

"It's not what she thinks," Corbyn told Riley, who offered no contradiction beyond a slow blink.

Yet Ellie hadn't been entirely wrong. He couldn't deny that Sadie had affected his routine, work habits, and even his tolerance for technology. What he wouldn't admit, even to his too-perceptive sister, was how he'd found himself noticing other things: the way Sadie tucked her hair behind her ear when concentrating, how her gray eyes sparked when she challenged one of his plot points, the quiet hum she made when reading a passage she particularly liked.

Small details that had no bearing on their professional relationship. Things he had no business cataloging.

Corbyn picked up the stylus again and tapped the tablet screen, bringing it back to life. The manuscript glowed up at him. It was still his words, but somehow he could see things more clearly in this format.

Time slipped away as he wrote. The words came faster than they had in months. It wasn't the painful extraction they'd become since the accident, but something closer to the rush he remembered. Not quite the same, nothing ever would be, but better. Easier.

When he finally looked up, he realized night had truly fallen, the grounds beyond the windows no longer visible. Glancing at the clock on the mantle, he was startled to see it was past midnight. He'd worked for hours without interruption, without the usual breaks forced by pain and frustration. He had been relaxed and focused, and his chest clenched when he thought of all the time he had spent allowing his anger and fear to control his decisions. He flexed his left hand experimentally. It ached, but not with the sharp, shooting pain that typically accompanied a long writing session.

Corbyn saved the document and watched as the word count updated. He'd written more tonight than in the past three days combined, and that realization brought a complicated mix of emotions.

Underneath his satisfaction at having successfully spent the night writing was the knowledge that Sadie had been right. She would know it immediately when she saw the new pages tomorrow, and she would get that look on her face—the one that said she'd been correct, but was too professional to gloat. One corner of her mouth would curve upward, gray eyes twinkling as she tried to avoid eye contact, as if somehow he wouldn't know exactly what she was thinking.

The thought didn't irritate him as it should have. Instead, he found himself almost looking forward to it. There was a warmth that spread through him as he pictured her smile, and he had to shake his head to clear the treacherous thoughts. This was a professional arrangement and nothing more.

Still, as he pushed up from his chair, Riley following him toward the study door, he couldn't shake the feeling that somehow he was fooling himself into thinking his heart was immune to Sadie Reed.

***

-Sadie-

Staring up at the ceiling in her room at the Roaring Stag, Sadie groaned in frustration. Once again, her mind was not focused on the manuscript she was trying to edit on the tiny screen of her phone for a freelance project. Instead, she had been thinking about Corbyn and what had transpired that afternoon, and even the simple act of remembering holding his hand in her own had her body responding in all sorts of inconvenient ways.

Shaking her head, she closed the manuscript file and pulled Jess's contact information. She needed a friendly voice, and Jess was the one person who could yank her out of an overthinking spiral. Her best friend's face lit up the screen in surprise on the second ring.

"Well, look who remembered I exist!" she exclaimed, her hair piled in a messy bun. Jess appeared to be in her apartment, and a glass of wine was visible at the edge of the frame. "The elusive Sadie Reed graces me with her presence!"

"I'm sorry, it has been way too long," Sadie admitted, settling more comfortably against her pillows. "I've meant to call, but everything has been such a blur."

"That bad, huh?" Jess asked, taking a sip of her wine. "Is Mr. Difficult still living up to his reputation?"

Sadie hesitated, unsure how to answer. The Corbyn Pearce who had greeted her on that first day—all cutting remarks and cold dismissal—seemed miles away from the man who had let her massage his scarred hand this morning.

"Actually," she began carefully, "he's not what I expected."

Jess raised her eyebrows. "Meaning he's worse? Because I can have you on the next flight home if he's being impossible."

"No, no, nothing like that," Sadie said quickly. "The opposite, really. Sure, he was difficult at first, but lately things have been... different. The edits and writing are going well. We might actually hit the deadline."

"Seriously? Thank God." Jess looked genuinely relieved as she told Sadie, "The board hasn't stopped asking for updates, and marketing has been hounding me daily about the launch. I've been running out of ways to tell them to be patient."

"Well, you can tell them to relax," Sadie grinned. "He's still protective of his work but receptive to feedback now, at least most of the time. We've actually made significant progress on the structural issues."

"Well, damn," Jess murmured, looking impressed. "You are a miracle worker, and I may build you a shrine if you get this book to the finish line."

Sadie laughed, shaking her head. "The book is good... *really* good. The plot just needed some untangling."

"And the author needed someone who didn't take his crap," Jess added with a knowing grin. "You always were good at standing your ground."

"Professionally, maybe," Sadie said, her gaze flicking away as she thought of Nate. "Not always in my personal life."

Jess's expression sobered immediately. "Has he been bothering you again? Because I swear to God, Sadie, if that asshole is still—"

"No, no, nothing like that," Sadie assured her quickly, resisting the urge to tuck her hair behind her ear. "Just... reflecting, I guess. On patterns." She took a breath, deliberately changing the subject. "You'll never believe what happened today, though. I got Corbyn to agree to experiment with a tablet and stylus this evening."

Jess nearly spat out her wine. "You what? The man who supposedly writes everything by hand with fountain pens imported from some artisanal shop in Paris? Who once told me technology was 'the death of authentic literary voice'? *That* Corbyn?"

"The very same," Sadie confirmed, a smile tugging at her lips at Jess's attempt to impersonate Corbyn's voice. "I showed him an app that converts handwriting to text. His left hand was really bothering him today—the rain makes it worse—and he couldn't type comfortably."

"And he just... agreed? To try it?"

"Well, not immediately," Sadie admitted. "But I left it with him with the promise to never bring it up again if he truly hates it."

"Huh," Jess said, studying Sadie's face through the screen. "That's... unexpected. Sounds like Mr. Difficult is softening."

Sadie felt heat rise to her cheeks. Jess had said the last part in a tone that left no doubt in Sadie's mind that she meant outside of their professional relationship. She stared at the screen as her sputtering mind tried to formulate a response.

"I have no idea what you mean," she said, hoping the dim light hid the blush that had spread from her cheeks to her neck and chest.

"You realize I can see through your bullshit, right?" Jess asked, clearly unconvinced. "You get this look when someone has your interest."

"That's ridiculous, I do not," Sadie said, though she could feel her blush deepening. "And even if I do have some look, I'm talking about his writing, not him personally."

"If you say so," Jess shrugged and took another sip of wine, her eyes never leaving Sadie's face. "But you know, it wouldn't be the end of the world if you were interested."

"Jess, no," Sadie said firmly. "I'm his editor, that's it. Plus, this assignment comes with an end date; it's not like I'm here forever."

"Right, because his writing is absolutely why you're turning the color of my wine right now," Jess teased. "Come on, Sadie. It's been what, two months since you left Nate? And years longer than that since you actually seemed happy with him. I know it hasn't been that long, but maybe it's time to put yourself out there again. As your boss, I know I should tell you to remain completely professional, but as your friend, I want to see you happy. Would it be so terrible to feel something for him?"

Sadie sighed, "It's not that simple."

"It never is," Jess agreed. "But sometimes it's not as complicated as we make it, either. Look, I'm not saying you should jump the poor man, but if there's something there, something real, maybe don't automatically shut it down because of timing, titles, or whatever other excuse your brain is manufacturing."

"There's nothing to shut down," Sadie insisted, though the memory of Corbyn's intense blue eyes meeting hers across his desk sent a flutter through her stomach that contradicted her words. "We're working well together. That's all."

"I'll have to take your word for it," Jess conceded, though her expression remained doubtful.

They chatted for another twenty minutes while Jess updated Sadie on the latest office gossip. When they finally disconnected, Sadie was unsettled by Jess's observations.

She couldn't deny the flutter of butterflies in her stomach when she thought of Corbyn's rare smile, nor the warmth that spread through her when he listened to her suggestions. Then, there was that strange charge that had passed between them when their eyes met over his desk. They were small moments that shouldn't matter, but somehow did.

The realization both thrilled and terrified her. She had sworn off relationships, convincing herself that her judgment was irreparably broken. Yet, every moment spent with Corbyn felt different from anything she had experienced. His gruff and grumbly exterior concealed a disarming gentleness.

Shaking her head, she opened the manuscript file once more. Working on her phone was inefficient and it strained her eyes, but she had no choice. Corbyn had to finish his book, and if that meant making do with her phone screen, it was worth the sacrifice.

"Just a few more hours," she murmured, the screen's glow harsh in the dimly lit room. She'd been pushing herself like this for weeks, the fatigue piling up, but she couldn't afford to turn down the work. Not when every extra penny meant getting closer to replacing her laptop and being able to afford her own apartment when she returned to New York.

The tiny text blurred as her eyes grew heavier. She blinked, forcing herself to focus on the line edits for a self-published fantasy novel, but each paragraph took twice as long to process as it should have. When the clock struck two, she finally admitted defeat, setting her phone aside with an ache between her shoulder blades. She'd have to finish tomorrow somehow, squeezed between sessions with Corbyn. As she turned out the light, she made a mental note to stop and see Maggie in the morning for an extra-strong coffee before heading to the estate.

March 1, 2025

-Sadie-

The persistent drizzle matched Sadie's mood as she made her way into the study. She had made her usual stop in the kitchen, knowing she would need a strong cup of tea to make it through the day. The previous night's work on her freelance projects had dragged until 3 AM. It was the fourth late night in a row, trying to juggle multiple freelance editing projects with impossible deadlines. The workload had snowballed, leaving her barely four hours of sleep each night this week. Her eyes burned, and her movements were slow. A dull pressure, usually an early warning of trouble to come, had settled at the base of her skull.

Sadie paused at the heavy oak door, drawing in a deep breath. Professionalism demanded she push through her exhaustion. Corbyn was making such good progress, and she wouldn't let a sleepless night derail their momentum. She'd learned long ago, especially with Nate, that admitting weakness only invited judgment or dismissal. This was no different.

"Just another day," she murmured, pushing the door open. "Morning," she called, her voice deliberately bright.

Corbyn sat at his desk, shoulders hunched over her tablet as he wrote. His dark brows were pinched together in concentration as the stylus moved across the screen. Riley was sprawled at his feet, and his tail gave a slow, sleepy thump at Sadie's entrance.

"Look who's still getting use out of that tablet," she said, unable to keep the satisfaction from her voice despite her exhaustion. She had hoped he might take to it when she'd left it with him after their session two days ago.

Corbyn glanced up, a hint of self-consciousness crossing his features before he schooled his expression, conceding, "Technology has its uses." He handed her the tablet so she could review what he had been writing, a little smirk tugging at his lips. "Though, I maintain that pen and paper are far superior."

"Still, a stunning admission from technology's greatest critic," Sadie teased, earning a huff that might have been the start of a chuckle.

They exchanged amused glances before she took her usual seat. She was shocked when she looked down at the screen and saw an entirely new chapter based on a conversation they had engaged in the previous day. A small, genuine smile spread across her face as she realized he wasn't just humoring her, but making real strides with the novel's progress.

"I'm impressed," she said. "You've been busy."

"Couldn't sleep," he responded with a shrug. "Thought I might as well be productive."

Riley pushed himself up from the floor, padding over to say hello to Sadie properly. She scratched behind his ears before he sprawled at her feet as they settled in for the day. The rain drummed steadily against the windowpanes, the sound easing the tension building behind her eyes. They passed the tablet back and forth for the next hour, discussing plot points and character motivations.

Gone was the adversarial tension of their early sessions. Corbyn still pushed back on specific suggestions, but now he didn't take issue with explaining his reasoning.

The morning slipped past and Sadie tried to ignore the steadily increasing pressure behind her eyes. She'd suffered migraines since college, stress-triggered monsters that occasionally knocked her out for days, but she couldn't afford to succumb today, not with so many people counting on her to help him get this book across the finish line.

Around midday, the clouds fully parted as the rain finally ended, sending a shaft of bright sunlight slicing through the study windows. The sudden glare hit Sadie's eyes, sending a spike of pain through her skull. She couldn't stop her flinch, nor the sharp breath she took as she turned away from the window.

"Reed?" Corbyn called, although his voice seemed to come from far away. "You alright?"

"Fine," she managed, but even she could hear the edge in her tone. "Just the sun in my eyes."

Corbyn said nothing, but she could feel his gaze lingering on her. Sadie forced herself to focus on the screen to avoid his eyes, though the words were becoming hazy, blurring at the edges. The symptoms were all too familiar: sensitivity to light, the low throb at her temples gradually intensifying, and faint nausea curling in her stomach.

She tried to push through, but her mind started tripping over details. When she read the same paragraph three times without absorbing its meaning, she knew there was no use denying it any longer. Eventually, she lowered the tablet to her lap, pinching the bridge of her nose as she closed her eyes briefly. She tried to breathe through the pain, feeling as if a vise were squeezing her head.

Corbyn's chair creaked as he leaned forward, and when she forced herself to look at him, his eyes were fixed on her. She had seen so many of his expressions over the last few weeks, but the concern that was etched on his face was new.

"What's wrong?" he coaxed, and she closed her eyes for another moment, trying to push down the guilt she felt for putting them in this position.

"Nothing. Just tired." She straightened, trying to project alertness she didn't feel. "Let's continue with…"

A particularly vicious throb of pain made her wince visibly, and she was forced to turn her head away from the windows and the sunlight that was currently streaming through them.

"That's more than just tired," Corbyn said, voice surprisingly gentle. "What's happening?"

She hesitated as another wave of guilt washed over her, realizing she couldn't push through and instead was letting him down. She admitted softly, unable to meet his eyes, "It's a migraine. I'll be fine."

Corbyn's eyebrows drew together, and she braced herself for his irritation that the rest of the day would be wasted. Instead, he rose from his chair, his voice soft when he asked, "How bad?"

The simple question, asked without skepticism, caught her off guard, and her grip on the tablet loosened.

"I've worked through worse," she said, though another stab of pain immediately made a liar of her.

"That's not what I asked," he insisted. Corbyn moved to the windows, drawing the heavy curtains closed. The room dimmed, and the sudden lack of light eased the pain enough for her to sink back into the chair. "Does light make it worse?"

Sadie blinked at him, surprised by both his actions and his knowledge.

"Yes," she said, finally looking up at him. "And sound, eventually."

Corbyn nodded as if confirming a theory before explaining, "Edie gets them occasionally. Bad ones. Lays her out for days sometimes."

He stepped toward his desk and turned off the lamp, leaving only the softer fireplace light illuminating the room. Riley's head came to rest in her lap as if sensing her discomfort.

"You should have said something sooner," Corbyn continued, but his tone lacked its usual gruffness.

"We have work to do," Sadie protested weakly. "The deadline..."

"Will still be there tomorrow." He cut her off with a dismissive wave. "Why are you so exhausted anyway? You look like you haven't slept in a week."

The direct question and momentary relief from pain caused Sadie's usual boundaries to waver.

"I was up late finishing a freelance project," she admitted, rubbing her temples and enjoying the momentary reprieve from the pain.

"You're taking on extra work? While handling my book?" he challenged, brow furrowing as he watched her from across the way.

Sadie sighed, pinching the bridge of her nose once more as the pain throbbed from the spike in her stress level before she replied, "I'm just saving up for a new laptop."

"What happened to your old one?"

The question hung in the air, seemingly innocent but weighted with things she wasn't ready to unpack. Sadie hesitated. This topic was so far outside the realm of a professional relationship. It wasn't even something she had really shared with anyone other than Jess.

"Nate... my ex... he smashed it against the wall during an argument," she told him, her voice low. "I had suggested he look for a steady job to help pay rent, since his writing career had stalled."

The silence that followed was thick with tension. Sadie kept her gaze fixed on the tablet in her lap, unwilling to see pity on Corbyn's face. It had been bad enough watching Jess flounder for words when she found out. When Corbyn finally spoke, though, his voice contained a tightly controlled anger that surprised her.

"He destroyed your computer? Deliberately?"

Sadie nodded, a slight movement that sent fresh pain radiating through her skull. Her cheeks burned with embarrassment as she once again was faced with admitting how bad things had been and how she had stayed despite so many warning signs.

"Not his finest moment. Or mine for pushing when I knew he was in one of his moods," she confessed with an attempt at a shrug. Downplaying was one thing she had mastered over the years.

"There's no excuse for that," Corbyn said, the words clipped as if trying to maintain his composure. "None."

The vehemence in his tone made her look up, wincing at the movement. His expression went cold, blue eyes blazing with an intensity that should have scared her. However, this wasn't anger directed at her, but on her behalf. It was protective rather than threatening, and she couldn't ignore the fact that it gave her a sense of security she had not felt in a very long time.

"It's in the past," she said softly. "I'm not with him anymore, that's all that matters."

Corbyn held her gaze for a long moment, something unreadable flickering in his eyes. Then he nodded once, sharply, as if coming to a decision.

"Go lie down on the sofa," he told her, continuing to surprise her with the sudden gentleness of his tone. "I'll be right back."

Before Sadie could protest, he was already striding toward the door, Riley trotting after him. The suggestion made sense; the sofa would be more comfortable than her chair. The fact that he had clearly been concerned with her comfort warmed her chest, and she carefully stood. Stretching out on the soft cushions, she closed her eyes.

She wasn't sure how much time had passed when footsteps announced Corbyn's return. She forced her eyes open to find him standing before her with a tray of supplies: a glass of water, what appeared to be medication, and a folded cloth.

"Edie keeps a pharmacy in the kitchen," he explained, setting the items on the coffee table. "Says these work best for her migraines. Ibuprofen, I think, but stronger than the regular kind."

Sadie accepted the pills gratefully, washing them down with cool water. "Thank you," she said, the simple words inadequate for the rush of gratitude she felt. "You didn't have to…"

"Don't," Corbyn cut her off, his voice gruff but not unkind. "Just… close your eyes."

He unfurled the cloth, which turned out to be a cold compress. With surprising gentleness, he pressed it to her forehead. The sudden coolness was a blessed relief against the pain, and she closed her eyes, unable to stop the quiet sound of contentment that escaped her.

"It's Edie's trick," Corbyn muttered, sounding almost embarrassed. "Hold it there. It helps, apparently."

Sadie complied, keeping the compress in place as Corbyn moved around the room, adjusting things to maximize her comfort. He stirred the fire to a lower flame, and even retrieved a soft throw blanket from a cabinet, draping it carefully over her legs.

"Is that… alright?" he asked, hovering above her with uncharacteristic uncertainty.

"Perfect," she murmured, the simple comfort nearly overwhelming in her vulnerable state. "Thank you, Corbyn."

The tenderness of these actions, so at odds with his usual brusque demeanor, brought a lump to Sadie's throat. She couldn't remember the last time someone had cared for her this way—certainly not Nate, who'd treated her migraines as inconvenient interruptions to his needs.

"You should rest," Corbyn said, still hovering awkwardly beside the sofa. "I can work quietly at my desk. Or leave if you prefer silence."

"No, stay," Sadie said quickly, unable to stop the blush that formed on her cheeks when she realized how desperate she must sound. "I don't want to run you out of your study… and the company is nice."

Corbyn nodded. "I'll just do some writing then. I don't need the light on with the tablet to work."

"Another point for technology," Sadie quipped softly. "I'm keeping a tally, you know. Soon, you'll be setting up Riley's social media account. 'Adventures of a Literary Hound.' It'll go viral."

A sound escaped him then. It was a low, rusty chuckle that surprised them both. It transformed his face completely, softening the hard lines around his mouth, making him look years younger.

"Now I know the migraine's affected your brain," he retorted, but there was a warmth in his voice.

Sadie smiled despite her throbbing head, oddly pleased at having coaxed that rare sound from him, and she smirked, "Mark it on the calendar, Pearce. I made you laugh. Proof that miracles do happen."

He shook his head, but that almost smile lingered.

Little by little, the medication dulled the pain, dulling its sharpness, and Sadie adjusted the compress before sinking deeper into the sofa. Riley had returned at some point and now lay on the floor beside her, his steady breathing centering her as she felt her eyes growing heavy.

"You know," she murmured, her voice soft in the quiet room, "I half expected you to tell me to walk it off."

Corbyn snorted from his desk, looking up from the tablet. "What kind of monster do you take me for, Reed?"

"A grumpy one," she replied, a hint of her usual spark returning despite the pain.

"Alright, that's enough clever remarks from you," Corbyn said, his tone gentler than his words. "Close your eyes and rest. The medicine won't work if you keep that brain of yours spinning."

"Such excellent bedside manner," she murmured with a faint smile. "Has anyone ever told you that you missed your calling as a nurse? So soothing."

The corner of his mouth lifted. "Go to sleep, Reed, before I reconsider my newfound patience."

Through half-closed eyes, she observed him at his desk. The way he held the stylus, the slight furrow in his brow as he concentrated, the occasional glance he cast in her direction when he thought she wasn't watching. There was a gentleness to him that he kept carefully hidden, a capacity for kindness that emerged only in these unguarded moments. Sadie's eyes drifted fully closed, consciousness slipping away.

The last thing she registered was the quiet rustle of Corbyn rising from his desk, his footsteps approaching the sofa. Then, the gentlest touch, fingertips lightly brushing hair from her forehead as sleep finally claimed her completely.

March 1, 2025

-Corbyn-

Corbyn tiptoed through the study, wincing at the floorboards creaking beneath his feet. He paused at the door, allowing himself one last look to make sure Sadie was still sleeping. The way her face had softened when he had given in to the temptation to brush the hair away from her face still lingered in his mind. She had looked so vulnerable, reacting with such trust as he'd cared for her. In the aftermath, there was a complicated tangle of emotions he wasn't ready to untangle.

"How is she?" Edie asked, her voice deliberately lowered, when he entered the kitchen.

Corbyn cleared his throat. "Still sleeping."

She nodded, turning back to her cooking. The kitchen was warm despite the early March chill that seeped through the old manor's walls. For as long as Corbyn could remember, this room had been the heart of the house—warm, loud, and lived in. It was Edie's domain where all needs, both physical and emotional, were tended to.

"Paul's just gone to fetch more firewood," she said, gesturing toward the back door. "This cold snap's set to continue through the weekend."

Corbyn nodded and crossed to the cabinet near the sink, automatically reaching for plates. The familiar routine of setting the table steadied him somewhat, giving him something to focus on aside from his thoughts of the woman sleeping in his study.

"Has Reed mentioned anything to you about her ex?" he asked abruptly, placing the silverware down more forcefully than necessary.

Edie turned from the stove, her expression shifting from concern to interest. "Not in detail. She mentioned she had been living with her boss after a breakup. Why?"

Corbyn's shoulders stiffened as he arranged the napkins. Just thinking about what Sadie had admitted to him earlier had him gritting his teeth and wishing he could tell the wanker exactly what he thought of him.

"Over the past few weeks, she's mentioned him a few times," he hesitated, weighing how much to share of Sadie's private confession. "Specifically, regarding his temper and penchant for destroying her things. Like her laptop."

The wooden spoon clattered against the pot's rim, and Edie's outrage was immediate. "He what? Deliberately?"

Corbyn nodded, his scarred left hand clenching reflexively. "Not to mention the manipulative texts and emails he's been sending. It's the kind of control that leaves no bruises but does plenty of damage."

The back door swung open, admitting Paul with an armload of logs and a blast of cold air. He shut the door behind him, stamping his boots on the mat.

"Weather's turned nasty," he grumbled, setting the wood on the log rack. "Frost already forming on the..." He stopped, reading the tension in the room. "What's happened?"

Edie shook her head, stirring the stew with more vigor than needed, as she told Paul, "I've just been hearing about Sadie's sorry excuse for an ex. That poor girl has been through hell with that git."

Paul's expression darkened as he muttered, "Some men shouldn't be allowed near decent women."

Corbyn finished setting the table, uncomfortably aware of Edie's sharp gaze following his movements. She had been more of a mother to him than the woman who had given birth to him, and he knew she could likely see through his attempt to seem calm.

"She'll... she'll need to stay here tonight," he said, his voice matter-of-fact. "The guest room should be made up still from when Ellie was last here."

"Of course," Edie agreed. "Though I wonder if we should put her in the blue room instead. It gets better morning light, and it's closer to your..."

"The guest room's fine," Corbyn cut her off, avoiding the knowing look she exchanged with Paul. "She'll need her things from the inn, though. I should..."

"I'll ring Maggie," Edie said, reaching for the phone.

"No, I'll do it." The words came out more sharply than he'd intended, and he took a breath, softening his tone. "I'll drive over. The fresh air will clear my head."

Paul and Edie exchanged another meaningful look that Corbyn pretended not to notice as he headed for the door. For as quiet as Paul was, he could be just as meddlesome as his wife.

"You sure?" Paul asked, crossing his arms over his chest as he watched Corbyn curiously. "Weather's turning."

"I won't melt," Corbyn replied, reaching for his coat.

The drive to the village was short, but Corbyn took his time, winding through the outskirts of the town. It provided a welcome distraction from the thoughts he was trying and failing to ignore. His mind wanted to drift back to the woman asleep in his study, and that look of peace on her face as she slept. How, in a short time, she had turned his entire world upside down.

The Roaring Stag stood at the village center, with its welcoming Tudor facade, and a wave of warm air washed over him as

Corbyn pushed open the heavy oak door. The pub was busy for a weeknight; locals crowded around the bar while a fire crackled in the massive stone hearth.

"Well, look what the wind blew in!" Maggie called from behind the bar, her surprised expression quickly masked with a grin. "Twice in one month? We're honored, Mr. Pearce."

Corbyn made his way to the bar, nodding awkwardly at the curious glances from villagers unused to seeing him in public.

"I need a word, Maggie," he said, lowering his voice. "About Reed."

Something immediately shifted in Maggie's expression, and concern replaced her teasing smile.

"Is she alright? She seemed peaky this morning when she left."

"She has a migraine," Corbyn explained, leaning over the bar to avoid being overheard. "It's a bad one. She's sleeping it off at the house."

"Poor love," Maggie clucked sympathetically. "Those late nights with the freelance work haven't been doing her any favors, I'd wager."

"No, they certainly have not," Corbyn agreed. "She'll likely sleep at the manor tonight. I thought I'd collect some things for her."

Maggie glanced around the busy pub and then called to a young woman wiping down tables, "Jenny, mind the bar a minute?" She turned back to Corbyn, nodding toward the back stairs and said, "Come on, then. I'll help you."

Relieved he wouldn't have to handle Sadie's personal items himself, Corbyn followed Maggie up the narrow staircase to Sadie's room. She produced a small set of keys from her apron pocket.

"It's room 7, just at the top of the stairs."

Room 7 was small but charming, with sloped ceilings and a window overlooking the village green. It was meticulously neat. The bed was made with hospital corners, books stacked precisely on the nightstand, and a phone charger coiled carefully. He'd watched her arrange her pens and notes each morning. Nothing about how pristine the room was surprised him.

"She's writing again," Maggie said, when his gaze lingered on a leather journal on the desk. "Started just after she arrived. First time in years, from what she's told me."

He watched Maggie add it to the duffel bag along with a change of clothes and other personal items. He knew the weight that journal held for Sadie, that for the first time in years, she was allowing herself to find her own voice instead of just editing the work of others. It was something to be encouraged, and he had a feeling Maggie understood that as well.

They returned downstairs, the duffel packed with everything Sadie might need for an overnight stay. The pub had grown busier in their absence, locals pressed around the bar where Jenny served drinks.

"She's all set then," Maggie said, tucking Sadie's phone charger into the side pocket of the duffel bag. She handed it to Corbyn with a sly smile. "Tell her to feel better soon. She's lucky to have someone looking after her."

"I couldn't very well let her continue trying to work herself into an early grave," Corbyn said, his tone more defensive than he'd intended.

"Of course not," Maggie replied, not bothering to hide her amusement. "I'm sure it's just professional courtesy."

"Thank you," Corbyn said, shifting the duffel to his good hand and trying to deflect any further comments. "For helping with this."

"Not a problem," Maggie assured him. "We look after our own here." She studied him for a moment, something softening in her expression. "That includes both of you, whether you like it or not."

Before Corbyn could respond to that loaded statement, Maggie was already heading back to the bar, calling greetings to new arrivals and slipping seamlessly into her proprietor role.

The drive back to the manor passed quickly despite his attempts to draw it out. He had hoped to find a little clarity, but instead his mind was even more muddled than when he had left. This was precisely the kind of complication he'd spent years avoiding. People were messy, relationships were messier, and he had no place for either in his carefully controlled existence.

By the time he reached the manor, darkness had fallen completely. Golden light glowed from the kitchen windows, and smoke curled from the chimneys against the star-strewn sky. He let himself in quietly, shaking off the cold as he hung his coat by the door. The smell of Edie's beef stew reminded him he hadn't eaten since morning, his stomach growling in response.

"That was quick," Edie called from the kitchen. "Dinner's nearly ready."

"I'll be right there," Corbyn said back, turning towards the study.

The room was nearly exactly as he'd left it. At some point while he was gone, Edie must have gone to check on Sadie, because a tray with a thermos of tea and what he assumed were scones under a covered dish sat on the coffee table.

Sadie had shifted onto her side on the sofa, one hand tucked beneath her cheek. Riley lifted his head as Corbyn entered, his tail thumping against the carpet in greeting.

"Good boy," Corbyn murmured, setting the duffel bag on the table next to the tray. "How's our patient?"

Corbyn crouched beside the sofa, studying her face in the firelight. Her breathing was slow and steady, each exhale lifting the strand of hair that had fallen across her cheek. He considered waking her since she hadn't eaten either, but the peacefulness of her expression stopped him.

Corbyn glanced around the room, eyes landing on the notepad he kept on his desk. Quietly, he moved to retrieve it and scribbled a quick note:

Reed,
*   Edie prepared a tray in case you're hungry, and Maggie packed you an overnight bag. Guest room is prepared when you're ready—top of the stairs, second door on the left.*
—C

He placed the note where she would see it upon waking, before turning to look at her one more time. That stubborn strand of hair still lay across her cheek. This time, he reached out and swept it back from her face with his good hand, the gesture light in hopes it wouldn't disturb her.

She stirred slightly, a small sigh escaping her lips, but didn't wake. Emboldened, Corbyn adjusted the blanket that had slipped down, carefully tucking it around her shoulders against the evening chill. It was so out of character for who he had become over the last four years, yet there was something about the intimate action that felt right.

"Keep watch, Riley," he whispered, giving the dog a final pat before straightening and heading back out of the study. He left the door open a crack before making his way towards the kitchen and the dinner Edie had prepared.

Letting out a long breath, he finally allowed himself to admit to the truth that he had been denying for days, if not weeks. He had grown to care for Sadie Reed.

March 2, 2025

-Sadie-

Sadie's eyelids fluttered open as the first light of dawn crept through the windows. As she took in her surroundings, her brow pulled together in confusion. This was not her room at the Roaring Stag.

The moment she realized she was still lying on the sofa in Corbyn's study, the events of the previous day came flooding back. Images of Corbyn taking care of her, fetching her medicine, and tucking her in sent warmth blooming in her chest. He had been the last person she had expected to treat her with such tenderness, and she bit her lip, unable to stop the blush from forming on her cheeks.

Stretching, she laughed when her hand brushed against something warm and furry beside the sofa. Riley lay belly up, his massive paws dangling in the air as he stared up at her sleepily.

"Good morning, handsome," she whispered, scratching his chest as Riley responded with a lazy thump of his tail. It was the only sound in the otherwise silent house. "Sounds like you and I are the only ones awake."

She pushed herself up, the blanket falling away as she swung her feet to the floor. Her gaze landed on a folded paper on the nearby coffee table. Even at a distance, she recognized the handwriting and reached for the note. Her pulse quickened for some unexplainable reason, and she shook her head at her own foolishness.

Reed,

Edie prepared a tray in case you're hungry, and Maggie packed you an overnight bag. Guest room is prepared when you're ready—top of the stairs, second door on the left.
—C

Tears prickled her eyes as she lowered the note to her lap. While she slept and recovered, the others ensured not only her comfort, but also that she would have what she needed when she woke. For most of her adult life, she'd been the one looking after everyone else. From the drudgery of trying to anticipate Nate's wants and desires, to stepping in every time Jess got overwhelmed with a work disaster, it had always fallen on her shoulders to fix things. Yet here, in this little town thousands of miles from home, she had met a group of people who were willing to step in when she needed them most.

Releasing a slow, measured breath, she lifted the cover that had been placed over the plate on the tray. Underneath, she found one of Edie's scones, and her stomach instantly growled in response. Picking it up, she took a bite and savored the taste, reminding herself to thank Edie later for her thoughtfulness.

Riley rolled rather ungracefully so his feet were back on the floor, then stared up at her hopefully. She chuckled as she reached out to scratch behind his ears, and the dog grumbled in contentment.

"Sorry, buddy, I promise I'll get you a treat later," she told him, and he heaved a sigh like he understood she wasn't planning to share her scone. Standing up, she took another bite and then asked him, "Feel like being my guide?"

While she retrieved her duffel bag, Riley stood and then did a perfect downward dog that would have made her yoga instructor back in New York swoon. With his rear in the air, he yawned loudly, and she shook her head at his dramatics.

"Lead the way," she told him when he was finished, and he seemed to understand perfectly as he padded toward the door.

The massive Irish wolfhound led her through the quiet house, up the staircase, and down a hallway lined with what looked like ancestral portraits. The guest room was exactly where Corbyn's note had said it would be. It was a spacious chamber with a four-poster bed and windows overlooking the estate's grounds. Sadie couldn't help but feel it was a shame she hadn't woken up earlier, so she could have sought refuge in the charming space.

In the adjoining bathroom, she found towels had been laid out along with various soaps to choose from. When Sadie caught sight of herself in the mirror, though, she froze. She looked... different somehow. The woman staring back had the same features, but there was a softness in her expression she hadn't seen in years. There were no worry lines between her brows or dark circles of exhaustion under her eyes. She was content and cared for.

"Get it together," she told her reflection as she turned away to start the shower, knowing exactly where her mind was going. "This is work. He's a client."

Stepping under the water, she closed her eyes, only to be greeted by the memory of bright blue ones staring back at her. Images of a winter in London, when she was seventeen, floated through her mind. The crowded Tube on New Year's Eve, a brush of hands with a stranger, the electric connection that had left its mark on her young heart. Then, as was usually the case these days, the young man became Corbyn, his eyes sparkling in much the same way on the rare occasions she could elicit a smile or a laugh.

"Ridiculous," Sadie muttered, trying to convince herself. "Thousands of men have blue eyes."

A short time later, she descended the stairs toward the kitchen and pulled her damp hair into a ponytail. She was immediately hit with the scent of fresh bread and could hear someone moving about in the kitchen. Edie stood at the stove, stirring a pot as she looked over toward Sadie.

"There you are," Edie said warmly, wooden spoon in hand. "Feeling better?"

"Much," Sadie replied, moving to sit at the kitchen's large island. "Thank you for everything. The guest room is lovely."

"Glad to hear it," Edie said, turning to stir whatever delicious concoction bubbled on the stove. "Porridge? You must be famished."

"That sounds amazing," Sadie admitted. Riley had disappeared during her shower, presumably through the dog door visible at the far end of the kitchen. "Is Corbyn around?" she asked, "I wanted to thank him for yesterday as well."

"He went for his morning walk about an hour ago. Said he needed to clear his head," Edie told her as she ladled a generous portion of porridge into a bowl and set it before Sadie. "Between you and me, he was up half the night checking on you."

"He was?" Sadie couldn't hide her surprise.

"Mmm," Edie hummed, setting a honey pot within reach. "I haven't seen him fuss like that since Ellie had a bad bout of flu a few winters back." Her eyes were kind as she studied Sadie's face. "You gave us a right fright."

Sadie stirred honey into her porridge, unsure how to respond. The idea of Corbyn watching over her while she slept stirred something warm and unfamiliar in her chest.

"I'm sorry about that," she said finally. "It's been ages since I've had a migraine that bad."

"No need to apologize, love," Edie assured her, sitting with her cup of tea. "Those wretched things have been known to keep me in bed for days. That's why Corbyn knew exactly what you needed to set you right."

They sat in comfortable silence for a few moments while Sadie ate. Through the kitchen window, she could see the frost still clinging to the grass, sparkling in the morning sunlight.

"He was unexpectedly kind," Sadie admitted.

Edie's expression softened, and she patted Sadie's hand. "He's a good man beneath all that grumbling he does. The accident changed him in many ways, but he still has a good heart." She paused, looking at Sadie thoughtfully before adding, "Life's hardships can either soften us or turn us brittle. Some scars don't show on the outside, but that doesn't make them any less real."

Edie fixed her with a stare, and a lump formed in Sadie's throat. Throughout their conversations, she had tried to keep the details of her relationship with Nate vague, but Edie often saw more than she let on.

"You know what might do you good after yesterday?" Edie asked, drawing Sadie from her thoughts. "A bit of fresh air. Corbyn and Riley usually walk down by the pond in the morning."

"That sounds perfect, actually."

Not only would the chance to stretch her legs help relieve the lingering stiffness in her muscles from sleeping on the sofa, but she also knew she needed a few quiet moments to speak with Corbyn before they started work for the day.

"Just follow the path past the old oak and take the right fork about five minutes in," Edie instructed, motioning to a spot outside through the window. "The morning light on the pond is quite beautiful."

Sadie thanked her and collected her coat from the hook by the door, wrapping her scarf around her neck and digging her gloves from her pockets. When she stepped through the door, Riley bounded up almost immediately from where he'd been investigating something in the garden, circling around her as if he had been waiting for her to emerge.

"So you're to be my escort, are you?" she asked, smiling as the massive dog trotted beside her. "Lead on, then."

Frost crunched beneath Sadie's boots as they made their way along the gravel path, and she could see puffs of steam from her breath. The cold snap transformed the estate grounds into an icy wonderland. The trees and bushes along the path sparkled with frost as they caught the morning light. After several minutes, the path curved around, revealing a small pond nestled in a natural hollow. Its edges were rimmed with ice, while the center was still liquid and reflected the sky above.

Corbyn stood at the water's edge, hands tucked into his coat pockets. Even from behind, Sadie saw he was relaxed and at peace. Missing was the tension that usually pulled his shoulders tight, the rigidness of his posture that never truly left when they were working. Here, alone with his thoughts, he seemed different, more at ease in his own skin.

Riley gave an enthusiastic bark, bounding ahead, and Corbyn turned at the sound. His gaze found hers almost immediately, and then something flickered across his features. She thought it might be surprise or relief, but then there was something warmer before he schooled his expression.

"Morning," he called as she approached, his voice carrying in the crisp air.

"Good morning," Sadie replied, suddenly feeling strangely shy, like she was invading some sort of morning ritual. "I hope I'm not intruding."

"Not at all," Corbyn said, his tone gentler than she was accustomed to hearing. "How are you feeling?"

"Better," she answered, standing beside him at the water's edge. "Thanks to you."

He shrugged, and she suspected he was trying to appear casual as he replied, "All I did was fetch some pills and darken a room. Hardly heroic."

"It was more than that," Sadie said quietly. "You could have just called me a car back to the inn. Instead, you..." She trailed off, uncertain how to articulate what his care had meant to her.

"Anyone would have done the same," Corbyn replied, though they both knew that wasn't true.

A comfortable silence settled between them as they gazed out over the pond. The surface rippled gently where Riley had ventured a paw into the shallows, breaking the ice and sending concentric circles spreading outward.

"Still, thank you for yesterday," Sadie said. "And for getting my things from the inn."

Corbyn kept his gaze on the water, his voice rough when he answered, "Seemed the practical thing to do."

"It was still thoughtful."

He glanced at her then, something unreadable flickering in his eyes. "Yesterday was..." he hesitated, seemingly struggling to find the right words. "I'm glad you're feeling better."

The simple statement contained more genuine concern than Sadie had heard from him before. It still surprised her how much Corbyn had changed since their first contentious meeting. He had gone from the prickly, dismissive author to someone who noticed when she was in pain and cared enough to help.

"You know, I realized this morning that I've been handling things alone for so long that I'd forgotten what it's like to have someone there when I needed them." She offered a small smile and added, "So thank you. For being there."

Something in Corbyn's expression softened further. The way he looked at her, like she was someone who actually mattered to him, had warmth running through her body, settling low in her stomach. Tucking a loose strand of still-damp hair that had escaped her ponytail behind her ear, she turned her gaze back to the pond, needing to break the spell.

Riley chose that moment to return to them, shaking water from his coat in a spray of droplets. The interruption lightened the mood, shifting them away from emotional territory, and Sadie's laugh rang out over the pond.

"Miscreant," Corbyn muttered, brushing water from his coat. "He knows perfectly well he's not supposed to get wet in this weather."

"He was just testing the ice for structural integrity," Sadie suggested with a smirk. "It's actually very scientific of him."

Corbyn's lips twitched in that almost smile she was coming to recognize. "Are engineers known for licking their testing equipment? Because that's his primary methodology."

"He's pioneering new techniques," she retorted with mock offense. "He's very innovative, our Riley."

"Our Riley," Corbyn repeated, something warming in his gaze. "He's certainly rather taken with you."

"The feeling's mutual," Sadie said, watching as the dog explored the shoreline.

She moved along the edge of the pond, and Corbyn fell into step beside her. Their silence was broken only by the sound of their footsteps and Riley's occasional snuffling when he caught an exciting scent.

"How did the writing go yesterday after I fell asleep?" she asked, keeping the conversation in safer territory. "Any breakthroughs?"

"Actually, yes," Corbyn replied. "I think I've found a way to tie in Shaw's relationship with his sister that gives the confrontation more emotional weight."

As Corbyn explained his narrative solution, Sadie was drawn into the creative discussion. There was an ease to their back and forth now that she had truly come to enjoy. It was refreshing to feel like he spoke to her as an equal, rather than an adversary.

They continued walking as Riley darted ahead to investigate something in the underbrush. The sound of the ground crunching under his paws grew softer as he wandered away from them.

"Sisters have this way of seeing through you," Corbyn remarked as they walked. "In fiction and in reality. My sister Ellie could always tell when I was hiding something, even as a child."

"Brothers, too," Sadie commented with a fond smile, seizing the opening. "What's your sister like?"

Corbyn's expression lightened with genuine affection, and he said, "Ellie's a force of nature. Brilliant doctor, terrible patient. Never stops moving, talking, pushing." He shook his head, but his tone was fond. "She'd like you."

"Oh? Why's that?"

"You're both bloody stubborn," he replied with a hint of humor. "And neither of you takes any of my nonsense."

"High praise indeed," Sadie laughed.

"She's been asking to meet you," Corbyn continued, his tone deceptively calm, but the clenching of his left hand suggested otherwise. "Quite insistent about it, actually."

"Oh? Why the interest?"

"Apparently, anyone who can get me to leave the estate and use modern technology warrants investigation," he said dryly.

"I bet she has more stories about you than Edie," Sadie laughed, watching his lips twitch as he tried to not appear amused.

"That's what concerns me," he replied, though his eyes held a spark that caused her heart to pound in her chest. "She wants me to bring you to London for dinner, perhaps." He kept his gaze fixed ahead as if the invitation were nothing significant and added, "After the manuscript deadline, of course."

The invitation hung between them, casual on the surface but laden with implications. This wasn't work-related but personal and a huge step across the carefully maintained line they'd drawn between them. It also meant he would have to leave the safety of the manor and Great Missenden to travel to London.

"I'd like that," Sadie said softly as they stopped once more along the pond, surprising herself with how much she meant it. She bit her lip, the mention of London taking her back fifteen years, and before she could talk herself out of it, she continued, "I haven't really visited London since I was a teenager." She observed his face as she continued, "I was seventeen, and on a school trip during winter break." She paused deliberately, waiting for any sort of recognition, and when there was none, she added, "We spent New Year's Eve there."

Something flickered in Corbyn's expression – so brief she might have imagined it if she hadn't been watching for it.

"New Year's Eve," he repeated, his voice suddenly rougher. He cleared his throat. "When was this?"

A strange tension coiled between them, and she felt her stomach clench with nervous energy when she answered, "2009." She tilted her head slightly, studying him. "Why do you ask?"

Corbyn had gone very still, his eyes searching her face in a way that made her breath catch. For a moment, just for a heartbeat, she thought she saw recognition there, confirmation of her own half-formed suspicions.

"Nothing," he said finally, though everything in his manner suggested it was something. "The city changes quickly, that's all."

But his eyes lingered on hers a moment too long, and Sadie felt sure there was more that he wasn't saying. Riley came bounding back before Sadie could press him, a stick clutched triumphantly in his jaws.

Sadie took the soggy stick, scratching Riley's ears before hurling it toward a distant tree. The Irish wolfhound took off like a shot, his tan form a blur against the frost-covered ground.

"Show-off," Corbyn muttered with a smirk. "He never runs that fast for me."

"Clearly, I'm the favorite," Sadie replied with a grin. "Can't blame him for having good taste."

They started walking once more, Riley returning with the stick several times, his enthusiasm never waning. They'd nearly circled the pond when a gust of wind cut through the trees. Sadie shivered, her coat doing little to combat the chill.

"Cold?" Corbyn asked, his brow furrowing with concern.

"A little," she admitted, blushing slightly as she realized she had brought this upon herself. "And my hair's still damp."

Corbyn shook his head, a mixture of exasperation and amusement. One corner of his mouth tugged into a smirk, and he reached into his pocket. He produced a soft gray knitted hat, his hand catching her elbow to stop her in her tracks. Even through the layers of clothing, that awareness she felt whenever he touched her was still there.

"Here," he grumbled good-naturedly. "You Americans have no sense of self-preservation."

Before Sadie could protest, he pulled the beanie over her head, his fingers carefully arranging it to cover her ears with surprising dexterity. The gesture was unexpectedly tender, and she found herself studying his face, taking in the way his expression softened as his fingers brushed against her skin.

"Thank you," Sadie murmured, intensely aware of his proximity.

Corbyn's hands lingered, his gaze dropping briefly to her lips. For a moment, Sadie thought he might lean in and close the small distance between them. She held her breath, and it felt like her heartbeat was so loud she was sure he would hear it. Everything seemed to slow, and Sadie swayed slightly forward, drawn by some invisible thread.

Just as Corbyn leaned in, Riley barreled between them, shaking pond water from his fur and drenching them both. Canine obliviousness had shattered the moment completely.

"Riley!" Corbyn sputtered, jumping back as droplets splattered his coat.

Sadie couldn't help laughing, the sound a mix of relief and disappointment. "Perfect timing," she quipped, wiping water from her cheek.

Corbyn shot the Irish wolfhound a look as he muttered, "You're sleeping in the garden shed tonight." Though she was quite sure it wasn't really a threat.

Completely unaware of the moment he'd interrupted, Riley gazed up at them both joyfully, tail wagging in enthusiastic circles.

"We should probably get back," Corbyn said, clearing his throat again, though his eyes still held a warmth that made Sadie's stomach flutter. "Edie will have my head if you catch a chill."

The moment had slipped away, but as they walked back toward the manor house, Riley trotting between them, Sadie couldn't help wondering what might have happened if Riley hadn't interrupted. The thought should have alarmed her; the complications it could bring were undeniable. Somehow, though, it didn't, and she couldn't find it in herself to stop those musings.

March 4, 2025

-Corbyn-

Pacing his study, Corbyn could feel the tension building in his shoulders as he waited to hear the sound of tires coming down the driveway. He'd been awake since dawn, his mind too restless for sleep, knowing what today would bring.

Two nights ago, once Sadie had gone back to the inn after recovering from her migraine, he had made an online late-night purchase. It had been an uncharacteristically impulsive move, and he told himself it was a moment of weakness brought on by the desire to avoid any more interruptions to their editing schedule. It certainly had nothing to do with what Sadie had shared about her ex smashing her laptop or the fact that he had almost kissed her by the pond.

At least, that's what he told himself as he entered his credit card information at 2 AM to purchase the newest model of the laptop Sadie had been looking at.

Now, waiting for her arrival, anxiety gnawed at his stomach. The order showed that it had been delivered to the inn, which meant she would have received it the previous night. He had sent it anonymously, but Sadie was smart, and she would inevitably figure it out. Rolling his shoulders, he made another lap around the study, stepping over Riley's massive form as he had stretched out across the width of the room.

He froze when the telltale sound of gravel under tires reached his ears. Riley immediately stood and trotted out of the room, leaving him alone with his anxiety. Tugging absentmindedly on the collar of his navy sweater, he forced himself to take his next breath through his nose as he sat. Turning on the tablet, he picked up the stylus in an attempt to look casual, like he had been working all morning instead of obsessing over her reaction to the gift.

The front door opened, and the tapping of nails on the wood floor told him Riley was enthusiastically greeting his new favorite person. He held his breath, waiting to hear the sound of her steps fading as she headed toward the kitchen for tea, only that wasn't what happened.

"Corbyn?"

Her voice rang out through the house, and he swallowed hard. When he noticed the subtle shake in his right hand, his eyes nearly rolled back into his head. He reminded himself he was in his mid-thirties, not a school lad with a crush on the girl sitting next to him.

"In here," he called, his throat suddenly dry.

Sadie appeared in the doorway, slightly breathless, her gray eyes stormy as she met his. Her dark blonde hair was windblown, a few strands escaping from her usually neat ponytail, and there was a noticeable crease in her brow. Under her arm, she carried a sleek package.

"Can you explain this?" she asked, stepping into the study and placing the box on his desk carefully. No greeting, no small talk, just straight to the point. "It arrived at the inn last night. No card, no note, just my name on the delivery label."

Corbyn shifted in his chair, his left hand unconsciously clenching in his lap, and he tried to sound surprised when he answered, "I'm not sure what you're implying."

"I'm not implying anything," she replied, placing special emphasis on the word implying. "I'm asking directly. Did you send this?" She gestured to the box, continuing, "Because this is a three-thousand-dollar laptop, and frankly, you're the only person I can think of who would both know I needed one and have the means to afford it."

Her gaze bored into him, unwavering, and he had to fight not to sink down in his seat. He shook his head, dropping the stylus so he could run his hand through his hair.

"What if I did?" he asked, trying to maintain a neutral tone. "Would that be so terrible?"

"Why, though?" she asked, and that crease in her brow deepened with her confusion. He gripped the armrests of his chair when he suddenly had the desire to get up and smooth it away somehow. "We've barely known each other for a month."

"You're working yourself to exhaustion with these side projects, Reed," he reasoned, forcing himself to drop his shoulders that had been creeping up toward his ears. "You're no good to me half-dead from migraines."

Her eyebrows shot up at his blunt assessment. Even though she was now looking at him like she might actually throw something at him, he was relieved to see the tension in her brow had disappeared.

"It's practical," he continued, forcing himself to look into the storm raging in her eyes. "You were kind enough to let me make use of your tablet, but it means you're stuck squinting at your phone screen trying to get other work done. That's not sustainable."

Sadie's expression remained guarded, though something flickered in her eyes—surprise, perhaps shock that he'd been paying such close attention. "So this is... what? A bribe to keep me focused solely on your book?"

"It's a gift to prevent a repeat of the other day," Corbyn replied, trying to ignore the fact that he knew that was only a secondary reason. "The book needs to be finished. You need to be functioning to help me finish it."

"I can't accept something like this," she insisted, but he didn't miss the way her voice softened. Her eyes met his again, and it seemed like the storm was passing. For a moment, her eyes turned bright, and he thought she might actually cry. "It's too much."

"It's not really a gift," he insisted, even though they both knew it was. The way she looked from him to the box on his desk, eyes wide and disbelieving, had him wondering how long it had been since anyone had done something like this simply because she deserved it. "Consider it a business investment. A tool for work." She started to open her mouth, and he continued on, "Before you say it, you will not be paying me back or whatever it was you were about to suggest. I want you at your best without worrying about finances or juggling late-night freelance work after our sessions."

Sadie shook her head, and her voice was thick when she told him, "That's not how this works. I'm your editor, not your..." She trailed off, as if uncertain how to finish the sentence. "I don't want charity because you feel bad about what I told you regarding Nate."

The room fell silent save for Riley's rhythmic breathing and the distant ticking of the grandfather clock in the hall. When Corbyn's shoulders dropped this time, it had nothing to do with trying to appear composed.

"Look," he said finally, his voice softening as he stood from his chair, moving around the desk so he was standing in front of her, "I know it seems excessive. But you're working yourself ragged, and you need proper equipment. Yes," he added, before she could interrupt, "what you told me about your ex destroying your laptop factored into it. But that's not the main reason."

Something in Sadie's expression shifted, curiosity replacing some of her wariness. He fought the urge to shy away as she studied his face, almost as if she was looking for some sign of deception. There was a pang in his chest at the realization that she didn't believe him, and he reminded himself that he wasn't the only one with a reason to have issues with trust. He realized in that moment that it was a very good thing Nate was thousands of miles away. Every time he thought about the prat, it triggered some long-buried protective instinct.

"Then what is?"

"I've spent four years struggling with this book," Corbyn replied, surprising himself with his honesty. "You're making it not just possible, but good. Better than I thought it could be. You shouldn't have to choose between your health and having the basic tools you need to do your job. This isn't charity or some grand gesture. It's practical. For both of us."

Finally, she sighed, and he saw her body relax; a small smile tugged at the corner of her mouth, and she chuckled. "You're impossible, you know that?"

"So I've been told," Corbyn said, relief easing the tightness in his own body, and he leaned back against the desk. "Frequently. By everyone who knows me."

"Regardless of what you said, I will pay you back over time," Sadie replied firmly.

"That's not necessary..."

"It is to me," she interrupted, her tone stopping him short. She could be nearly as intimidating as Edie when she wanted to be. "I accept the gesture, Corbyn. I appreciate it more than I can say, but I need to maintain some... boundaries."

The word hung between them. Boundaries. Each day, they carefully navigated those invisible lines that seemed to blur and reform as she slowly broke down his walls. He was beginning to detest that word.

Corbyn nodded though, knowing he had no choice but to agree as he responded, "Alright. If that's what you need."

A smile bloomed across Sadie's face, genuine and warm. "Thank you. For understanding. And, well, for this." She gestured to the laptop box and added, "It really is thoughtful, even if it's way over the top."

She took a step forward and time seemed to stand still as she closed the small distance between them and brushed her lips against his cheek. His right cheek was closest to her, and she didn't shy away from the scars that ran along his jaw.

He was acutely aware of everything about that moment. The scent of her shampoo, the way she placed a hand on his arm to steady herself, the warmth that spread through him at the soft touch of her lips. He found himself wishing time really had stopped when she pulled away, a shy smile tugging at her lips as she looked up at him.

"You're welcome," Corbyn said, his voice rough, a tingling feeling running down his spine.

A blush was creeping up her neck and blooming across her cheeks, and he was pretty sure his own were a similar shade of pink. They stared at each other for a moment, her gray eyes searching his blue, as if looking for a sign he might react poorly to the gesture. A few weeks ago, he would have sent her packing back to the inn, likely back to New York. Now, though, all he could think about was that inexplicable pull between them.

He unconsciously turned so he was facing her, his right hand reaching up to brush a lock of hair away from her face, tucking it behind her ear. He heard her breath catch, her pupils dilating slightly as he traced her jaw. She bit her lip, and his eyes were immediately drawn to the action. A little voice in the back of his mind was saying something about boundaries and how the last thing she needed was someone as damaged as he was. Yet he still leaned in slowly, giving her time to pull away.

"I brought you two tea and pasties." Edie's voice called just before she appeared in the office door.

They broke apart quickly, Sadie reaching for her bag and busying herself with retrieving her red pens, her head ducked.

Corbyn, his own cheeks warm once more, turned to retreat behind his desk, trying to calm his pounding heart and shaking hands.

"Thank you, Edie," he said, clearing his throat when his voice sounded hoarse. "The pasties smell delicious."

He risked a glance up at Edie, who was still standing in the doorway, looking between him and Sadie, a little smirk playing at her lips. When she met his eyes, she quirked an eyebrow before moving to the coffee table to set down the tray. Her gaze flickered to the laptop box on Corbyn's desk, then back to them with obvious amusement as she said, "I see you've been having an interesting morning."

"Edie..." Corbyn began, a warning in his voice.

"Don't mind me," she chirped, heading back toward the door. "I'll just leave you both to your work. Wouldn't want to distract you from such an important... literary collaboration."

The emphasis she placed on 'collaboration' was subtle but unmistakable. He was all too aware of the way Sadie's cheeks flushed again as Edie disappeared down the hallway. The silence stretched between them, and from the corner of his eye, Corbyn saw Sadie shift in her seat, tucking a strand of hair behind her ear.

Riley, oblivious to the tension, stood with a resounding yawn before crossing to sit near the coffee table, eyes darting between the pasties and the two humans in the room. Corbyn cleared his throat and made his way over to the coffee table, thankful for the distraction.

"And everyone says I'm the impossible one," he sighed, though there was fondness in his voice.

"She means well," Sadie replied, turning to reach for one of the teacups. Neither of them seemed to be willing to address what had nearly happened directly, but for once, they weren't pretending like it was nothing. "I'm getting used to her particular brand of... interference."

"She has had years of practice," Corbyn muttered, absently breaking off a piece of pasty for Riley, who accepted it and flopped to the floor once more. "Should put a bell on her apron so we can hear her coming."

Sadie chuckled softly, adding, "Nothing gets past her." She took a sip of her tea, and he glanced over, surprised to find her looking back at him. He had expected her to shy away as she had on the other occasions they had gotten caught up in the moment. "At least the pasties are still warm."

Corbyn cleared his throat. Part of him was eager to move on to safer ground, his shoulders starting to ache as he realized they had once again crept up toward his ears. He forced himself to relax, to not focus too much on the disappointment he was trying very hard to ignore.

"Right, shall we?" he asked, gesturing toward the tablet sitting on his desk. "You mentioned last night you had thoughts about chapter twenty?"

"Yes," Sadie said, and he saw the way her shoulders relaxed as well now that they were back to discussing the book. "There's a pacing issue in the interrogation scene that I think we can fix."

Work. That was safe territory. They could navigate it without the dangerous undercurrents that seemed to pull at them whenever they strayed too close to something personal. He felt his chest clench when he reminded himself he needed to be careful. Sadie was here temporarily, and she would return to New York once the book was finished. Not to mention, what could someone like her possibly see in someone like him? Scarred, damaged, difficult. The laptop sat in its box on the corner of his desk, a reminder that he'd already crossed lines he shouldn't have.

But as Sadie began to speak about character motivation and scene structure, her voice steady once more, Corbyn couldn't quite silence the part of him that had felt her breath catch when he'd touched her face, nor could he forget how she hadn't shied away from his scars. Behind all the walls he had erected around his heart, there was a tiny glimmer of hope that he couldn't quite snuff out.

March 4, 2025

-Sadie-

The door of The Roaring Stag creaked open, and a rush of warm air chased away the chill as Sadie stepped inside. The pub hummed with the usual early evening conversations, the locals having their pints as a fire crackled in the stone hearth. Over the last several weeks, many of them had gone from glancing at her warily to giving her a friendly smile and wave as she passed.

She spotted Maggie behind the polished oak counter, phone pressed to her ear, her expression tense. The usual warmth in her eyes was gone, replaced by an unease that settled low in Sadie's stomach. She motioned for Sadie to come over to the bar.

"She just arrived," she said into the receiver, and Sadie felt a pit in her stomach.

"Thank goodness you're here," Maggie said, covering the mouthpiece briefly. "Just give me one moment, love." Turning back to her conversation, she continued, "Yes, she's here now. I'll handle it... No, I think it's better if... Alright, but give me a few minutes first."

Sadie approached the bar, setting the laptop box down. Shrugging out of her coat, she could feel an ache forming between her shoulder blades. Maggie's tone had set her on edge.

Maggie ended the call and immediately moved toward her, her voice strained. "I've been trying to reach you all afternoon."

"Sorry." A wave of guilt washed over her, and her shoulders dropped as she set her coat on a bar stool. "I had my phone turned off. I kept getting calls from a number I didn't recognize. What's going on?"

Maggie's lips pressed into a thin line, arms crossed over her chest. "I think I know who your mystery caller is. Some bloke's been asking for you, says he's your fiancé. He's been hanging about since teatime."

The words hit Sadie like ice water. "My fiancé?" she whispered, her knees threatening to give way. Her hands felt clammy, and her eyes darted around the room, trying to find the one man who would claim such a thing.

"Dark hair, hazel eyes, glasses? Kept ordering shots of whiskey and getting tetchy when I wouldn't tell him when you'll be back." Maggie shook her head as she spoke. "He seemed charming enough, but I can always tell when they're trying too hard."

"Where is he now?"

"Said he was going for a walk, but that was twenty minutes ago. Could be back any moment." Maggie leaned closer, lowering her voice, adding, "I don't like the feel of this, Sadie."

Before Sadie could respond, the pub door opened again. The chill of the wind had her shivering, and the next sound she heard over the murmurs of the other patrons made her draw in a sharp breath.

"Sades?"

She knew that voice. It had whispered both sweet nothings and cruel barbs in her ear for years.

"Nate... what are you doing here?" she asked, turning to face the man she had hoped to never see again.

Nate stood just inside the doorway, his hazel eyes holding a softness she recognized from the times his behavior had been so atrocious that he couldn't possibly shift the blame. The way his shoulders curved forward, hands shoved in the pockets of his charcoal pea coat. The coat had been left open to reveal the green sweater she'd given him two Christmases ago. Soft cashmere she'd saved for months to afford, all while making sure the bills got paid.

"I just want to talk," he said, crossing to her, his voice taking on an intimate tone, one hand reaching up to cup her cheek. "To make things right between us."

A wave of nausea washed over her, the scent of his cologne, something she once loved, now made her want to vomit. His hand was icy when he touched her cheek, and she quickly took a step back, shaking her head.

Behind her, Sadie heard the soft clinking of glasses as Maggie moved about her work. Out of the corner of her eye, she noticed Fergus, one of Maggie's part-time helpers, wiping down tables that already looked spotless. His massive frame was positioned strategically behind Nate. Several of the regulars had paused their conversations, eyeing Nate with suspicion. She took her first full breath since walking through the door, knowing the people here were watching out for her safety.

Curiosity, and perhaps a need for closure, got the better of her. She knew this was simply another attempt to manipulate the situation, to hook her back into his orbit. Still, she looked back at Nate and jerked her head toward the courtyard door.

"Fine. We can talk outside. I'll give you five minutes and then you're going back to New York."

"Sadie, love, I don't think that's wise..." Maggie began, but Sadie shook her head.

"Five minutes," Sadie assured her, "that's all he gets. Leave the courtyard door unlocked."

The March air bit at her cheeks as they stepped outside. Cobblestones glinted beneath their feet, slick from the afternoon rain shower. The soft glow of fairy lights lit the space, and Sadie flipped on one of the outdoor heaters, hoping to ease her shivers.

"Alright," she said with a sigh, turning to face him, "you've got five minutes. Talk."

"I miss you," he said. "I miss... us." He stepped closer, his hand reaching out to tuck a wayward strand of hair behind her ear.

She flinched at the contact. Just hours ago, Corbyn had done something similar, but where his touch had felt tender, Nate's was possessive, as if he still had the right to touch her without consent.

"I've been thinking about everything we talked about. I accepted a position at NYU, and I start next month. We could afford a brownstone. There's one available that's pet-friendly, and we could get that golden retriever you wanted. You always said you wanted one like your childhood dog, Buddy." His smile turned almost shy as he leaned his forehead against hers. He whispered, "And it has a spare bedroom that could be perfect for... you know. Eventually. When we're ready for a family."

For a fleeting moment, Sadie closed her eyes and allowed herself to indulge in the fantasy his words painted. Cozy writing nooks, exposed brick walls, the patter of a dog's paws on hardwood floors, maybe someday the sound of a child's laughter. Everything she'd once thought she wanted, all the dreams she'd only ever voiced in their most vulnerable moments.

Stepping back, she shook her head, trying to chase away those treacherous thoughts. She wasn't the same woman who had left him months ago, and she squared her shoulders, expression hardening. The man before her was a master of manipulation, and she refused to fall for his tricks.

"How did you find me, Nate?"

He shrugged, guilt flickering across his face, and he replied, "You let it slip when I called you. Remember? You mentioned working with Corbyn Pearce." A smug smile played at his lips. "Wasn't hard to look him up. Then I found your email still logged in on my laptop, and I saw the confirmation for The Roaring Stag."

Sadie blinked a few times, stammering for words. "You read my emails?"

"What else was I supposed to do?" Nate argued, familiar petulance creeping into his tone. "You wouldn't respond... I tried calling, texting, and even emailing. You wouldn't answer, so I had to come all this way!"

Sadie could hear his voice starting to rise in volume. This was the Nate she knew best. The one who could twist any situation and make himself out to be the victim. Crossing her arms over her chest, she looked away, letting out a slow, tense breath.

"You could have, I don't know, maybe just accepted that we're over instead of stalking me halfway across the world," she pointed out, her voice still quiet.

The word 'stalking' triggered something in Nate. His expression cracked, and with it the soft, pleading look. It was replaced with something that had Sadie taking another step back, trying to angle herself so she could easily escape back into the pub.

"I prefer to think of it as keeping tabs on what's mine," he retorted, countering her retreat by moving closer once more.

"What's yours?" Sadie spat with a humorless laugh. "I'm not some object for you to possess. Go home, Nate. There's nothing here for you."

She turned to leave, but he grabbed her arm, spinning her back around. His grip on her arm tightened as she tried to pull away, and a soft cry of pain escaped her, knowing there would be bruises.

"Let me go, Nate," she demanded, but he only pulled her closer, capturing her other wrist. Trying her best to show no fear, she threatened, "One scream from me and you'll be dealing with Fergus."

"I came here having done everything you asked," he said, his voice hard, and she saw a muscle in his jaw tick. "I took the teaching job, I looked into new apartments... I'm trying to give you everything you ever wanted, and your response is to spit in my face."

"Everything I wanted?" Sadie repeated, stilling for a moment as she blinked at him. It was inconceivable to her that after nearly a decade together, he still didn't know anything about her, not really. "What I wanted was a partner, not someone who acts like a child when he's angry."

Something ugly flickered across Nate's face, and when he leaned closer, she could smell the whiskey on his breath.

"So that's what this boils down to? You're actually going to throw everything we had away because of *one* time when I lost my temper?" he practically snarled at her, and Sadie couldn't stop the disbelieving huff that escaped her. "I said I was sorry, but you're going to hold that over me again, and hold yourself out there as blameless and perfect?"

"You and I both know it wasn't just one time," she fired back, angrily trying to yank her arms away, which only brought forth a hiss of pain. "I never said I was perfect, but I do think I deserve better than living in fear of you destroying things in a fit of anger."

Nate's eyes narrowed, and a cruel laugh escaped him. "Is that why you're so caught up on this Pearce guy? Because you think he's so much better?" His grip tightened, and he leaned over her, making her shrink away. "Tell me, Sadie, are you screwing him?"

She had to fight the urge to drive her knee into his groin. The muscles in her leg had tensed as if preparing to deliver the blow, but she forced herself to take a breath. Escalating the situation further would only make it worse.

"Nate, I need you to listen to me," she said, keeping her voice soft and her eyes pleading as she tried to placate him. "Maggie is going to come looking for me any minute. Just let me go... please."

"When I'm finished saying what I have to say," he sneered, his face close to hers. She tried once more to step back, only to be pulled against his chest. "You think he cares about you? He's isolated in his fancy house and probably hasn't had a woman look at him twice since his accident. You're convenient, Sadie. That's all you are to him."

The words hit like a physical blow, each one aimed at her most profound insecurities. That, despite all the evidence to the contrary, the people in her life only wanted her around when she could be of use.

"I'm trying to save you from making a mistake," Nate continued, one hand releasing her wrist to grip her chin so she couldn't look away.

"The only mistake I made was staying with you as long as I did," she snapped, and his face turned red.

It didn't register that he had shoved her until she slammed into the glass table behind her, sending it tumbling to the ground along with her. The sound of shattering glass echoed through the courtyard, and she reached out to try to catch herself so her face wouldn't hit the cobblestones.

She came down hard on her side, her hip absorbing most of the impact as pain radiated down her leg. When her forearm hit the ground, a different kind of pain registered in her mind. This one was sharp, almost stabbing, and a loud cry escaped her. She had landed in the glass left behind by the table shattering, and one of the few larger shards had cut through her sweater and embedded itself in her arm.

The door that led to the pub flew open almost immediately. Corbyn appeared first, and Sadie saw his body instantly go taut when he saw her on the ground. His jaw tightened, and before either could say a word, he moved quickly between Sadie and Nate, shoving the other man violently back with his right hand.

"Touch her again..." Corbyn warned in a tone that would have made her afraid for Nate's safety, were that possible.

Maggie appeared at Sadie's side, offering her a hand up and taking care around the broken glass. Reaching out, Sadie took the other woman's hand and slowly stood, trying not to grimace when her bruised hip protested the movement. Maggie wrapped an arm around her for support, and Sadie cradled her injured arm to her chest. She could feel the blood oozing beneath her sleeve, and her breath became ragged.

Fergus and another man, whom Sadie only knew as one of the pub regulars, had followed them. Fergus stepped up next to Nate, massive hand gripping Nate's shoulder as he said, "You've made a big mistake coming here, mate."

"So this is who's been keeping you so busy, Sades?" Nate taunted, trying to look smug as he stared at Corbyn. She could hear a hint of fear in his voice. "Tell me, Pearce, how long has it been since you actually published anything worth reading? Three years? Four? Must be nice having someone around to make you feel like you still matter, given that face is the only thing people talk about now."

Sadie wasn't sure if Nate's insult landed as intended, but she felt her own body tense. She took a breath, ready to defend Corbyn, but the strange man spoke first.

"I wouldn't say another word if I were you," he said, and Sadie saw him produce a black wallet and hold up what appeared to be a government ID. "I'm Police Constable Jones."

Nate went pale; the man's badge and identification card finally penetrated his rage-clouded mind. His eyes darted around the courtyard as if seeing it clearly for the first time—the witnesses, the shattered glass, the bloodstain that was spreading on Sadie's sleeve. This time, no amount of fake charm would spare him.

The constable turned toward Sadie, eyes softening with pity. Heat rushed into her cheeks, and she looked down at her feet. She could already hear all of their unspoken thoughts. How long had she allowed this to go on? Why hadn't she left sooner? They were the same questions she asked herself every time she thought of Nate.

"Miss," he said softly, and Sadie forced herself to meet the constable's eyes, "would you like to make a formal complaint?"

She could feel four pairs of eyes fixed on her. The only person in the courtyard not looking at her was Corbyn, and she realized his glare was still locked on Nate. She wanted to vomit, her body starting to tremble as the reality of what had just occurred settled in. Maggie's embrace was the only thing keeping her standing, and for a moment, she had to look away to blink back tears.

"It's your call, Reed," Corbyn said, without looking at her after she hesitated.

After spending so many weeks in Corbyn's study, she knew that tone. It was the same one he had used days earlier when he counseled her not to let Nate pull her back into his orbit, not when she had come so far. It became easier to breathe as her body slowly relaxed against Maggie. She blew out a slow breath, straightening her spine as she glared at Nate. He had come here to try to get her back, to try to make her believe she was alone. What he hadn't counted on was the fact that the people here had taken her in as one of their own.

"I just want him to go back to New York," she told the constable. "If he leaves, there's no need to file a complaint."

"Come on, Sades, don't do this," Nate pleaded, that tender look returning to his face. He tried to take a step toward her, but Corbyn blocked him, countering the movement. She watched as Nate was forced to look up slightly so he could narrow his eyes at Corbyn. "This has nothing to do with you, Pearce."

"But it does," Corbyn countered, leaning forward slightly and forcing Nate to shrink back. "You are not fit to lick her boots, and if you ever come near her again, I will move heaven and earth to make sure you regret it."

"Time for you to go, mate," Constable Jones added, and Fergus gave Nate a slight shove in the direction of the door. Looking back at Sadie, he said, "We'll make sure he leaves, miss. And if he shows up here again, don't hesitate to call and make a complaint."

No one else moved as Fergus and Constable Jones herded Nate through the door to the pub. It was only once it closed that Corbyn finally turned to face her, his expression immediately melting into concern. He took a step closer, Maggie giving them space as he gently took hold of the arm she was cradling against her chest.

"You're bleeding," he murmured, his brow furrowing as he examined the wound.

"I'll live," she managed, her voice shaky as she tried her best to give him a half smile. Her forearm throbbed, warm blood still seeping through the torn fabric, and she knew she would have an ugly bruise on her hip come morning.

"Let's get you inside," Maggie said, taking charge of the situation. "That cut needs bandaging."

Sadie hissed as she took a step, her body protesting the movement. When Corbyn took hold of her uninjured arm to steady her, his left hand coming to rest on the small of her back, she felt her breath catch. She glanced over at him to try to assure him that she was fine, but the way he was looking at her with a mix of tenderness and concern caused the words to die on her lips. No one had ever looked at her like that, and there was a sudden tightness in her chest.

They made their way back through the courtyard door into the warmth of the pub, and his hand remained on her back, sending a jolt along her spine. Maggie directed them to a corner table away from curious glances before disappearing into the back to retrieve a first aid kit.

"What are you doing here?" she asked softly as she settled into one of the chairs.

He pulled out a chair beside her, seating himself before answering. She noticed he angled himself so he could see both her and the door, leaning close enough that only she could hear him.

"Maggie called," he told her, his voice calm though the crease in his brow hinted at what he was truly feeling. "She said she had a bad feeling about some man who'd been asking for you."

"You came because Maggie had a feeling?" she asked, her brows raising.

She saw a blush creeping up his cheeks, and he sat back in the chair, clearing his throat. For a moment, she thought he wouldn't answer her question, that perhaps she had pushed too far. Her shoulders started to curve inwards as she prepared to apologize.

"I came," he began, his eyes finally meeting hers once more, "because after everything you've told me about him, I needed to be sure you were alright."

The simple honesty of his words sent warmth blooming in her chest; this time, her own cheeks burned with a blush. Tears welled in her eyes, and she did her best to blink them away before he noticed. When she had recovered enough to trust her own voice, she reached across the table to place her hand on his. She saw his eyes drop. That now familiar spark ran through her, and she welcomed the feeling.

"I'm glad you came," she whispered, and his gaze snapped back to hers, the crease between his brow finally easing.

Maggie appeared with her first aid kit, and Sadie pulled her hand back. She didn't miss Maggie's quirked eyebrow or the little smirk on the other woman's face as she looked from her to Corbyn.

"Right then, let's have a look at this," Maggie said, carefully cutting away the torn fabric. Her face fell, and Sadie held her breath, knowing that wasn't a good sign. "Oh, love, this needs a doctor. There's still glass in the wound... you'll likely need stitches."

"I'll call Ellie," Corbyn said immediately, already standing and reaching for his phone. "She can meet us at the estate."

"It's late... I don't want her making a trip just for me," Sadie protested, but she fell quiet when he placed his hand on her shoulder.

"Ellie won't mind. In fact, she'd be furious if I didn't call her for something like this," he told her, lips lifting in a comforting half-smile. "I'd rather not have to face her wrath for the next several weeks."

"He's right, love," Maggie chimed in. "I'll clean and bandage this as best I can, but you'd better let Ellie take a look."

Corbyn stepped away, phone already to his ear, while Maggie cleaned the wound as best she could without disturbing the large piece of glass. Sadie hissed at the burn of the antiseptic, and Maggie murmured her apologies as she worked. She was just finishing the bandage around Sadie's arm when Corbyn returned.

"Ellie will meet us in an hour," Corbyn said firmly, in a tone she had learned meant there would be no reasoning with him. "She said to try to make some sort of sling to keep her arm elevated." Maggie nodded, heading over to the bar, her head disappearing as she began looking for something underneath. Corbyn shifted, rubbing the back of his neck before adding, "And I think it would be best for you to stay at the house for at least the next few days."

"That's excessive," Sadie insisted, hating that they were fussing over her like this. She looked down at the bandage on her arm, wanting nothing more than to go to bed and wake up to find it was all a bad dream. "I'm fine right here."

"And what if he comes back?" Corbyn countered, and a heavy sigh left Sadie's body. "You got lucky tonight, Reed. What would have happened if no one knew what was going on?"

"As much as I hate to admit it, you should listen to him, love," Maggie chimed in, a scarf thrown over her shoulder. Sadie's eyes widened, realizing that she was outnumbered. Maggie gently positioned her injured arm and began creating a sling from the scarf as she continued, "I'd sleep better knowing the tosser can't get to you again."

Her eyes began to prickle, and she had to look away while Maggie tied the scarf behind her neck. She blinked rapidly, willing herself not to let the tears of frustration overwhelm her. The sound of a chair scraping against the floor and a large, warm hand covering hers had her closing her eyes for a moment. She took a slow, measured breath before finally meeting Corbyn's eyes.

"After what just happened, you could use someone watching your back," he said softly, his thumb brushing over her knuckles. The action had her sucking in a quick breath, but it was his following request that set her heart pounding. "Sadie, please don't fight me on this."

In all their time together, he had never called her by her first name. It had always been Reed, even in those moments when all the lines seemed to blur. The way he was looking at her now, like she was someone precious, someone he would do anything to protect, made the last of her defenses crumble to dust.

"Okay," she whispered, managing a tiny smile.

"Good," Corbyn said, relief evident, and she felt his hand squeeze hers.

When the door to the pub opened, Sadie held her breath for a moment, a pit forming in her stomach. She only relaxed when she saw Fergus walk through the door alone. He made his way through the crowd, the other patrons watching with curiosity. Sadie was sure they'd be the topic of local gossip tomorrow.

"He won't be bothering you again, lass," he said when he reached the table, and Sadie managed a grateful smile.

"Fergus, would you grab Sadie's things from behind the bar?" Maggie asked, then turned back to them. "You two had better get going. I'll send someone over with a bag of your things later."

As Sadie stood, she felt one of Corbyn's hands land on the small of her back again, the other taking hold of her good arm as if to keep her from toppling over. She took a breath, ready to insist she didn't need help, that she could pack her own belongings, but the look on his face had her falling silent with another sigh. Arguing with just Corbyn or Maggie was difficult enough; the two of them on the same side would be impossible.

"You take care of yourself," Maggie said, giving Sadie's shoulder a gentle squeeze. Then, she fixed Corbyn with a stern look. "And you, Mr. Pearce, you look after her, you hear?"

"Yes, ma'am," Corbyn replied, a touch of amusement softening his features, and he took the laptop box and Sadie's coat from Fergus.

Outside, Corbyn's Range Rover waited at the curb. He helped Sadie into the passenger seat, ensuring she was settled before walking around to the driver's side. The leather interior still held warmth from the heater, and Sadie sank into it gratefully.

As he pulled away from the curb, she noticed Corbyn hesitate for a moment, then reach across the center console with his left hand. He found hers in the darkness, and he allowed their fingers to intertwine.

The significance wasn't lost on Sadie. It was the hand he usually kept hidden. It was a physical manifestation of all his vulnerabilities. Yet now, he reached for her with it without hesitation. His grip was different—more cautious, more measured—but the level of trust the action took was profound.

"Thank you," she whispered, looking over at his profile as he drove, taking in the strong angles of his face. "For coming tonight. For everything."

Corbyn glanced at her briefly, his blue eyes serious in the dim light from the dashboard, and gave a slight nod as his hold on her hand tightened. That simple action had her eyes welling again. Eventually, she knew she'd have to deal with all the emotions that had built up tonight, but the thought wasn't as terrifying as it once would have been. Mostly because she was no longer navigating this alone.

The weight of Corbyn's hand in hers, the steady presence of him beside her—it all combined to create a sense of safety she hadn't felt in years. The crisis had burned away any remaining pretense or hesitation, and there was no going back. They had moved beyond tentative attraction into something deeper—something that felt like a homecoming.

"Sadie?" Corbyn's voice was soft in the darkness.

"Mm?"

"You're safe now. You know that, right? Not just tonight, but..." He paused, seeming to search for words. "I won't let him near you again. None of us will."

The simple declaration made it hard to speak. She'd felt alone for so long, even when she was with Nate. Alone in her fear, alone in her shame, alone in the careful lies she told to maintain the illusion of normalcy. Even when Jess had offered her help, it hadn't felt like this. Tonight, a community had rallied around her without question, the people she had come to care for showing up when she needed them the most.

"I know," she whispered, and realized that she meant it.

March 4, 2025

-Corbyn-

Corbyn couldn't sit still. He paced the length of the kitchen, glancing at his watch again and again. Nearly an hour had passed since the inn incident, and the panic he'd stifled for Sadie's sake threatened to boil over. His left hand trembled in his pocket, every tick of the clock tightening something in his chest.

At the kitchen table, Edie sat beside Sadie, gently coaxing her to drink the tea she'd prepared. Sadie held the mug in one hand, occasionally drinking when told, but she mostly stared down at the steaming liquid. Her face was pale, features drawn with tension, and she'd barely spoken since they'd arrived at the manor. She was in shock, and he hated feeling helpless.

"Steady now, love," Edie murmured, her voice carrying the same tone she'd used when Corbyn and Ellie were children with scraped knees. "Sugar helps with the adrenaline crash, dear. My gran always swore by it."

Sadie managed a slight nod, taking another sip. Her eyes remained distant and unfocused, sending another wave of worry through Corbyn's mind.

"You're making me nervous with all that pacing, lad," Edie said, casting him a concerned look. "Why don't you make yourself useful and fetch some biscuits from the pantry? They're on the second shelf."

Grateful for an excuse to do something, Corbyn nodded and slipped to the pantry. His hands shook so badly he nearly dropped the tin. Riley padded over and pressed against Corbyn's legs, warm fur a comforting anchor.

"Good boy," Corbyn murmured, running his hand through the dog's wiry coat. The familiar gesture helped steady him, though his mind kept replaying the scene at the inn, and Sadie's terrified face as she looked up at him.

He returned with the tin, setting it on the table while trying to keep his hand from causing it to rattle. The sight of Sadie there, looking hollow, arm still in a makeshift sling, and her sleeve cut away to reveal a stark white bandage, sent his chest into a fresh spasm of guilt and protectiveness.

"There we are, love," Edie said softly, opening the tin and handing a biscuit to Sadie. "Try to eat something."

"Thank you," Sadie said quietly, taking the biscuit but not biting into it.

Edie patted her shoulder, soothing, "Nothing to thank me for. We look after our own here."

The words sent a fierce, unfamiliar rush of heat through Corbyn's chest. Our own. When was the exact moment Sadie became that? When had she stopped being merely his editor and become someone this household would protect? Someone they considered part of their little family?

Car headlights swept across the kitchen window, and Riley's ears perked up. Corbyn felt his shoulders drop, and he took a deep breath for the first time since Maggie's phone call.

"That'll be Ellie now," Edie said, rising from her chair. "She'll set you right, don't you worry."

The door opened to reveal Ellie, with her dark hair in a ponytail and a medical bag slung over her shoulder. She was wearing jeans and a thick jumper beneath her winter coat, the lack of scrubs suggesting she had not been at work. She took in the scene, eyes sweeping quickly around the room.

"Evening, all," she said, shrugging out of her coat and draping it over a chair. She gave Corbyn's arm a quick squeeze as she passed. "How are we holding up, Corbie?"

"Fine," he replied automatically, though they both knew it wasn't true.

Ellie nodded to Edie with a warm smile before turning toward Sadie and settling into the chair Edie had vacated.

"Right then, you must be Sadie," she continued, setting her bag on the table. "I'm Ellie, Corbyn's infinitely more charming younger sister."

He noted how Sadie's eyes became more focused as Ellie went about her work. His sister pulled on a pair of gloves before untying the scarf around Sadie's neck and carefully unwrapping the bandage. Sometimes it still caught him by surprise to see his baby sister, who had tormented him growing up, slip into this role of gentle caretaker.

Sadie's lips quirked, and he saw the start of a smirk tugging at her lips when she responded, "It's nice to finally meet you."

"You as well, although I had hoped it would be under better circumstances. I hear you managed to drag my brother into this century," Ellie quipped. She glanced up at Corbyn with mock amazement before adding, "I didn't think it was possible. What sort of trickery did you use?"

"Sheer will," Sadie replied, and Corbyn was relieved to hear a hint of her usual dry humor returning. "I out stubborned him."

"Well, Corbie has always been unable to resist a good battle of wills," Ellie said with a grin, as she started examining the injury. "The good news is this looks like a clean cut, and there doesn't appear to be any major internal damage. I can remove the glass and get you stitched up. It could have been much worse; you got lucky."

"Lucky," Sadie repeated with a dry laugh. "Right."

Ellie's brow creased as she processed Sadie's bitter tone, her eyes flicking briefly to Corbyn. Her gaze was questioning, but he could see her putting together pieces—the late-night call, Sadie's injury, the apparent tension in the room.

"Well, you're here now, and that's what matters." Ellie turned to Corbyn, asking, "Fetch me that lamp from the sitting room? I need better light."

Corbyn hurried off, Riley at his heels. When he returned, Ellie was preparing a local anesthetic, chatting easily with Sadie, who seemed to be slowly coming back to the present. Her eyes were sharper, a small smile ghosting across her mouth, and for that alone, Corbyn knew he would put up with any amount of teasing from his sister.

"So tell me truthfully," Ellie said, positioning the lamp to illuminate her work area, "has my brother been a beast to work with? He gets sulky when his routine's disrupted."

"I'm right here," Corbyn protested, flustered by the sudden shift in conversation.

"Oh, we know," Ellie replied cheerfully, beginning to clean the wound more thoroughly. "We're talking about you, not to you. There's a big difference."

Sadie actually chuckled at that and when she glanced over at him, his heart rate spiked seeing the tiny smirk that was playing at her lips.

"He's just... very committed to it," she admitted, that smirk growing a bit before she turned her gaze back to Ellie.

"That's the most diplomatic way anyone's ever described him," Ellie replied, and she began numbing the area around the cut. "Did he tell you about the time he got stuck in a tree at age twelve trying to rescue a cat that didn't need rescuing?"

"Ellie," Corbyn warned, but his sister ignored him completely.

"Fire brigade had to come get him down," she continued, extracting the piece of glass while she kept Sadie distracted. "The cat, meanwhile, had already climbed down and was having a lovely nap in the garden. He'd been up there for three hours being a hero to no one."

"That's... oddly fitting," Sadie chuckled, and the ache that had been living in Corbyn's chest for the last hour finally started to ease.

"Isn't it just?" Ellie agreed, opening a suture kit. "You'll barely feel this, by the way—just a little pressure."

Sitting back in his chair, Corbyn could hear Edie bustling about upstairs, likely making sure the room she always referred to as the Blue Room, due to the decor, was ready for Sadie. This time, when she had mentioned having Sadie stay there instead of the usual guest room, he hadn't argued.

"You know, Sadie," Ellie said conversationally as she worked, "you've been here for weeks and haven't been to London, have you?"

"Not really," Sadie admitted. "I've been pretty focused on the manuscript."

"That's unacceptable!" Ellie declared, glancing pointedly at Corbyn. "Corbie, you should take her to the city. Why not next week? I could remove these stitches at the hospital, and then we could make a day of it."

"I wouldn't want to impose," Sadie said quickly, though Corbyn caught the flicker of interest in her eyes.

"Nonsense," Ellie replied firmly. "You've been cooped up in this village for ages. A change of scenery would do you good. Both of you, actually," she added with a meaningful look at Corbyn.

He started to object, but one glance at Sadie shut him up. Their relationship had evolved drastically, and part of him felt like a tosser for having kept her practically locked away at the manor. Ellie, despite her tactless approach, was absolutely right.

"We'll see," he said finally, which earned him a grin from Ellie, who already knew she had won.

"There we are," she announced, applying antibiotic ointment to the neat row of stitches before rebandaging it. "Keep it dry for the next few days, and it should heal beautifully."

Sadie glanced down at her arm, eyes fixed on the bandage as she said, "I can't thank you enough for coming out so late."

"Think nothing of it," Ellie replied, removing her gloves and beginning to pack up her supplies. "Anyone important to Corbie is important to all of us."

Shaking his head, Corbyn stood with an exasperated sigh, and grumbled, "Stop calling me that, Eleanor."

"Don't you two start with that nonsense," Edie interjected with exasperation from the bottom of the stairs before turning her attention to Sadie. "Let's get you settled upstairs, love. You've had quite enough excitement for one evening."

As the two women fussed over Sadie, helping her to her feet and gathering supplies for her injured arm, Corbyn found himself watching from the periphery. There was something about watching Ellie and Edie, the two women who had stuck by him through everything, tend to her. The aching knot in his chest loosened, allowing him to take a full breath.

"I've put you in the Blue Room," Edie was saying as their voices faded up the staircase, Riley padding up the stairs behind them. "It's just down the hall from Corbyn's room, so if you need anything in the night..."

Corbyn remained in the kitchen, suddenly alone with his thoughts. The adrenaline was finally beginning to ebb, leaving him feeling drained and oddly hollow. He poured himself a cup of tea, but instead of drinking it, he simply stood there staring into the amber liquid. Ellie was right. Sadie had become important to him, and he knew he had to tread carefully while she was staying under his roof.

"Right," Ellie's voice startled him from his thoughts. She'd returned to the kitchen and was leaning against the door frame, arms crossed, studying him with a look he knew all too well. "Now tell me what really happened tonight."

Corbyn took a sip of tea, buying himself time. "What do you mean?"

"Don't play dumb with me," Ellie said bluntly. "On the phone, all you said was that Sadie had cut herself and needed stitches. But I know what it looks like when someone is in shock after a traumatic experience. So I want the whole story, Corbie."

He sighed, recognizing that tone. It was the one that meant his sister wouldn't be deterred.

"Maggie called and said there was a man at the pub claiming to be Sadie's fiancé and asking a lot of questions. She had a bad feeling about it."

"Fiancé?" Ellie's eyebrows rose.

Corbyn's jaw tightened as he continued, "Ex-fiancé. She had mentioned him when he tried to contact her while we were working, but, obviously, the situation was more serious than she let on."

Ellie studied him as he recounted the events of the evening to her, from Maggie's frantic call to bursting into the courtyard and finding Sadie on the ground. The memory made him flinch.

"You really do care about her, don't you?" Ellie asked, raising an eyebrow as he set the cup down with hands that were shaking once more.

"Of course I do," he said, the words coming out rougher than he'd intended. "You don't work with someone every day without coming to care about their well-being."

"I think it's more than that," Ellie pressed, "because from where I'm standing, you look like a man who's been through a war. You're still shaking, Corbie."

"I'm fine," he protested, though even he could hear how unconvincing it sounded.

"Bollocks," Ellie retorted, crossing her arms in defiance as she stared up at him. "I saw how you looked at her tonight, like you were afraid she was going to break into a million pieces at any moment." She paused, studying his face. "When's the last time you left this house for something that wasn't necessary?"

Corbyn opened his mouth to protest, then closed it again. Before Sadie had been thrust into his life, he couldn't remember the last time he'd gone anywhere that wasn't a doctor's appointment or some other unavoidable obligation.

"I don't know what you want me to say," he said, a heavy sigh leaving him. His sister knew him entirely too well.

"I want you to be honest with yourself," Ellie replied. "You've been different since she arrived. Less isolated. More... present. Edie's mentioned it several times."

As if summoned by her name, Edie appeared in the doorway. "She's settled," she announced. "Riley's appointed himself guardian and stretched out right across her doorway." She glanced between the siblings, raising a suspicious eyebrow before asking, "Everything alright down here?"

"Just having a chat about feelings," Ellie said lightly, though her eyes never left Corbyn's face. "You know how much Corbie loves that."

"Ah." Edie shook her head. "Well, don't keep him up too late. He's had quite enough excitement for one evening."

She disappeared down the hall toward the rooms she shared with Paul, leaving the siblings alone. Corbyn could hear her footsteps fade into the familiar sounds of the house settling.

"Bring her to London," Ellie said gently. "I'm serious about that, and not just for her sake."

"What's that supposed to mean?"

"It means you've been hiding here for four years, and maybe it's time to remember there's life beyond these walls." Ellie reached out and squeezed his shoulder. "And she needs to see that you're not just the hermit author she's been working with."

"I don't know if she'd want..."

"Ask her," Ellie interrupted. "What's the worst that could happen? She says no, and you continue working together exactly as you have been. But if she says yes..." She let the possibility hang in the air.

Corbyn nodded slowly, though his mind was already spinning with logistical concerns. London meant crowds, meant exposure, meant all the things he'd been avoiding since the accident. But the thought of Sadie seeing the city, of showing her places that mattered to him, was surprisingly appealing.

"I should go," Ellie said, glancing at her watch. "Early surgery tomorrow. But Corbie?" She waited until he met her eyes. "Whatever this is between you two, don't overthink it to death. Some things are worth taking a risk for."

She kissed his cheek and gathered her medical bag, leaving him alone in the kitchen with his thoughts. Upstairs, Sadie was settling into sleep, safe and protected, and this allowed him to breathe a little easier.

When he finally made his way upstairs, he found Riley exactly where Edie had said he'd be, stretched across the threshold of the Blue Room like a furry sentinel. The dog lifted his head as Corbyn approached, tail thumping once against the floor in greeting.

"Good boy," Corbyn whispered, bending to scratch behind Riley's ears. "Keep her safe."

Riley's warm brown eyes held a steady, knowing calm, and he settled back down with a contented sigh.

As he finally retreated to his own room, Corbyn felt something shift inside his chest—a loosening of the tight control he'd maintained for so long. Ellie was right, even if he'd never admit that out loud. Some things were worth taking a risk for.

And Sadie Reed, he was beginning to realize, might just be worth risking it all.

March 5, 2025

-Sadie-

Sadie jolted awake just before dawn with Nate's voice still ringing in her head. She inhaled deeply, counting to four, then exhaling for four. It was a technique her therapist had taught her for panic attacks, and she continued the pattern until her pulse began to slow. The Blue Room's unfamiliar ceiling came into focus, and all the memories from the previous night rushed back.

A soft squeak drew her attention to the door where Riley's massive head appeared. His eyes met hers, and he pushed his way inside, the hinges groaning in complaint. The Irish Wolfhound rested his chin on her mattress, his gaze unwavering until she scratched behind his ears.

"I'm alright, boy," she whispered, ignoring the quiver in her voice.

The bandage on her arm caught her eye in the dim light, and the wound throbbed. It wasn't terribly painful, but it was a persistent reminder of everything that had happened. Less than twelve hours ago, she'd been giving herself a mental pep talk about maintaining boundaries where Corbyn was concerned, and now... now she was staying in his home in a room just down the hall from his own.

Through the now-open door, Sadie could hear the sounds of someone moving about the kitchen and smell coffee beckoning her. Her stomach fluttered, but it wasn't due to hunger. Everyone in this house had seen her at her most vulnerable last night, and they had taken care of her as if she were part of their family.

The concept of a found family was something she had only ever read about. It was clear, though, that the bond between the Pearce siblings and Edie and Paul was unbreakable. Last night had given her a tiny glimpse into what it would be like to be a part of that, and the memory of Ellie and Edie taking care of her had a slow warmth unfurling in her chest.

A short while later, she emerged from the ensuite bathroom dressed for the day. Riley gave a little grumble as she approached, moving behind her to give her back a little shove with his snout. It was clear his loyalty was being tested by the promise of breakfast.

"Alright, handsome," she laughed, scratching under his chin. "Let's see who else is up."

She found Corbyn in the kitchen, standing at the counter with his back to her, methodically measuring coffee grounds with his right hand while his left rested at his side. He'd dressed in dark jeans and a thick gray sweater, his hair slightly mussed as if he'd been running his fingers through it. She found her own fingers itching to do the same, but she pushed that thought aside.

"Morning," she said softly, not wanting to startle him.

Corbyn turned, and she caught the flicker of relief that crossed his features when he saw her.

"You're up early. Couldn't sleep?"

"Not really." Sadie moved further into the kitchen, drawn by the rich aroma of brewing coffee. "You?"

"Same." He reached for a second mug without asking, adding it to the counter beside his own. "Bad night for both of us, I guess."

There was something in his tone that made her study his face more closely. Dark circles shadowed his eyes, and she realized he'd probably slept even less than she had. Her shoulders drooped as it suddenly occurred to her that last night had not simply affected her but everyone who was involved.

"I'm sorry for bringing all this drama into your life," she told him softly, not knowing what else to say.

"Don't." Corbyn's response was immediate, and the intensity in his eyes stopped her cold. "Don't apologize for being the victim of someone else's poor choices."

Turning away, he poured coffee into both mugs, the steam rising between them. Sadie added a bit of milk and sugar before wrapping both hands around the mug and letting the heat seep into her hands. Riley had planted himself between them, head practically resting on the counter as his gaze moved back and forth.

The buzzing of the phone in her pocket broke the silence, and Sadie jumped in surprise. She pulled it out to find Jess's name on the screen, and her stomach immediately clenched. It had to be nearly midnight in New York.

"I should take this," she said apologetically. "It's Jess."

Corbyn nodded, and she retreated into the living room with her coffee for a bit of privacy. If Jess was calling at this time of day, it couldn't be good.

"Jess?" she answered, holding the phone to her ear.

"Thank God," came Jess's voice, tight with worry, and Sadie froze in place. "I've been trying to reach you since yesterday afternoon. When you didn't answer your phone, I started imagining all sorts of terrible scenarios."

"I'm sorry," Sadie said, sinking onto the sofa in defeat. "I had to turn off my phone, and then... things got complicated."

"Complicated how? Are you alright?"

Sadie closed her eyes, trying to find words for what had happened. With a sigh, she decided to keep it simple and told her, "Nate showed up."

"What do you mean, showed up? At the inn?"

"He tracked me down. I guess my email login was still saved on his computer, and he found out where I was staying... he researched Corbyn." The words came out in a rush, and Sadie realized her hands were starting to shake again. "He showed up at the pub yesterday asking all kinds of questions."

"Shit," Jess swore, and she could almost picture the tips of her friend's ears turning red in anger. "Sadie, that's stalking. Please tell me you called the police."

"I... I didn't have to." Sadie set the coffee mug on the table, anxiety gnawing at her stomach once more. "Corbyn and some of the locals stepped in, and a police officer escorted him out of town."

"What do you mean, stepped in?" Jess asked, surprise coloring her voice. "You know what, we'll circle back to Corbyn in a minute... Nate was apparently very busy yesterday, because I called to tell you that he talked to our HR department. Apparently, he's claiming he's worried about your mental health and he believes Corbyn is taking advantage of you."

The words slammed into her, and had she not been sitting, she was sure her knees would have given out.

"He's what?"

"I shut it down immediately," Jess told her, but it didn't ease the tension that had crept into her shoulders. "But he was persistent and manipulative... it took all day for me to convince HR not to pull you off this assignment and launch an investigation."

She closed her eyes, trying to will away tears. An investigation would likely ruin Corbyn's chances of his book ever seeing the light of day, regardless of what they found. It had the potential to ruin them both, even though they had done nothing wrong.

"Maybe I need to come home," she said, the words causing a pit to form in her stomach. "So I can put an end to this."

"Absolutely not," Jess replied firmly. "That's exactly what he wants. You stay where you are, finish the assignment, and let me handle things from this end. I'll get legal involved if necessary."

"But—"

"No buts. You're safe where you are, and the book is almost done, right? I'll handle Nate." There was a pause, and then Jess continued, "But Sadie, you need to document everything. Every time he contacts you, texts, emails, calls... make a note of it. If he continues, we'll need a paper trail."

"Okay," Sadie said quietly, though the thought of cataloging Nate's behavior made nausea climb up her throat.

"Sadie, you need to take this seriously," Jess told her, her tone stopping Sadie from arguing or downplaying the situation. "The stalking, the manipulation—this is a dangerous pattern and you're on the other side of the Atlantic alone."

"Well, about that," Sadie began shyly, heat burning her cheeks, "I'm... actually staying at Corbyn's."

There was a pause on the other end of the line again, and then Jess replied, voice softening, "As your manager, I'm going to forget you told me that. As your best friend, though, I'm relieved you're somewhere he can't get to you."

"I should let you get some sleep," Sadie said, trying to be aware of the time in New York. "But Jess... thank you. For having my back."

"Always," Jess replied firmly. "And Sadie? Stay safe."

Sadie ended the call and sat there for a moment, trying to process it all. Nate, his behavior last night, his attempt to discredit Corbyn. It made her stomach twist uncomfortably, and her attempt to take a deep breath was shaky and uneven.

"Everything alright?" Corbyn asked, his voice drawing her from her thoughts as he settled on the sofa. He was close enough that she could feel his warmth and smell his now familiar scent, but still left a respectful amount of space. She tried to ignore the way her chest clenched, thinking he might retreat once he learned what Jess had relayed.

"After he left yesterday, Nate started making phone calls to my office's HR department," Sadie said, staring down at her hands, trying to work up the courage to tell him the rest.

"About?" Corbyn let that single word hang between them, waiting for her to continue.

"You," she said softly, not daring to meet his eyes. "He tried to tell them that you were taking advantage of me." In her peripheral vision, she saw his posture stiffen, and she pressed on, "Jess handled it, but... I'm so sorry, Corbyn. I don't want him to ruin this for you... and if you want me to go back to New York, I would understand."

She blinked back tears and then forced herself to look up. She mentally prepared herself for the very real possibility that he might have finally had enough of the drama she had brought his way. That he might agree and send her packing. Nate's words from the previous night, about how she was a convenience, echoed through her mind. At a certain point, whether she was good at her job or not, her presence in his life wouldn't be worth the additional stress.

"Stop apologizing for him," he replied, his voice tight with anger. "You are not responsible for what that tosser does."

She shook her head with a sigh, staring back down at her phone in her hand. "Maybe not, but if it weren't for my poor choices, you wouldn't have been dragged into this mess."

"He's a manipulator," Corbyn told her, and she looked up to find him wearing that serious scowl that he usually reserved only for when he disagreed with her suggestions during editing sessions. "He's trying to convince the world he's worried because he cares, so he'll ultimately appear to be the victim. And you're doing exactly what he wants—blaming yourself instead of him."

The directness of his words made her flinch, but there was something else in his expression now, something that went deeper than simple frustration that had her waiting silently for him to continue.

"It's how they operate," he continued, and the sudden roughness of his voice didn't escape her notice. "They twist everything until you can't tell which way is up, and you're apologizing for their actions. If they're angry, it's because you provoked them. If they're sad, it's because you're not supportive enough. If they're destructive, it's because you pushed them to it."

"And now that I'm trying to move on with my life..." she began, her voice trailing off.

"He's lashing out in any way he can," Corbyn finished for her, turning on the sofa so he was facing her more directly. "I want you to answer a question for me. What is it you want? Not what I want or what Jess wants or what you think you should do to appease Nate... but what you want?"

"I want to stay and finish what we started," she whispered, her voice trembling.

For the first time, she wasn't entirely sure she meant the book, and that thought had her looking away as her eyes prickled once more. When she dared to glance his way again, he was watching her silently, his brow furrowed with worry.

"Don't look at me like that," she told him, voice still soft.

"Like what?" he asked, slowly reaching out to brush her hair back from her face and tuck it behind her ear. The tenderness of the action caused her to blink rapidly. All of the emotions she had been trying to force down were starting to bubble to the surface. When he wiped away an escaped tear with his thumb, though, something inside her broke.

Looking away, she tried to regain control, but another tear fell. Her breathing was becoming ragged as she fought against the rising tide, and her chest felt tight, like she couldn't get enough air.

"I'm sorry. I just need a minute..."

Her voice caught on the last word, thick with tears. She wrapped her arms around herself, trying to hold the pieces together, willing herself not to crumble in front of him.

"Sadie," he whispered, and the way he said her name, like it was precious, was the final straw.

His arms wrapped around her slowly, as if he were afraid she might bolt, and he pulled her into an embrace. The sob that escaped seemed to come from somewhere deep in her chest, raw and wounded. Sadie buried her face against his sweater, her shoulders shaking as the tears ran down her face.

At first, Corbyn's posture was stiff, but slowly she felt him relax. Without any hesitation, she melted against him, and his arms tightened around her as if he could shelter her from the pain.

"It's alright," he whispered, his breath warm against her hair, his cheek resting against the top of her head. "You're safe now. He can't hurt you anymore."

Sadie clung to him, her fingers clutching at his sweater, the solid warmth of him anchoring her as the storm raged. "I'm sorry," she hiccuped between sobs.

Corbyn held her tighter. "Don't." His hand made slow, soothing circles on her back. "You haven't done anything that you need to apologize for."

She felt something then, so light she might have imagined it—the gentle press of his lips against the crown of her head. Warmth flooded through her, that simple action bringing more comfort than words ever could.

Gradually, her sobs began to subside, becoming hiccupping breaths and then just the occasional shuddering sigh. As her crying quieted, Sadie became acutely aware of other things—Corbyn's warmth surrounding her, the steady beat of his heart against her cheek, the way his hand had found its way into her hair. His shirt was damp where her tears had fallen, and she could smell his cologne mixed with something uniquely him.

Embarrassment began to creep in. She pulled back slightly, looking up at him through damp lashes. His blue eyes were soft with concern, the lack of judgment she found there making her breath catch.

"Thank you," she said, her voice hoarse. Heat crept up her neck as she noticed the wet spot on his sweater. Her fingers brushed over the damp material, and she managed a soft, "Sorry."

Corbyn's hand caught hers, and when she looked up, his lips quirked into a half smile, and there was something almost teasing about the way he said, "Stop apologizing, Reed. I won't melt from a few tears."

Despite everything, Sadie couldn't help but laugh, the sound watery but genuine as he released her hand. Turning away, she grabbed a tissue from a nearby box, wiping at her cheeks as she said, "God, I must look a mess."

"You look like someone who's been through hell and is still standing," Corbyn said softly, drawing her gaze back to his. "That's the furthest thing from a mess."

For a moment, she forgot how to breathe. Nervously, she reached up to tuck her hair behind her ear, and she feel her hands trembling. No mental pep talks about boundaries were going to save her from falling for this man if he kept saying things like that.

Thankfully, Riley saved her from having to respond when he let out a grumble on his way to stand by the front door. They both laughed, and she shook her head, the moment broken.

"Someone needs his morning walk," Corbyn told her. "Why don't you join us? Fresh air might do us both good. And after that, we can spend the day discussing the final chapters of the book. No editing or revisions."

She gave him a little smile, aware of what he was doing and also extremely appreciative. His suggestion allowed them both to take it easy today, to recover emotionally from all the turmoil. It was exactly what they both needed.

"That sounds perfect," she said, standing to get her coat.

"It's going to be complicated," Corbyn warned, a slight smirk tugging at his lips as he followed her.

"The best ones usually are," Sadie replied, and felt the truth of that statement settle around them.

March 15, 2025

-Corbyn-

The drive to London had been uneventful. Corbyn's knuckles, though, had remained white on the steering wheel for most of the journey. He'd made this trip countless times since the accident, but not for a social visit.

Sadie sat beside him and, as if sensing his emotional discomfort, would find ways to distract him whenever the tightening in his chest grew overwhelming. She would comment on landmarks or ask questions about the book. At one point, she had even reached for his left hand, threading her fingers through his, and sent his pulse into a different kind of frenzy.

Ellie's hospital offered a sanctuary of sorts. In the private wing where she worked, Corbyn's shoulders finally relaxed. Here, no one stared; scars were expected instead of being seen as an anomaly. When Ellie snipped the last stitch from Sadie's arm and pronounced her healing "textbook perfect," Corbyn had exhaled fully for the first time in days.

That relief evaporated in Covent Garden's early evening bustle. He noticed every stare, every whisper. Corbyn found himself performing a dance he'd mastered years ago: angling his damaged profile toward brick walls and shadowed corners, presenting the unmarred side of his face to the world. They'd spent the afternoon exploring Ellie's carefully curated slice of the city. Sadie had been enchanted by it all, her delight infectious, and it made him wish he'd been the one to make the effort despite his discomfort.

Corbyn watched his sister as she pointed out landmarks, noting how animated she'd become. This was Ellie in her element. She was confident, knowledgeable, and genuinely happy in a way that had nothing to do with anyone else's validation.

"She's really come into her own here," he murmured, watching Ellie's confident stride as she moved ahead to check the gallery hours.

Sadie nodded. Their shoulders brushed as they walked close enough that he caught the faint scent of her citrusy shampoo. "It suits her," she said. "The energy of it all. Visiting London as a teenager made me fall in love with the idea of living in a city."

Corbyn's heart stuttered in his chest, but he remained silent. She'd mentioned her school trip to London once before, specifically that she had been in the city on New Year's Eve. He had also been in London on that day in 2009. It had been his first holiday season in the city, and he had just purchased his flat, where he spent a great deal of time working. After weeks of locking himself away, a group of his friends from university had convinced him to come to their party, and so, he had found himself riding the Underground in the middle of rush hour.

"I'd never experienced anything like the public transportation here before," she continued, completely lost in her own memory. "I grew up in a small town, and the closest city was hours away. Now, after living in New York for so long, it no longer fazes me, but being surrounded by so many people on New Year's Eve... I felt so out of my depth."

"Must have been quite an experience," he managed, when the pause in their conversation started to stretch too long.

He told himself there was no way this woman next to him had been on the same train car that day. That she couldn't possibly be the beautiful redhead whom he had forced himself to believe would never be more than a memory. It was simply a coincidence, her stormy gray eyes, the jolt he felt when they touched... it couldn't possibly be her.

"It was," Sadie agreed, already moving on as Ellie gestured toward their restaurant. "And one I never forgot."

They settled into a corner table at Rules, Ellie insisting on celebrating Sadie's successful recovery at a historic location. The dining room was warm and intimate, all dark wood paneling and soft lighting that made Sadie's eyes gleam like silver.

"This place has been here since 1798," Ellie announced, perusing the wine list. "Dickens used to eat here. So did H.G. Wells, Evelyn Waugh..."

Corbyn rolled his eyes, exchanging a look with Sadie. Ellie was doing what she did best, meddling. Despite that, he found himself relaxing as the evening went on. The wine helped, as did watching Sadie's genuine enjoyment of Ellie's company.

"So," Ellie said, settling back in her chair with her second glass of wine. "I think it's time for some properly embarrassing stories about my dear brother. Sadie, you need to know what you're dealing with."

"Ellie," Corbyn warned, but his sister ignored him completely.

"Did he tell you about his brief career as a teenage detective?" she asked, her eyes sparkling with mischief.

"You wouldn't dare," Corbyn said, though he was fighting a smile.

"Oh, I absolutely would. Picture this, Sadie—fifteen-year-old Corbyn, convinced that our elderly neighbor Mrs. Pemberton was running some sort of criminal enterprise because she had too many visitors and received mysterious packages."

"And was she?" Sadie asked, already chuckling into her wine glass.

"She was teaching piano lessons and ordering sheet music through the post," Ellie finished triumphantly. "Meanwhile, our budding Sherlock Holmes spent three weeks taking detailed notes about her 'suspicious activities' and even followed the postman to see if he was involved in the conspiracy."

"I was being thorough," Corbyn protested, his cheeks warming. "And her lesson schedule was unusually irregular."

"Because she taught school children in the evenings," Ellie pointed out. "Which you would have discovered if you'd simply asked instead of launching a full surveillance operation."

Sadie burst into delighted laughter. Corbyn felt warmth spreading through his chest at the sound, and he was sure it had little to do with the wine.

"Well, that certainly explains your choice of writing genre," she said, grinning at Corbyn. "You've been plotting mysteries since you were fifteen."

"I prefer to think of it as early research," Corbyn replied with mock dignity, which only made both women laugh harder, Sadie's smile causing a flutter in his chest. "And I think that's enough stories, Eleanor."

Ellie narrowed her eyes in his direction, and he couldn't stop the satisfied smirk that formed on his lips. As much as he detested her old nickname for him, he knew she hated the use of her full name even more.

"Do you have any siblings, Sadie?" Ellie asked, turning her attention away from Corbyn. "Any annoying older brothers back home?"

"A younger one, actually," Sadie said, although there was fondness in her eyes. "My little brother Lucas definitely kept me on my toes. I'm five years older than him, so keeping him out of trouble fell to me a lot of the time."

Taking a sip of his wine, Corbyn saw the soft look on Sadie's face while she talked about her brother. It was clear the siblings had been close growing up, much like he and Ellie.

"He's also the reason I go by Sadie," she continued, pausing to sip her own wine. "He couldn't pronounce Alessandra when he was little, and it came out sounding like Alesadie, which my parents shortened to Sadie, and... it stuck."

Corbyn froze with his wine glass halfway to his lips. Alessandra. His fingers went numb against the stem. The restaurant's chatter faded to a dull hum as blood rushed to his ears. That name was confirmation of something he hadn't dared to allow himself to hope for. Fifteen years of wondering about the girl with gray eyes and red hair on the Underground, and here she sat across from him, laughing with his sister. His chest tightened as memories crystallized: her hand brushing his on the metal pole, that electric current he'd never felt with anyone else, the way her smile had started in just one corner of her mouth exactly as it did now.

Ellie was watching him with growing concern, her own glass suspended in midair as she took in his expression.

Sadie noticed the sudden tension immediately, her gaze moving between the siblings with growing confusion.

"Is everything alright?"

"Fine," Corbyn said quickly, his voice rough. He cleared his throat, setting the glass back on the table. "Just... surprised you have such an unusual name. Alessandra's beautiful."

"It's Italian," Sadie explained slowly, still looking puzzled. "My grandmother was very insistent about preserving family traditions, even though that side of my family had been in America for three generations by then."

"How lovely," Ellie managed, though her voice sounded strained. "Family traditions are important."

Corbyn was only half listening as the conversation continued. His mind was reeling, trying to remember all the signs he had ignored. When Sadie excused herself to visit the loo, Ellie immediately leaned across the table.

"Corbyn?" she whispered urgently. "You look like you've seen a ghost. What just happened?"

"I've met her before," he said quietly, his voice barely audible. Ellie's eyes narrowed in confusion, so he continued, "Fifteen years ago, I had just graduated from university, and I was living here in the city. I was on my way to a party and I met an American girl on the Tube named Alessandra."

"Wait, isn't that the girl you prattled on about in your journal?" Ellie breathed, her eyes bright with amazement. "This isn't a coincidence, Corbyn. This is fate. You have to tell her!"

"You read my journal?" Corbyn's eyes narrowed, his whisper gaining a bit of an edge. Between his sister and Edie, he had no hope of ever keeping anything a secret.

"Of course I did, I'm your sister," Ellie responded, waving it off like it was the most natural thing in the world for her to have done. "You've been pining for her ever since. You have to tell her."

"Firstly, I don't pine," Corbyn said desperately, glancing toward the direction Sadie had gone. "Secondly, she just ended a relationship with a man who would use anything at his disposal to manipulate her feelings. What if she thinks that's what I'm trying to do?"

"Or maybe she'll see how it explains everything," Ellie countered. "You two are perfect together. And tonight, watching you two..." She shook her head, leaning forward, and she enunciated each word, "You have to tell her."

"When the time is right," Corbyn said firmly. "If there is a right time. This is too important to handle poorly."

Ellie studied his face, and he could see her trying to formulate her next argument, but Sadie reappeared at the table. She slipped back into her seat with a smile that made Corbyn's pulse thrum with a mix of longing and fear.

They finished dinner as the restaurant began to empty around them, conversation flowing easily once more. As they gathered their coats and stepped out into the crisp London evening, Corbyn found himself hyperaware of every glance Sadie cast his direction. There were several times she even started to say something before changing her mind.

"This has been perfect," Sadie said finally as they approached the garage where Corbyn had parked the car. "Thank you, Ellie. For everything. I feel like I've seen a completely different side of London."

"And of my brother, I hope," Ellie replied with a meaningful look at Corbyn that had him wanting to hide. "He's actually quite sweet when he puts his mind to it."

"I'm learning that," Sadie said softly.

His thoughts swung between Ellie's insistence about fate and his own mounting terror, as they continued to walk. What if telling Sadie about their past connection destroyed the careful trust they'd built? What if she thought he'd been manipulating her all along, using some romantic fantasy to influence their working relationship?

But he also couldn't help but think, what if Ellie was right? What if Sadie also remembered that night and that connection? And what might happen if she had spent the last fifteen years chasing that memory, too?

They were just turning the corner toward the garage elevator when the crash happened. Corbyn's body registered the sound before his mind could process it—that sickening crunch of metal folding against metal. A delivery van had collided with a street vendor's cart at the intersection ahead. The cart spun wildly, its contents scattering across the pavement. Then came the hiss, the whoosh, and suddenly the night split open with fire.

Brilliant orange flames shot skyward. Four years collapsed into nothing. Corbyn was back there again—trapped in the twisted wreckage, left hand crushed between the steering wheel and dashboard as fire licked at the edges of his peripheral vision. The smell of his own burning flesh filled his nostrils. Someone was screaming. Was it him? Was it the vendor? He couldn't breathe. Couldn't move.

"Corbyn?" Sadie's voice seemed to come from very far away.

Suddenly, he was fleeing, both from the sight and the memories as his feet carried him down the nearest alley. His chest constricted, breathing shallow, and the world spun out of focus. Behind him, he could hear Sadie calling his name, but the sound of the fire crackling in the distance kept his feet moving.

The alley was dark and narrow, lined with overflowing bins and the back entrances to shops. Corbyn pressed his hands against the brick wall, trying to let the feel of the roughness against his skin ground him as he fought to breathe.

Footsteps echoed behind him in the alley, growing closer, but he couldn't bring himself to look up. He couldn't face the concern he knew he'd see. He couldn't explain why the accident had reduced him to this trembling wreck of a man.

March 15, 2025

-Sadie-

The sound hit Sadie first. Metal against metal, followed by the sickening crunch of impact and the whoosh of something igniting. She spun toward the intersection just in time to see the delivery van overturn a vendor cart, and flames erupted from the ruptured propane tank in a brilliant orange column.

But it was Corbyn's reaction that stole the air from her lungs.

He'd gone rigid beside her, his face draining of all color as his breathing became rapid and shallow. For a heartbeat, he stood frozen, staring at the flames with an expression of pure terror. Then, without a word, he bolted.

"Corbyn!" Sadie called, but he was already disappearing down the nearest alley, his steps faltering.

Around them, people were running toward the accident—some to help, others to gawk. Sadie could hear someone screaming, whether from pain or panic, she couldn't tell. The vendor was on the ground, clutching his arm, while flames licked higher from his overturned cart.

"Ellie!" Sadie grabbed the other woman's arm as she started after her brother. "Help the vendor, I'll find Corbyn."

Ellie held Sadie's gaze for a moment before nodding and moving quickly towards the injured man.

Sadie ran after Corbyn, her heeled boots clicking against the pavement as she turned into the narrow alley where he'd disappeared. The sounds of the street faded behind her, replaced by the hollow echo of her footsteps between the brick walls lined with overflowing bins and service entrances.

She found him halfway down the alley, braced against the brick wall as if the bricks were the only thing holding him together. His chest heaved with each gasp, fingers splayed and shaking against the rough surface. The sight made her breath catch, and she understood immediately what he was going through. The way time folded in on itself during panic attacks, how the world narrowed to the desperate struggle for the next breath, how escape seemed impossible even as your mind screamed for it.

Sadie's stomach ached. She'd never seen him this vulnerable, this completely stripped of the careful control he always presented to the world. She approached him slowly, not wanting to startle him further. When she was beside him, she reached out and placed her hand on his shoulder, feeling his muscles tense under her touch.

"Corbyn," she said softly, "it's just me... It's Sadie."

His eyes shot open, wide and unfocused, and his gaze darted over her face. Sweat beaded on his forehead despite the cold evening air, and she could see the rapid pulse beating in his throat.

"You're not there anymore," she continued, her hand dropping to rub a comforting circle on his back. "You're here with me, in London. It's Tuesday evening, March fifteenth. We came here to see Ellie..."

Corbyn's gaze locked on hers, though his breathing remained ragged. She could see him trying to fight his way back to the present. It was a struggle she had fought many times herself.

"I need you to breathe with me," Sadie said, keeping her voice steady and calm, drawing on her own experience. "Try to breathe in for four, hold for four, and then breathe out for six."

She demonstrated the breathing pattern slowly, exaggerating her movements so he could follow. It took several cycles, but gradually his breathing began to slow, syncing with hers. The rigid tension in his shoulders eased fractionally, though she could still see his hands shaking against the wall.

"Now tell me three things you can see," Sadie said gently, a grounding technique that had saved her more than once when her own memories threatened to overwhelm her. "Just three things, right here in this alley."

Corbyn's gaze moved shakily around their surroundings. "The... the brick wall," he managed, his voice hoarse. "A green door. You."

"Perfect. Now, what are two things you can hear?"

He closed his eyes briefly, listening. "Your voice. Traffic from the street."

"And one thing you can touch."

He turned, leaning his shoulder against the wall, one trembling hand reaching out to brush a stray lock behind her ear. Sadie felt tears prick her eyes as she leaned into the touch. Her hand came up to cover his, where it rested against her cheek; she could feel the warmth of his skin against her own.

His throat bobbed. "The fire," he whispered suddenly, his voice breaking. "I couldn't get out. The door was jammed, and the smoke was so thick, and I thought... I thought I was going to die."

Sadie squeezed his hand gently, her heart breaking for the terror he'd endured.

"But you didn't die," she said firmly. "You're here. You survived."

"Sometimes I can still smell it," Corbyn continued, the words pouring out now as if a dam had burst. "Burning rubber and leather and..." He shuddered. "I wake up choking on smoke that isn't there."

"I know," Sadie said gently, and something in her tone made him look at her more closely. "I know what it's like when your body remembers trauma your mind tries to forget."

"You do?"

Sadie nodded, thinking of the nights she had been jarred awake at the sound of a door slamming, confident Nate was coming for her. The way her hands would shake when men raised their voices, even in casual conversation. The hyper-vigilance that had left her exhausted.

Corbyn's breathing had steadied now, his hand slowly dropping back to his side as he asked, "How do you make it stop?"

"I don't think it ever truly stops," Sadie said honestly. "But you learn how to bring yourself back to the present, how to calm your mind. You learn that you can survive it." She studied his face, seeing exhaustion and vulnerability there. "You've been dealing with this alone for four years?"

"Mostly," Corbyn told her, turning to lean his back against the wall and running a hand over his face. "Ellie knows, of course. And Edie suspects. But I've gotten good at avoiding triggers, at controlling my environment."

"Until tonight."

"Until tonight," he agreed with a humorless laugh. "I'm fine now, you don't have to stand here trying to take care of me."

"I don't mind," Sadie said, and realized she meant it entirely. "We take care of each other. That's what..." She paused, unsure how to finish the sentence. *That's what friends do? That's what people who care about each other do?* Neither felt adequate for what was happening between them.

The silence hung in the air between them, loaded with meaning she hadn't allowed herself to truly examine. In the distance, they could hear sirens approaching. Still, the sound seemed muffled and unimportant compared to the intensity of this moment—Corbyn's defenses completely down, Sadie's own walls crumbling as she recognized how much this man had come to mean to her.

Corbyn turned to face her once more, his hand coming up to cup her cheek. His thumb traced along her cheekbone, making her breath catch, and he leaned his forehead against hers. He closed his eyes, and they both stood there, lost in their moment of stillness.

A siren wailed past the mouth of the alley, the sound making Corbyn tense reflexively. But when Sadie squeezed his hand, pulling him gently back into the here and now, he relaxed again, his shoulders settling as she saw his eyes focus on her face instead of the distant emergency sounds.

"We should go back," Sadie said, though she made no move to pull away from him. "Ellie will be worried."

"I know." Corbyn took a deep breath, steadying himself. "Just... give me another moment."

They stood together in the quiet alley, foreheads pressed together, processing what had shifted between them. The careful boundaries they'd maintained for weeks now completely swept away, replaced by this raw honesty that felt both terrifying and inevitable.

"Are you okay?" she asked, studying his face for signs of lingering panic.

"Getting there," Corbyn replied, his color slowly returning to normal. "The attack... it was bad, but not the worst I've had. Having you here... It helped. More than you know."

"Good," Sadie said simply, giving his hand one final squeeze. "Ready?"

Corbyn nodded, pulling away, and she could see the toll the panic attack had taken in the way his shoulders drooped. As they walked back toward the street, his hand found hers, fingers intertwining like it was the most natural thing in the world.

When they emerged from the alley into the harsh riot of emergency lights and gathering crowds, Sadie realized that whatever came next, they would face it together.

March 15, 2025

-Sadie-

Ellie had taken one look at Corbyn's still pale features and insisted they shouldn't drive back that evening. For once, Corbyn hadn't argued, telling Sadie he had a place where they could stay for the night. Now, as they descended into the underground garage beneath a Bloomsbury apartment building, Sadie watched Corbyn's jaw tighten with each turn of the steering wheel. By the time he guided the car into a space and cut the engine, she half expected him to crack a tooth. In the silence, his shaky exhale seemed to fill the entire car.

"Are you sure about this?" she asked.

"I can't keep running from my past forever," he said without looking at her, his voice tight.

The lift carried them up to the third floor, neither of them speaking. Her hand found his as he led her down the corridor, his fingers tightening almost imperceptibly around hers. He unlocked the door, and then they stepped into a space that felt like a museum exhibit—frozen in time, waiting for its owner to return.

Dust motes danced in the light as Corbyn flicked on the switches, illuminating a sitting room that belonged to the man he'd been before the accident. Books lined every wall, and there were stacks on every table. A vintage leather sofa faced tall windows that looked out over a tree-lined square. On the mantelpiece sat framed photographs. There was a photo of Corbyn with friends, captured in profile as he laughed at some long-forgotten joke. There was also a photo of two children dressed in stiff formal clothes, which she assumed were him and Ellie, and even one with Paul and Edie standing on the porch of the manor.

"This is beautiful," Sadie said, running her fingers along the spine of a well-worn copy of *Persuasion* that sat on a shelf. A fine layer of dust covered everything, but she could still see glimpses of him in every carefully chosen detail.

"It was beautiful," Corbyn corrected, moving to open the windows and let in fresh air.

As he passed a side table, he quietly turned a framed photograph face down without saying a word. She had briefly caught a glimpse of a dark-haired man and a blonde woman. She assumed the man was him, but the woman's identity was a mystery.

Dropping her bag on an accent chair, Sadie spotted a crystal decanter on the kitchen counter and reached for the matching glasses. Her fingers trembled slightly as she poured two fingers into each glass, careful not to spill. The familiar ritual steadied her, gave her hands something to do while Corbyn stood frozen by the window. She watched his shoulders rise and fall with each measured breath, knowing some ghosts couldn't be exorcised with words.

"I can't believe I'm here," he said at last, turning back to her as she sat on the sofa, a glass in each hand. "Part of me thought I'd never set foot in this place again."

He crossed to her, settling on the sofa, his knee brushing against hers. He took one of the glasses when she offered it to him, and that spark she always felt ran down her spine when their fingers brushed.

"It must feel strange, being back," she replied.

"It does," he told her, taking a long sip of whiskey before setting the glass on the coffee table. "I was happy here once. I wrote my first book at that desk by the window." He paused, swallowing hard. "My ex-fiancée and I were supposed to build a life here."

He had never mentioned an ex-fiancée before, and she realized that there was still so much she didn't know about him. He'd lived a whole life before his accident, with successes and heartbreaks she'd never really considered. She glanced at the face-down photograph, wondering what color the blonde woman's eyes had been, whether she'd helped choose the books that lined these shelves.

"Do you miss it? That life?" she asked finally, pushing aside that particular train of thought and taking a sip of her own whiskey.

"I used to think I did," Corbyn said slowly. "Everything changed so quickly. I went from planning a wedding and a future to a hospital bed in the blink of an eye. And Claire, my ex, she wouldn't even look at me most of the time because it was a reminder of everything she had lost."

Sadie's chest tightened as the weight of his words settled between them. She thought of Claire, this woman she'd never met, making promises she couldn't keep when reality turned harder than expected. She had taken his pain, his tragedy, and twisted it until it became about her. Turning on the sofa so she was facing him, her hand found his, pulling it into her lap so she could intertwine their fingers.

Another piece of the Corbyn Pearce puzzle clicked into place. Before she could stop herself, Sadie said, "Claire is why you understood Nate so well, isn't she?"

Every time they had discussed Nate, he had instantly seen through her ex's manipulation in a way only someone with experience could. Initially, she had thought it was because he had spent so many years writing flawed and emotionally complex characters, but she had been wrong. His fingers tightened their grip on hers, confirming her theory.

"Everyone around me saw it before the accident, but I was too proud—and too in love—to listen," he admitted, looking at their hands. "She loved the idea of the life I could give her—the money, the parties, the connections—more than she did me."

Sadie looked down at their hands, the way her smaller one seemed to fit so perfectly in his. Neither of them could fix the hurts the other had suffered in the past, but she found herself wanting to prove to him that he was worthy of so much more than Claire had given him.

"I was so angry for a long time," he continued, still not looking up at her. "I felt like I had truly lost everything."

When he did look, his voice trailed off, the hand she wasn't holding coming to rest on her cheek. She leaned into the touch, her eyes never leaving his. Turning her head, she placed a soft kiss on his palm, and she heard him take a shuddering breath.

"And now," she prompted.

"Now, I'm starting to believe in second chances," he replied, his thumb stroking her cheek. "I need to tell you something."

She gave a small nod, and his hand fell away from her face, his arm coming to rest on the back of the sofa. Her stomach fluttered with nerves as his expression grew serious. The only sign of his nerves, of how vulnerable he felt, was the way his fingers tightened around hers.

"Earlier, at dinner, when you told that story about your brother not being able to pronounce Alessandra," he began, and she noticed he was watching her expression carefully as he spoke. "I...it took me back...to New Year's Eve, fifteen years ago."

"Less ballroom, more doom," she whispered, quoting the man she had met years before on the Tube. His eyes snapped up to hers, confirming her suspicions. "It was you. When I mentioned my high school trip before, you never said anything."

Her breath caught when he looked at her with a combination of hope and fear. For a moment, he was the young man from her memories, the one she had been thinking about nearly daily since arriving in England.

"I... I was scared," he admitted, looking down at their joined hands. "I'm not that man anymore. But you've made me feel things that I haven't felt in a very long time... you make me feel like maybe I'm not as broken as I thought."

Sadie's heart ached at the raw honesty in his voice. In the short amount of time they had known each other, he had come so far. Not only professionally by finding his voice once more, but in every aspect of his life. Reaching out with her free hand, she lifted his chin so he would look at her.

"You're not broken," she said firmly. "You're the strongest person I know."

"I don't feel strong," he admitted. "I feel terrified. We've both carried this memory for fifteen years, and I can't live up to whatever version of me it is you've had in your mind all this time."

"That man isn't real. You are, and that is so much better than any fantasy I could have conjured up."

From the way he clenched his jaw, she knew he was still struggling with the feelings of self-doubt that haunted him, especially in this apartment that was nothing but a window to the past. That familiar inner voice echoed his uncertainty. Fifteen years ago, she had been confident and fearless. Life and heartbreak had changed them both.

"I'm not some idealized version of that girl from your memories either," Sadie told him, slowly pulling her hand away so she could stand. "I've spent so long believing I couldn't trust my own feelings, couldn't trust anyone else either. But with you...I trust you."

She crossed to where she had left her bag, opening it and pulling out her leather journal. Taking a slow breath, she tried to calm her sudden nerves as she turned back to him. His brows were furrowed in confusion, and she could sense him tracking each movement as she opened it to a page she had previously marked.

"You know I haven't written anything in years, and it's been even longer since I showed my writing to anyone," she told him, turning the journal and holding it out for him to take as she returned to her seat on the sofa. "Lately, though, I've been working on something that could possibly turn into a book...someday. I want you to read it."

The way his eyes widened as he glanced down at the page and then back up at her told her he understood how important this moment was. He studied her face for a moment, and she gave him a small smile, trying to hide fear. Every anxious instinct screamed at her to snatch the journal back from his hands and hide it away again, but she refused to obey her own insecurities.

"Are you certain?" he asked, his voice rougher than usual.

She gave a small nod, and as he began to read, she mentally recited what was on the page. While the main character was fictional, the chapter he was reading told the story of the day they met. A young woman visiting a large city for the first time—alone, overwhelmed, and very aware of the blue-eyed stranger beside her. A young man with a literary background who changed her world with just a touch.

All Anna wanted was to get off the train. Sweat trickled down her back as more passengers squeezed into the already packed Northern Line train car in London's Underground.

The Tube's musty dampness clashed with the floral perfume wafting from a group of women nearby, ready for a night out. She clung to the cold metal pole for balance, the books in her Foyles shopping bag digging into her hip as the carriage jolted forward. Around her, she could hear her friends' chatter, their voices a low hum beneath the train's rumble as they headed back to their hotel to celebrate New Year's Eve.

"You wrote about us," he breathed, his gaze meeting hers again.

"You were always meant to be a part of my story," she replied, "both on and off the page."

"There's a lot of potential here," he said after a moment, and she felt the knot in her stomach loosen. "It's engaging, and the descriptions are vivid. Romance is far from my usual genre, but I think you're off to a strong start."

"Thank you, I appreciate that more than you know, but that's not the reason I showed it to you," she told him softly, taking the journal so she could set it on the coffee table. "I showed it to you because I want you to know how much I trust you. The real you. The man who showed up when I needed him...the one who makes me feel safe."

"You matter to me," Corbyn said quietly. "Even then, when I was still trying to convince myself you were just my editor. I couldn't bear the thought of you being hurt."

"That's exactly my point," Sadie replied, her fingers reaching to trace the scars on his cheek with reverence. "This is just skin. But your heart, your soul—that's what matters. That's what I fell for, not the fantasy."

His hand caught hers, and he turned and pressed a kiss to her palm. His eyes remained locked on her own, burning with an intensity she had never seen before. Her breath caught, the simple action sending a tingling sensation down her spine.

"When did you know you were falling for me?" Corbyn asked, his confidence in her, in what she felt for him, noticeably growing with each passing moment.

Sadie couldn't help but smile, telling him, "Remember that day when Riley got out and we went looking for him together? You were so worried. And when we found him at the park playing with the children, the way your whole body relaxed..." She smiled at the memory. "I think that's when I knew you weren't just some difficult author. You were someone with a huge capacity for love who'd been hurt badly enough to hide it away."

"And that made you fall for me?"

"That made me want to earn your trust," Sadie corrected. "The falling came later, gradually, and now it's impossible to pretend otherwise. Even if this complicates things."

"Only if we let it," he replied, a slight smirk forming on his lips. "You don't have to make outlines and storyboards for real life, Reed."

"I'll have you know that storyboard I made for you for act three was a masterpiece," she teased back, biting her lip, enjoying this more playful side of him.

Corbyn's gaze dropped to her mouth, his thumb brushing her lip and freeing it from her teeth. That simple action had heat spreading through her body, and when he looked back up, she thought her heart might beat right out of her chest. He leaned forward and their lips met. The kiss was soft and hesitant. It was careful, exploratory, a question posed by lips against lips and answered by the way Sadie melted into him, her free hand coming up to fist in the fabric of his shirt.

When they finally broke apart, both breathing unsteadily, Corbyn took her hands in his own. Bringing them up to his lips, he brushed a kiss across her knuckles, a grin tugging at his lips.

"I should have brought you to London sooner," he told her, his eyes twinkling with mischief, something she had never seen before.

"Why is that?" she answered, her smirk matching his.

"There's no Riley or Edie here to interrupt me when I'm trying to do this..."

That first kiss had been gentle, almost chaste. This kiss, however, was the opposite. His fingers curled in her hair, gently tugging her head back to give him better access, and she gave it willingly.

His lips burned against hers, stealing her breath. She gasped, and something shifted—his hesitation vanished. His tongue traced the seam of her lips, and she opened to him without thought. Everything else faded away, leaving only this—his scarred palm cradling her jaw, the taste of whiskey, and the rightness of being exactly where she was.

They settled into comfortable silence after that, the whiskey forgotten on the coffee table as they held each other on the old leather sofa. Her head rested against his shoulder, and she savored every detail. How she seemed to fit so perfectly against him, the way the smell of his cologne had come to feel like home, how she wanted to freeze time and stay in this moment as long as it could.

"Can I ask you something?" Sadie said, her voice just above a whisper as she traced an invisible pattern on the soft fabric covering his chest.

"Anything."

"That first day, when I arrived and you were so angry I was here... what changed? When did it shift from you wanting me gone to... this?"

Corbyn was quiet for a moment, his fingers combing gently through her hair. A sigh of contentment escaped her, and she relaxed even more into his warmth and the safety she felt in his arms.

"I think it started changing the moment you stood up to me," he said finally. "You didn't back down or apologize for doing your job, you just looked me in the eye and told me exactly what you thought of my attitude and my writing." He smiled at the memory. "No one had done that in a very long time. You saw that I was hiding behind my pain instead of dealing with it, and you called me on it." Corbyn's expression grew more serious as he continued, "And then later, when you saw my scars for the first time, you didn't flinch. You didn't look away or pretend they weren't there. You just... accepted them as part of me."

"They are part of you," Sadie said softly, reaching up to trace the line of scars along his jaw. "But they're not the most important part. Underneath all your brooding, you're kind, and you care about the people in your life."

"I don't brood," he insisted, although she could see the hint of a smirk tugging at his lips.

"Says the man who glares out his office window for an hour whenever I win an argument," she quipped, poking his side gently as she laughed. That elicited a chuckle from him, a smile spreading across his face and making her heart tumble in her chest.

A yawn escaped her as the emotional upheaval of the day finally began to catch up with her. The whiskey and the warmth of his embrace were making her eyelids heavy.

"I should probably find something to sleep in," Sadie murmured, then blushed slightly. "I didn't exactly pack for an overnight stay."

Corbyn's expression grew tender. "I think I can help with that." He rose from the sofa and gestured for her to follow. "Come on."

He led her into a large bedroom, a space that felt even more personal than the sitting room. A large bed dominated the room, its navy duvet slightly rumpled as if he'd just been sitting on it, even though he hadn't been here in years. Of course books were stacked on both nightstands, and through the open wardrobe, she could see the clothes he'd left behind—expensive suits and casual shirts hanging like ghosts of his former life.

Corbyn moved to the chest of drawers and pulled out a soft gray t-shirt and a pair of navy sweatpants.

"These will be enormous on you, but they're clean," he said, holding them out to her.

"Thank you," Sadie said, accepting the clothes with a grateful smile. The fabric was soft and worn from washing.

"Bathroom's just through there," Corbyn said, pointing to a door across the room. "Take your time."

When she emerged a few minutes later, the clothes were indeed swimming on her; the t-shirt fell nearly to her knees, and the sweatpants were rolled up several times at the ankles. Corbyn had changed as well, and when he looked up from where he'd been folding back the duvet on the bed, something in his expression shifted. His eyes darkened as he took in the sight of her, and she felt heat rise in her cheeks.

"You look..." he started, then cleared his throat. "I like seeing you in my clothes," he admitted, his voice rough. "More than I probably should."

"They're very comfortable," Sadie said, heat creeping into her cheeks. "And warm."

"Good," Corbyn said, rubbing the back of his neck.

They stood there for a moment, the weight of everything that had happened settling between them. Sadie could see the exhaustion in his face, the emotional toll of returning to this place, of everything they'd shared.

"I should probably let you get some rest," she said eventually, though she made no move toward the door.

"Sadie? Stay. Please."

His voice was soft when he said it, almost unsure. She knew he wasn't asking for anything more than this—no expectations, no pressure—and the thought of falling asleep in his arms had her nodding and moving toward the bed. Once they had settled, he shifted so he was behind her, his chest pressed against her back, and an arm wrapped around her waist. She could feel his breath tickling the skin of her neck, and she couldn't stop the contented sigh that escaped her lips.

"Is this okay?" he asked, and she could hear the vulnerability in his voice.

This moment felt precious, and she wasn't going to ruin it by overanalyzing it to death. They could figure out the details in the coming days, but tonight, she wasn't going to pretend she didn't want to fall asleep in his embrace.

"This is perfect."

That was the last thing she said before drifting off to sleep, wrapped up in Corbyn's arms and, for the first time, completely and unquestionably at peace.

March 22, 2025

-Sadie-

Returning to the Roaring Stag felt like a homecoming. Sadie sat beside Corbyn at their corner table, their fingers entwined on the bench. He'd steered her to the banquette that ran along the wall, settling in close enough that their knees occasionally brushed, sending a spark through her.

In the last week, the flame that had been simmering between them had started to burn brightly, and she had been left breathless on more than one occasion when their work had ceased for a stolen kiss. All of it had led up to this—whatever this night would become.

Part of her still couldn't believe he had suggested having dinner at the pub. During their morning walk with Riley, he had glanced over at her while they were stopped by the lake, and something in his expression had softened just before he spoke.

"Have dinner with me," he'd said, voice low.

Sadie's brow furrowed in confusion and she replied, "I have dinner with you every night."

Since coming to stay at the manor, she had become a regular at the dinner table in the evenings. His answering smirk had her raising an eyebrow, her confusion only growing.

"I meant have dinner out, Reed. I'm asking you on a date."

"Well, well, look what we have here," Maggie's familiar voice cut through her reverie as she approached with menus tucked under her arm, wearing a cat-who-got-the-cream smile. "Corbyn Pearce, out for dinner and with the lovely Sadie Reed, no less."

"Good evening, Maggie," Sadie managed, hyperaware of how Corbyn had tensed slightly beside her at being the center of attention. A flush rose at the knowing gleam in Maggie's eyes.

"Evening, love," Maggie replied warmly, then turned to Corbyn with her hands on her hips. "About time you brought this one out for an actual date instead of hiding away with your manuscripts and brooding." She gestured around the pub, adding, "Half the village has been wondering when you'd work up the nerve."

"Maggie," Corbyn warned, but there was no real edge to it, more like fond exasperation, similar to the tone he took with Edie when she refused to mind her own business.

"Oh, don't you 'Maggie' me," she laughed, placing menus in front of them. "This is exactly where you belong, the pair of you. Now, what can I bring you to drink?"

Sadie felt her face burning as Maggie fussed around them, adjusting the single daffodil in its small vase as if trying to ensure that not even a petal was out of place. Glancing around, the entire pub seemed to be watching with interest, as if they'd all been waiting for this.

Once they had their wine and ordered their dinners, the other patrons at the pub seemed to settle back into their own discussions. They fell into their usual easy conversation, but there was something charged humming beneath the surface. Every accidental brush of their fingers, every shared laugh, every moment their eyes met and held just a beat too long, Sadie's body buzzed with anticipation. Something inside her reached for him, hungry and new.

"It feels like the entire village is here tonight," Corbyn said, nodding toward the bar where Mr. Davies was holding court. "I haven't seen Mr. Davies in years."

"I met him when I stumbled upon his farm by mistake," she recalled. "According to Edie, he's the one you go to for the latest village news."

"That's his reputation, though he'll deny it," Corbyn told her with a genuine laugh that turned her smirk into a grin. "When I was about twelve, I ordered something rather embarrassing from a catalog. I can't even remember what now... probably some terrible fantasy novel I was too mortified to buy in person. For weeks afterward, Davies would give me these knowing looks whenever he saw me in the village."

"No," Sadie gasped, delighted to glimpse this softer side of him.

"Oh yes. And then one day, he pulls me aside and says, very seriously, 'Nothing wrong with a bit of escapism, lad. Though you might try Tolkien, classier than whatever rubbish you're reading.'" Corbyn shook his head at the memory. "Turned out he'd been a fantasy reader himself. Used to slip me books on the sly after that."

Right on cue, Mr. Davies appeared beside their table, his stealthy approach causing Sadie to stifle a chuckle as she suddenly realized how he had learned so much of the village's gossip.

"Pearce," he said gruffly, studying Corbyn with sharp eyes. "Good to see you out and about."

"Davies," Corbyn acknowledged with a nod.

The older man's gaze shifted to Sadie, and he continued, "Heard you've been working miracles up at the house."

"I don't know about miracles," Sadie said, charmed despite his bluntness.

"Nonsense," Mr. Davies declared. "Haven't seen this one venture into the village in years. Must be doing something right." He fixed Corbyn with a stern look before turning his gaze back to her. "Is he treating you well? None of that brooding nonsense?"

"I'm sitting right here," Corbyn said dryly.

"So you are," Davies agreed, completely unrepentant. "Which is why I'm asking. Man needs reminding sometimes." He turned back to Sadie. "You need anything, you let me know. And mind you, if he puts a foot wrong, I'll hear about it before the milkman."

"I'll keep that in mind," Sadie said, fighting back a smile.

Davies gave them both a satisfied nod before returning to his spot at the bar, raising a pint to his lips.

"Subtle as always," Corbyn muttered, but Sadie could see the warmth in his eyes, the way the tension had eased from his shoulders. These people, his people, had accepted him back into their fold even after his years of isolation. They had also accepted her and them as a couple without question or judgment.

"I like him," she said simply.

"You would," Corbyn replied, but he was smiling. "He used to let me hide in the barn with the lambs when I was avoiding my tutors. Said every boy needed a bolt-hole."

Their food arrived, and the conversation continued. They shared stories of their childhoods, getting to know each other in a way their work hadn't previously allowed. Occasionally, she would see him sneaking glances at her, the heat in his eyes making something low in her belly tighten.

"I sometimes forget," Corbyn said quietly, during a lull in conversation, "what it's like to just... be. Without feeling like everyone's staring at the scars, wondering about the story behind them."

Sadie shifted slightly closer on the banquette, her thigh pressing against his. "They're not staring tonight," she observed. "They're just... glad to see you happy, I think."

He was quiet for a long moment, his fingers playing with the stem of his wine glass. "You know what," he said finally. "I think I am. For the first time in... God, years."

The admission hung in the air between them, raw and honest in a way that made Sadie's breath catch. She reached over, covering his restless hand with hers.

"Corbyn," she began, not sure what she meant to say.

"Sadie, wait..." he said, taking her hand in his. He leaned forward, voice quiet so only she would hear, and she felt his breath ghost across her skin. "You know I'm terrified of this, of us, of letting anyone close enough to matter again, but I can't imagine not being with you. This thing between us... We've blown past every boundary we had—and I don't regret it."

His honesty struck her, and her pulse spiked; her heart suddenly pounded in her chest. The realization that they had been given a second chance, whether by fate or some other unknown force, had made them both brave and led them to this moment. Around them, the pub's patrons carried on, unaware of the enormity of Corbyn's admission. She heard the laughter and conversation, the clink of glasses and scrape of chairs, but all of it felt distant.

"I suppose we have," she said softly, giving his hand a squeeze. She turned on the banquette to face him more fully, her leg brushing against his. Leaning forward, she whispered, "I don't know what happens next, but I think I'm done with boundaries."

She watched Corbyn's entire body relax as if a weight had been lifted from his shoulders, his eyes darkening as he took her in. Releasing her hand, he brought his up to cup her cheek, and she leaned into the touch. Then his lips brushed against hers. It was sure and unhurried, a quiet declaration for anyone watching. The kind of kiss that would be village gossip by morning, discussed over garden fences and in the post office queue with delighted speculation.

When they pulled apart, the pub had fallen quiet, as if everyone were holding their breath. It broke after a moment, and the conversations resumed with renewed vigor. Someone near the bar let out a low whistle of appreciation, quickly hushed by their companion, and a smile tugged at Sadie's lips.

They lingered over the last bites of dessert, Sadie's fork tapping against the plate. Neither of them brought up the complications this could bring to their situation, and Sadie knew that, for her at least, she didn't want to burst the cocoon of warmth and happiness that was surrounding them.

The drive home wound through narrow country lanes, and it seemed to take longer than usual as the anticipation built. Corbyn reached across the console, his scarred hand covering hers. His thumb brushed over her knuckles, and Sadie felt heat spread through her body. She watched his profile, the strong line of his jaw working as if he were holding back words.

He parked in the circular drive but made no move to get out. Instead, he turned to her in the driver's seat, moonlight painting his scars silver and his eyes dark with want.

When he kissed her this time, it was nothing like the sweet declaration in the pub. This was hunger and need and weeks of careful restraint finally snapping. Sadie found herself leaning across the center console, her hands fisting in his shirt, pulling him closer even though the awkward angle made her neck ache.

"Not in the car," Corbyn breathed against her mouth, but he didn't pull away. If anything, his arms tightened around her, one hand tangling in her hair while the other pressed against the small of her back.

"No," Sadie agreed, even as she traced the line of his jaw with her lips. "Definitely not here."

It took another five minutes of heated kisses and wandering hands before they finally managed to separate enough to make their way into the house. The manor was quiet, and Riley greeted them with a yawn.

At the landing, they paused. The Blue Room lay to the left, Corbyn's suite to the right. The moment hummed between them, and she realized he was giving her one last chance to pull away and retreat to her own room.

She knew the smart choice was to go to the Blue Room alone. It meant no additional complications, no possible repercussions on their careers, and less heartache when she had to return to New York. It was the safe choice, but she had been making those for most of her life.

Letting out a slow breath, she took Corbyn's hand in hers and turned right.

His door opened to reveal a spacious and masculine room, with dark wood furniture and windows overlooking the moonlit grounds. He led her through the threshold, closing the door behind them, leaving Riley looking forlorn in the hall.

"Are you sure?" he asked, even as his hands framed her face like she was something fragile and precious.

"I've never been more sure of anything," Sadie whispered, and meant it.

He kissed her again, with a tenderness that undid her completely. His arm wrapped around her waist, pulling her closer, and Sadie knew with bone-deep certainty that nothing would ever be the same. It was beautiful, irrevocable, and precisely as it was meant to be.

March 22, 2025

-Corbyn-

Sadie's fingers traced along his arm as he pulled her closer, one of his hands tangled in her hair, the other settling on her waist. Corbyn felt his pulse quicken, and for once it wasn't from the all-too-familiar feeling of panic, but something more profound, like finding a haven in a storm.

They had been standing like this for minutes now, the need for air forcing them to pull apart after another heated kiss. When she looked up at him, her eyes were soft, and he found himself leaning his forehead against hers without conscious thought.

"Corbyn," she reached up to frame his face. The gentle touch grounded him in this moment, allowing him to believe this was real. She was here with him, her skin soft against his, and so much better than anything he'd ever imagined.

He caught her hands, holding them against his face for a heartbeat.

"I've wanted this," he said quietly, "wanted you for weeks now."

"I know," she said, a small smile playing on her mouth. "So have I."

He captured her lips with his once more, but this kiss was different from their desperate moments that had brought them here. This was exploration, slow and deep, a promise built on discovery. His hand traveled down her side to her waist once more, fingertips brushing the strip of skin where her sweater had lifted. He felt her shiver at the delicate contact as goosebumps rose on her flesh.

"I've seen the way you look at me when you think I'm not watching," she whispered against his mouth. "You're not as subtle as you think you are."

He huffed a laugh, whispering back, "Who said I was trying to be subtle?"

She pulled him in for another kiss, and this time, his hands were bolder. They slid under her sweater to span her back, relearning the language of touch. A soft sigh, and the hint of a moan, escaped her lips. It made his body hum with need. When her fingers went to his shirt buttons, though, he pulled back suddenly.

"Wait," he said as she reached the third button. At her questioning look, he took a breath. "I know you've seen them before, but I..." He trailed off, unable to finish the thought.

"But what?" she asked softly, her fingers stilling on his shirt. When he didn't answer immediately, she added, "We can stop if you're not ready."

He shook his head, not willing to entertain that idea. Instead, he finished unbuttoning the shirt himself, muscle memory compensating for his left hand's weakness.

She didn't gasp, and she didn't pull away. Instead, he watched her fingers trace the air above his skin, not touching, but close enough to feel her warmth.

"May I?" she asked, looking up to meet his eyes, seeking his permission.

He nodded, remembering how she'd touched his hand that day with the arnica cream, how gentle she'd been. Now he stood still, letting her explore.

"That morning by the pool," she said quietly, her fingertips finding the most prominent scar. "I need you to know that the scars weren't all I saw. They weren't even the first thing I noticed." She looked up at him. "I saw your strength. Someone who keeps going despite everything. Who still swims and stays active. Someone who still pushes forward."

He shivered—the nerves there were damaged, sensation dulled in some places, hypersensitive in others. His voice was rough when he answered, "You looked away so quickly. I thought..."

"I looked away because I was trying to be professional," she said, her fingers growing bolder as they mapped the geography she'd only glimpsed before. "Because you seemed so guarded, and I didn't want to make it worse."

"I was. But not anymore," he told her, catching her hand and resting it over his heart. "Not with you."

She rose to kiss him then, her lips claiming his. She only lingered there for a moment before he felt her lips trail along his jaw, pressing soft kisses across his skin. She followed the line of his throat, her teeth grazing his skin.

"Sadie," he breathed, his body going taut.

She continued tracing downward, her mouth finding the place where neck met shoulder, then lower still. The first scar she encountered was where the fire had kissed his skin more gently. It was pink and smooth, the texture like silk that had been crumpled and pressed flat again. He felt her lips coast over the marred flesh, a soft touch that had him tense for a moment on instinct before his body relaxed.

The next was angrier, where the flames had bitten deeper. It was ridged and ropy, the skin puckered and tight across his collarbone. This one she traced with her tongue, and a low moan escaped him at the sensation, at the way she was claiming every inch of him.

Finally, she reached the scar over his heart. There, the flames had been the hottest. The skin here was a landscape that spun a story of survival, mottled and rippled like candle wax. She pressed her lips there, lingered, felt his chest rise and fall with shuddering breaths.

Something cracked open in his chest at that touch, that complete acceptance.

"These are stories too," she whispered. "Stories of survival. Of strength." She looked up at him, her eyes hooded, pupils blown wide. "Of a man who could have given up but has decided to live."

His voice was a raspy whisper and he breathed, "Sadie..."

She looked up at him through her lashes. "Bed?"

"God, yes."

They moved together, her sweater finally joining his shirt on the floor, and the sight of her in the moonlight made his mouth go dry. All that creamy, pale skin he'd imagined more times than he cared to admit was more beautiful than any description he could craft.

"You're staring," she said, but there was pleased warmth in her voice.

"I'm committing every detail to memory," he told her, allowing a devilish half smile to tug at his lips.

He pressed her into the bed, but when he moved to cover her body with his own, his left hand gave out on him—trembling, then buckling beneath even that slight pressure. The familiar flash of frustration burned through him, cheeks burning with embarrassment.

"Damn it," he breathed, his jaw tightening as he shifted his weight.

When Sadie's eyes met his, though, he saw no pity in them, only understanding.

"Here," she whispered, moving deliberately until his stronger side could bear most of his weight, her body arching to meet his. "Better?"

"Perfect," he said, and meant it. It would be different than before, but she was here, warm and willing beneath him, and that was all that mattered.

He lowered his mouth to her throat while maintaining this position; no longer merely receiving but participating in their dance of desire. Her pulse fluttered under his lips, and when he nipped the spot where neck met shoulder, she gasped.

"Still good?" he asked, hyperaware of his weight, his balance.

"Better than good," she breathed, her hands mapping the mostly unmarked skin along his back. "Don't stop."

He didn't. He took his time learning her—every detail of her body—a slow exploration filled with soft sighs and sharp intakes of breath as they teased one another's skin with their fingers and tongues. He marveled at the tender spot behind her ear that made her sigh when his lips brushed it, and the curve of her collarbone that had her arching her back when he gently bit down. His body might move differently now, requiring thought where there once was instinct, but it still wanted her with an intensity that almost frightened him.

They undressed each other with care; each new expanse of skin revealed felt like a gift. When nothing remained between them, he paused, braced above her on his good arm, drinking in the sight of her in the moonlight.

His voice was rough with want when he asked, "Are you sure?"

She pulled him down for a kiss that left no room for doubt, and then whispered against his lips, "I've never been more sure of anything."

Still, he held back, his forehead pressed to hers.

"Are you?" she asked this time, her eyes searching his face.

"Completely."

"If something hurts, if a position isn't working, you tell me immediately," Sadie said, her hands framing his face. "No suffering in silence, no pushing through pain. We're in this together, which means you have to trust me enough to be honest."

He swallowed hard. The vulnerability of it, the partnership she was offering, he had never expected to find someone who made him feel like this again. And if by some miracle he did, he had certainly never expected they would want him in return.

"I promise."

The faith in her eyes undid him. When he finally joined with her, he watched her face for any sign of discomfort or regret. Instead, he found desire and something that looked very much like love.

They moved together, taking their time exploring what worked. When the skin along his ribs protested a certain angle, she shifted with him without comment. For weeks, they had been building toward this moment, and he intended to savor every touch and every feeling.

"You're thinking too hard," she murmured at one point, her fingers brushing the hair away from his eyes.

"I want this to be good for you," he admitted, hips stilling for a moment.

"Corbyn." She kissed him quietly. "You're here. You're with me. Trust me, it's already good."

Time loosened around them. The moonlight traced across the floor as they explored each other with hands and mouths, whispering words. When she moved above him, the sight of her in the silver light made his breath catch.

"Still with me?" she asked, reading something in his expression.

"Completely," he said, and meant it. His hands found her hips, the right one steady, the left lighter but still present, still participating. "God, Sadie, you're..."

Words failed him as she moved, as they found rhythms that had nothing to do with his limitations and everything to do with connection. When she shattered above him, her face transformed by pleasure, Corbyn felt the last of his walls crumble.

His own release followed, overwhelming after years of isolation. She held him through it, whispering his name like a prayer, and he might have wept if he'd had any breath left.

After, they lay tangled together, both breathing hard. His ribs ached, and his left hand had gone partially numb, but the discomfort felt distant, unimportant compared to the woman in his arms.

"Are you okay?" Sadie asked, tracing careful fingers over his chest. "Was it... did I..."

"It was perfect," he interrupted, catching her hand. "I'll have a few aches tomorrow, maybe, but it was worth every single one."

She smiled, settling against his side with a contented sigh that made his chest tight.

"For someone worried about what he could do..." she murmured, her fingertips tracing the edge of a scar on his shoulder, her touch featherlight yet grounding.

He pressed a kiss to her hair, breathing in the faint scent of her shampoo—citrus and something uniquely Sadie. The simple intimacy of it struck him more profoundly than the passion they'd just shared.

The telltale thump of Riley settling against the door interrupted their silence.

"He's judging us," Corbyn chuckled softly.

Sadie traced a line across the smooth skin of his forearm. Her laugh tickled his neck, sending a shiver through his body.

"Let him," she laughed, and he could feel her grin against his chest.

Corbyn held her tighter, pulling her close. All his careful analysis, all his planning, meant nothing against this simple, quiet certainty: here, now, they were real, regardless of what the coming weeks might bring. The future could wait.

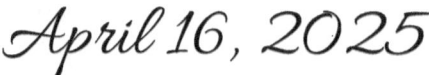

April 16, 2025

-Sadie-

The last sentence stared at them from the tablet's screen on the desk. The study glowed with the late afternoon light filtering through the tall windows as they stared at the culmination of their months of work.

Sadie leaned forward, studying the words. She felt like she was saying goodbye to an old friend, a wistfulness settling in her chest. After countless hours spent within these four walls, the arguments, the breakthroughs, and the slow, careful building of trust, Detective Inspector Shaw's story was complete.

"That's it, then," Corbyn said quietly, his voice carrying a strange mix of satisfaction and melancholy that made Sadie's chest tighten. His hand still hovered over the screen with the stylus, clearly equally as affected by the end of this chapter of their lives. Both had been avoiding the topic of what came next, but there would be no hiding from it now.

She watched his profile in the amber light. The sharp line of his jaw, the way his dark hair fell across his forehead, the slight furrow between his brows that appeared whenever he was feeling something deeply. She'd memorized these details over the months they had been together, but somehow they still had the power to make her breath hitch.

"Wait," Sadie said, an idea forming in her mind as she tapped her red pen against her lips. She saw his eyes instantly land on her mouth, and watched as they darkened. "This transition could be smoother. The emotional beat needs more weight."

She shifted her chair closer to his, the wheels catching slightly on the worn Persian rug, using the capped end to point to a particular spot on the screen. She was close enough that their shoulders brushed, sending a familiar tingling sensation through her body. "What if Shaw's final thought connects back to the opening chapter? Full circle?"

Corbyn considered this, his head tilting in that way that meant he was truly listening and not just waiting to argue. She had learned to tell the difference, unlike their early days. He picked up the stylus, and Sadie smiled at how natural the action had become. It was no longer the foreign object he'd glared at with suspicion, but a tool he'd mastered, just as he'd learned so many new things these past months.

"Like this?" he asked, writing the revision directly on the tablet screen with fluid strokes. His handwriting had evolved, too. It was less cramped, as if the stress and tension of trying to find the perfect prose had somehow eased during their partnership.

"Perfect, but..." Sadie found herself leaning across him to point at the tablet, drawn by an invisible force she'd stopped fighting. Her body angled over his arm, which brushed against her side, sending a shiver down her spine. She could feel the warmth radiating from him, the solid presence that had become her anchor. "Actually, can you move that part down one line? It'll give the revelation more breathing room."

She stood, her arm coming to rest on his shoulder as she ran her fingers through the hair at the nape of his neck. The arm of the chair pressed against her hip, and she was acutely aware of every point of contact between them. When she leaned forward again to suggest another small change, Corbyn's right arm came around her waist, and she felt her breath catch.

"Come here," he murmured, his voice dropping to that low register that never failed to make her knees weak. Before she could protest—not that she wanted to—he'd pulled her into his lap. She found herself facing the desk, her back against the solid wall of his chest. When her hand came to rest on his wrist, she could feel his pulse, quick and strong, betraying the calm facade he presented to the world. His breath stirred the hair at her temple, and she had to close her eyes for a moment, the combination of the rightness of the moment and the uncertainty about the future threatening to overwhelm her.

"This is hardly professional," she said, though her protest was thoroughly undermined by the way she immediately melted into him, letting the side of her head rest against his cheek.

"Good thing we're nearly finished then," he replied, each word sending a warm brush of air that had tingles running through her body. She felt him smile as he picked up the stylus again with his right hand, his left arm remaining securely around her waist, fingers splayed possessively across her ribs.

When she had first arrived in Great Missenden, she never could have imagined them sitting like this. Back then, she'd been determined to maintain professional distance despite the inexplicable pull she'd felt from their first meeting. But now it felt as natural as breathing, as right as the final sentence of a perfectly crafted story.

They made the final adjustments together, her suggestions flowing seamlessly with his execution, until the manuscript truly was complete. When Corbyn finally saved the document and turned off the tablet, silence settled between them, each lost in their thoughts. They both jumped when the door to the study opened, and Ellie's excited voice cut through the silence.

"Edie told me you were finishing the book today, so I thought I'd..." Ellie trailed off abruptly as she took in the scene before her. Her eyes widened in surprise, taking in their intimate position with obvious delight. "Oh."

The single syllable hung in the air, a sly grin spreading across Ellie's face. Sadie immediately moved to stand, heat flooding her cheeks in a rush at being caught in such a compromising position, but Corbyn's arm tightened around her waist, holding her in place.

"Stay," he murmured against her ear, and the combination of his voice and his breath against her skin sent a shiver through her that Ellie definitely noticed—her smirk and arched eyebrow gave her away.

"Behave," Sadie whispered back, swatting at his hand as he tried to pull her back down. But she was smiling despite her embarrassment, unable to resist his newfound playfulness.

"We've just finished the final chapter," Corbyn told his sister, trying to appear nonchalant, although Sadie could see the slight flush creeping up his neck above his collar.

"I can see that," Ellie replied, her eyes dancing with undisguised delight as she fully entered the room and closed the door behind her, her gaze fixed on her brother with a wicked little grin. "Very... collaborative finishing technique you've developed there, Corbie. Is this the sort of thorough editing process they teach in university these days?"

"Don't..." Corbyn began, but his protest was doomed from the start.

"Because if so," Ellie continued blithely, settling herself in the worn leather armchair across from them with the apparent intent to stay, "I might need to reconsider my career path. Medicine suddenly seems terribly dull."

Sadie bit back a laugh, returning to her chair. Corbyn could growl and grumble all he liked, but she knew he had a soft spot for his sister. They had a dynamic she had come to enjoy watching, Ellie's sharp wit a match for her own.

"We were working," Corbyn said with as much dignity as a man could muster while his sister's grin threatened to split her face in half.

"Oh, I'm sure you were," Ellie said solemnly. "Tough work, by the looks of it. Quite hands-on. I do hope Sadie's getting proper compensation for such... dedicated editorial services."

"Don't start," Corbyn warned. Sadie had learned to read the subtle differences in his tone. This was exasperated affection, something that was common when he was dealing with Ellie.

"Start what? I'm impressed by your commitment to the collaborative process," Ellie laughed, crossing her legs with a triumphant smile. "In fact, I think we should celebrate the completion of the book with a toast!"

"Edie keeps a bottle of good champagne hidden in the back of the refrigerator, 'just in case,'" Corbyn quoted, glancing over at Sadie, the hint of a smile forming as his shoulders relaxed once more. "She thinks no one knows it's there."

"Well, why don't I get it while you two catch up?" Sadie said, pushing up from the chair to stand. "I think Edie's still in town shopping, so I won't have to be too sneaky."

Heading out of the study, Riley followed her into the kitchen. When she opened the cabinet door to retrieve three champagne flutes, he nudged her back with his nose, eliciting a laugh. She turned to look at him, and a little whine escaped him as he looked hopefully in the direction of the tin where Edie kept his dog biscuits.

"You know, handsome, Edie is going to hide these if she catches me sneaking them to you," she told the dog as she set the glasses down and rewarded him with a treat. Taking it from her gently, he trotted off back toward the study. With a shake of her head, she muttered fondly, "Well, I see your loyalty is short-lived."

For a moment she stood in the middle of the kitchen, soaking in the familiar sights and scents. The scones Edie had baked that morning sat on the counter under a covered dish, everything in its place exactly as she liked it. Paul's toolbox sat by the back door, and her coat was mixed among those of the others on the hooks just above it.

Reality surged through her, and she found herself rapidly blinking back tears. Her assignment was over. She was expected to return to New York, to go back to a life that no longer felt like her own. To leave behind the people who had become her family.

She sank into one of the chairs at the table, champagne and celebration forgotten. Her chest ached at the thought of never sipping tea and getting words of wisdom from Edie, never throwing another stick for Riley, never waking up in Corbyn's arms again. They hadn't discussed the future, which meant he hadn't asked her to stay.

A few days ago, she had a video call with Jess. True to her word, her best friend had handled Nate, getting the legal department to send a cease and desist letter and arrange for a restraining order. That should have made her happy, to know that she had someone in New York looking out for her safety, but it had just been another reminder that her time here was coming to an end.

The sound of nails on the hardwood floor drew her attention and she looked up to find Riley padding back into the kitchen. The dog let out a low whine before going to her. He sat, tall enough that his head came to rest against her chest. Wrapping her arms around him, she buried her fingers in his fur as the tears finally escaped.

"It's over, handsome," she whispered softly, wiping her cheeks with the sleeve of her sweater. "Tomorrow I'll make arrangements to go back to New York."

Riley let out a sigh, leaning his head more firmly against her, and the simple act of unconditional love broke something inside her. Closing her eyes, she leaned her head down against his, letting the tears fall silently. The hound, her furry sentinel, simply stood there, letting her draw comfort from his silent presence.

She wasn't sure how long she sat there, just letting herself feel everything that had been building since the very first time she arrived at the manor. When she heard familiar heavy footsteps coming down the hall, she sat up, wiping her face once more with her sweater. Standing, she hurried to the refrigerator, trying to hide the fact that she had been crying.

"Did Edie catch you and throw you in the dungeon, Reed?" Corbyn asked, his teasing tone almost making her lose her composure.

"No, Riley conned me into belly rubs before I could look," she answered, hoping he wouldn't notice the way her voice was still thick with emotion, or the sound of her sniffles when she tried to inhale.

His footsteps stopped short though, and she swore internally. Unaware was not a word she would use to describe Corbyn, and she should have known she wouldn't be able to fool him. Closing her eyes, she took a slow breath, trying to prepare herself for the conversation to come.

"Sadie..." he said softly, moving closer. "Look at me."

Biting her lip, she straightened, closing the refrigerator door slowly. She allowed herself one more breath before she turned to face him, knowing what he would see. The redness of her eyes and the blotchy patches on her nose and cheeks gave her away every time.

"What's wrong?" he asked, closing the distance. His hand came up, and he wiped away a stray tear with his thumb. She leaned into the touch, like it was the most natural thing in the world, because after the last few weeks, it was.

"I'm fine," she replied softly. "It's just the reality of the book being finished hitting me. After all the hard work, it's strange that it's over."

276

He raised an eyebrow at her, his hand still resting against her cheek. She couldn't meet his gaze, not sure what she would find there. Not sure if she would be able to keep herself from crying again if she did look up into his eyes.

"And of course there's a lot to do over the next few days," she continued, pulling away, and turning to look out the window. "Packing... travel arrangements."

"Travel arrangements?"

There was surprise in his voice, and she felt him step closer again. The warmth radiating from his body and the familiar scent of his cologne wrapped around her. She closed her eyes.

"Yes," she replied, trying to sound casual about the whole topic. "I mean... the book is done. The plan was always for me to go back to New York when that happened."

She could feel the sudden tension radiating from him. He gently turned her toward him, and she didn't resist. He was looking at her with that intensity she had come to know so well, his brow creased as he worked through her words.

"Indeed, it was," he said, raising an eyebrow at her. "Is that what you want?"

"My job is there," Sadie replied, matching his energy. "New York is my home."

"Home isn't a place, Reed. It's a choice," he told her. She had noticed he reverted back to her last name when he was being playful or felt like he was on unstable ground. This was definitely the latter. "It's a choice to be with the people you love. So, let me ask you again, is going back to New York what you want?"

"I can't stay here forever," she responded, not answering the question. "My visa will expire eventually... plus I can't just pretend like I don't have a job."

"Answer the question, Sadie," he said, his tone telling her he was losing patience with her stubbornness. "Visas and work... we can figure all of that out. Do you want to go back to New York?"

"No."

Her voice came out as a breathy whisper, and she saw his shoulders drop as some of the tension left his body. She bit her lip to try to stop the fresh tears from falling, trying not to feel utterly ridiculous for being so emotional. His hand came up to rest on her jaw, his thumb sweeping across her lower lip and causing her to release it.

"The people I love... they're all right here," she said, once she was sure she could speak. "It's Maggie and the villagers, and Ellie, and Paul, and Edie... and you."

His forehead came to rest against hers and she could see the smile tugging at his lips. She closed her eyes for a moment, allowing herself to soak in the comfort of his presence. She felt Riley bump her with his nose, and she pulled away just enough to look down at him with a chuckle.

"And you too, handsome."

"Then you belong right here," he said, drawing her attention back to him. "I watched you walk away once, Reed. I couldn't bear to do that a second time."

Corbyn pulled her in for a kiss, one to seal the promise of their future. It was a perfect ending to the story she was living, and for the first time in a very long time, she had no desire to edit a single line of it.

Epilogue

-Sadie-

Sadie sat at the kitchen island, sipping tea and listening to Corbyn pace by the front door. Glancing at Edie, who had paused kneading dough to look in his direction, they shared a look. The post was due any minute and Corbyn had been impatiently lurking in the front room for the last hour.

Riley picked his head up from where he was sleeping by the hearth, and a moment later they heard tires crunch over the gravel. Setting her tea down, Sadie tried to push away her own nerves, taking a steadying breath before joining Corbyn in the living room.

"It's about bloody time," she heard him mumble, and a soft chuckle escaped her.

"It's not like the postman has other stops to make before he gets here," she teased, and he narrowed his eyes at her.

Going to him, she placed a quick kiss on his cheek. He had been like this all morning, from the moment they had gotten the notice that the package from the publisher had been loaded onto the mail truck. There had been no talking him down from his restless pacing.

They watched through the window as the postman got out of the truck, a large box in his arms. Paul intercepted him before he could get too far, and she felt Corbyn let out a frustrated sigh beside her as Paul engaged in a brief conversation with the other man.

Finally, Paul turned toward the house, and Corbyn pulled away to open the door. They both followed Paul into the kitchen where he set the box on the counter, and Sadie bit her lip, fighting a grin. The arrival of the box meant the book was finally a real, tangible thing and not just some file on a computer.

"Well? Would you like to do the honors?" Corbyn looked at her with his own barely suppressed grin.

Grabbing the scissors from the drawer, she made quick work of the tape holding the box closed. Setting them on the counter, she paused for a moment, glancing at Corbyn. He gave her a small nod of encouragement, which she found herself returning before pulling open the flaps.

The moment she saw the books inside, her vision blurred.

The Northern Line by Alessandra Reed.

As she pulled out one of the books, Corbyn wrapped an arm around her, pulling her against his side. Her fingers brushed over the title as her mind tried to accept that it was real. She had done it. She had written and published her first book.

"I'm so proud of you, love," he whispered, and she felt him place a kiss on the top of her head.

"I couldn't have done this without you," she said softly, looking up at him. In her peripheral vision she saw Paul and Edie busying themselves with other tasks in the kitchen, giving them the illusion of privacy. "I love you."

A laugh escaped Sadie when Riley shoved his way between them, eyes darting between them as they looked down at him. Corbyn reached down, scratching the dog behind the ears.

"Menace," he grumbled before turning his attention back to Sadie. "I love you, too."

Leaning over, he pulled her in for a kiss, and Sadie knew their story was just beginning.

Acknowledgments

First, thank you for going on this journey with Sadie, Corbyn, and all of the rest of the characters from *Between the Lines*. This story has been living in my mind and heart for some time, and I can not tell you how thankful I am to each and every person who reads it.

I could not have done this without the help of some truly fantastic people.

- My husband, Randy: The first person I trusted with this story. Thank you for giving me encouragement and feedback, and helping me make sure this book could become reality.

- My Mom and Dad, and my son, Cameron: Thank you for putting up with me shutting myself away in my office for hours on end.

- Morgan, Cindy, Millie, Jesske, and Gabrielle: Thank you for being my amazing beta readers who gave me such wonderful feedback!

- Nora and Julieonna: Thank you for your editing and proofreading skills. You were both amazing!

Kickstarter Backers

Angie
Ariel
Cassandra
Cassie
Erin
Jessica
Juliana
Katie
Katy
Kourtney
Kristen
Linda
Melody
Michael
Morgan
Ruth
Sabrina
Sara
Sharon
Stacy
Victoria

Thank you!

About the Author

Tracey Magruder is a debut author of contemporary romance, bringing her first magical romance novel, *Between the Lines*, to life. Tracey's passion for storytelling began long before she put pen to paper. As a professional music instructor, she understands the rhythm and emotion of compelling narratives. She finds joy in helping others discover their voice, whether through teaching song or in weaving the quiet, captivating magic of a romance novel. Tracey believes that every love story is a song waiting to be written and that magic can be found in the most unexpected places. When she's not reading or dreaming up future books, Tracey loves spending time with her husband and son.

Instagram & TikTok: @traceyreadsandrambles
https://traceymagruder.com